BmC

Large Print Sto
Stout, Rex, 1886-1975.
The red box /

dmg 9-13

THE RED BOX

Also Available in Large Print by
Rex Stout:

Fer-De-Lance
The Rubber Band
The League of Frightened Men

Nero Wolfe

THE RED BOX

Rex Stout

G.K.HALL&CO.

Boston, Massachusetts

1981

Library of Congress Cataloging in Publication Data

Stout, Rex, 1886-1975.
  The red box.

    At head of title: Nero Wolfe.
    Large print ed.
    Reprint of the ed. published by Jove Publications,
New York.
    1. Large type books. I. Title: Nero Wolfe, The
The red box.
  [PS3537.T733R4 1981]   813'.52   80-29555
  ISBN 0-8161-3223-2

Published in Large Print by arrangement with
the estate of Rex Stout

Set in Penta/Linotron 202 18 pt Times Roman

THE RED BOX

1

Wolfe looked at our visitor with his eyes wide open — a sign, with him, either of indifference or of irritation. In this case it was obvious that he was irritated.

"I repeat, Mr. Frost, it is useless," he declared. "I never leave my home on business. No man's pertinacity can coerce me. I told you that five days ago. Good day, sir."

Llewellyn Frost blinked, but made no move to acknowledge the dismissal. On the contrary, he settled back in his chair.

He nodded patiently. "I know, I humored you last Wednesday, Mr. Wolfe, because there was another possibility that seemed worth trying. But it was no good. Now there's no other way. You'll have to go up there. You can forget your build-up as an eccentric genius for once — anyhow, an exception will do it good. The flaw that heightens the perfection. The stutter that accents the eloquence. Good Lord, it's only twenty blocks, Fifty-second between Fifth and Madison. A taxi will take us there in eight minutes.''

''Indeed.'' Wolfe stirred in his chair; he was boiling. ''How old are you, Mr. Frost?''

''Me? Twenty-nine.''

''Hardly young enough to justify your childish effrontery. So. You humored me! You speak of my build-up! And you undertake to stampede me into a frantic dash through the maelstrom of the city's traffic — in a taxicab! Sir, I would not enter a taxicab for a chance to solve the Sphinx's deepest riddle with all the Nile's cargo as my reward!'' He sank his voice to an outraged murmur. ''Good God. A taxicab.''

I grinned a bravo at him, twirling my pencil as I sat at my desk, eight feet from his. Having worked for Nero Wolfe for nine years, there were a few points I wasn't skeptical about any more. For

2

instance: That he was the best private detective north of the South Pole. That he was convinced that outdoor air was apt to clog the lungs. That it short-circuited his nervous system to be jiggled and jostled. That he would have starved to death if anything had happened to Fritz Brenner, on account of his firm belief that no one's cooking but Fritz's was fit to eat. There were other points too, of a different sort, but I'll pass them up since Nero Wolfe will probably read this.

Young Mr. Frost quietly stared at him. ''You're having a grand time, Mr. Wolfe. Aren't you?'' Frost nodded. ''Sure you are. A girl has been murdered. Another one — maybe more — is in danger. You offer yourself as an expert in these matters, don't you? That part's all right, there's no question but that you're an expert. And a girl's been murdered, and others are in great and immediate peril, and you rant like Booth and Barrett about a taxicab in a maelstrom. I appreciate good acting; I ought to, since I'm in show business.

But in your case I should think there would be times when a decent regard for human suffering and misfortune would make you wipe off the make-up. And if you're really playing it straight, that only makes it worse. If, rather than undergo a little personal inconvenience —"

"No good, Mr. Frost." Wolfe was slowly shaking his head. "Do you expect to bully me into a defense of my conduct? Nonsense. If a girl has been murdered, there are the police. Others are in peril? They have my sympathy, but they hold no option on my professional services. I cannot chase perils away with a wave of my hand, and I will not ride in a taxicab. I will not ride in anything, even my own car with Mr. Goodwin driving, except to meet my personal contingencies. You observe my bulk. I am not immovable, but my flesh has a constitutional reluctance to sudden, violent or sustained displacement. You spoke of 'decent regard.' How about a decent regard for the privacy of my dwelling? I use this room as an office, but this house is my home. Good day, sir."

The young man flushed, but did not move. "You won't go?" he demanded.

"I will not."

"Twenty blocks, eight minutes, your own car."

"Confound it, no."

Frost frowned at him. He muttered to himself, "They don't come any stubborner." He reached to his inside coat pocket and pulled out some papers, selected one and unfolded it and glanced at it, and returned the others. He looked at Wolfe:

"I've spent most of two days getting this thing signed. Now, wait a minute, hold your horses. When Molly Lauck was poisoned, a week ago today, it looked phony from the beginning. By Wednesday, two days later, it was plain that the cops were running around in circles, and I came to you. I know about you, I know you're the one and only. As you know, I tried to get McNair and the others down here to your office and they wouldn't come, and I tried to get you up

5

there and you wouldn't go, and I invited you to go to hell. That was five days ago. I've paid another detective three hundred dollars for a lot of nothing, and the cops from the inspector down are about as good as Fanny Brice would be for Juliet. Anyhow, it's a tough one, and I doubt if *anyone* could crack it but you. I decided that Saturday, and during the weekend I covered a lot of territory." He pushed the paper at Wolfe. "What do you say to that?"

Wolfe took it and read it. I saw his eyes go slowly half-shut, and knew that whatever it was, its effect on his irritation was pronounced. He glanced over it again, looked at Llewellyn Frost through slits, and then extended the paper toward me. I got up to take it. It was typewritten on a sheet of good bond, plain, and was dated New York City, March 28, 1936:

TO MR. NERO WOLFE:
At the request of Llewellyn Frost, we, the undersigned, beg you and urge you to investigate the death of

6

Molly Lauck, who was poisoned on March 23 at the office of Boyden McNair Incorporated on 52nd Street, New York. We entreat you to visit McNair's office for that purpose.

We respectfully remind you that once each year you leave your home to attend the Metropolitan Orchid Show, and we suggest that the present urgency, while not as great to you personally, appears to us to warrant an equal sacrifice of your comfort and convenience.

With high esteem,
WINOLD GLUECKNER
CUYLER DITSON
T. M. O'GORMAN
RAYMOND PLEHN
CHAS. E. SHANKS
CHRISTOPHER BAMFORD

I handed the document back to Wolfe and sat down and grinned at him. He folded it and slipped it under the block of petrified wood which he used for a paperweight. Frost said:

"That was the best I could think of, to get you. I had to have you. This thing has to be ripped open. I got Del Pritchard up there and he was lost. I had to get you somehow. Will you come?"

Wolfe's forefinger was doing a little circle on the arm of his chair. "Why the devil," he demanded, "did they sign that thing?"

"Because I asked them to. I explained. I told them that no one but you could solve it and you had to be persuaded. I told them that besides money and food the only thing you were interested in was orchids, and that there was nobody who could exert any influence on you but them, the best orchid-growers in America. I had letters of introduction to them. I did it right. You notice I restricted my list to the very best. Will you come?"

Wolfe sighed. "Alec Martin has forty thousand plants at Rutherford. He wouldn't sign it, eh?"

"He would if I'd gone after him. Glueckner told me that you regard

Martin as tricky and an inferior grower. Will you come?''

''Humbug.'' Wolfe sighed again. ''An infernal imposition.'' He wiggled a finger at the young man. ''Look here. You seem to be prepared to stop at nothing. You interrupt these expert and worthy men at their tasks to get them to sign this idiotic paper. You badger me. Why?''

''Because I want you to solve this case.''

''Why me?''

''Because no one else can. Wait till you see —''

''Yes. Thank you. But why your overwhelming interest in the case? The murdered girl — what was she to you?''

''Nothing.'' Frost hesitated. He went on, ''She was nothing to me. I knew her — an acquaintance. But the danger — damn it, let me tell you about it. The way it happened —''

''Please, Mr. Frost.'' Wolfe was crisp. ''Permit me. If the murdered girl was nothing to you, what standing will there be for an investigator engaged by you? If you could not persuade Mr. McNair and the others to come to me, it would be futile for me to go to them.''

''No, it wouldn't. I'll explain that —''

''Very well. Another point. I charge high fees.''

The young man flushed. ''I know you do.'' He leaned forward in his chair. ''Look, Mr. Wolfe. I've thrown away a lot of my father's money since I put on long pants. A good gob of it in the past two years, producing shows, and they were all flops. But now I've got a hit. It opened two weeks ago, and it's a ten weeks buy. *Bullets for Breakfast*. I'll have plenty of cash to pay your fee. If only you'll find out where the hell that poison came from — and help me find a way. . . .''

He stopped. Wolfe prompted him, ''Yes, sir? A way —''

Frost frowned. ''A way to get my cousin out of that murderous hole. My ortho-cousin, the daughter of my father's brother.''

''Indeed.'' Wolfe surveyed him. ''Are

you an anthropologist?''

''No.'' Frost flushed again. ''I told you, I'm in show business. I can pay your fee — within reason, or even without reason. But we ought to have an understanding about that. Of course the amount of the fee is up to you, but my idea would be to split it, half to find out where that candy came from, and the other half for getting my cousin Helen away from that place. She's as stubborn as you are, and you'll probably have to earn the first half of the fee in order to earn the second, but I don't care if you don't. If you get her out of there without clearing up Molly Lauck's death, half the fee is yours anyhow. But Helen won't scare, that won't work, and she has some kind of a damn fool idea about loyalty to this McNair, Boyden McNair. Uncle Boyd, she calls him. She's known him all her life. He's an old friend of Aunt Callie's, Helen's mother. Then there's this dope, Gebert — but I'd better start at the beginning and sketch it — hey! You going now?''

Wolfe had pushed his chair back and

elevated himself to his feet. He moved around the end of his desk with his customary steady and not ungraceful deliberation.

"Keep your seat, Mr. Frost. It is four o'clock, and I now spend two hours with my plants upstairs. Mr. Goodwin will take the details of the poisoning of Miss Molly Lauck — and of your family complications if they seem pertinent. For the fourth time, I believe it is, good day, sir." He headed for the door.

Frost jumped up, sputtering. "But you're coming uptown —"

Wolfe halted and ponderously turned. "Confound you, you know perfectly well I am! But I'll tell you this, if Alec Martin's signature had been on that outlandish paper I would have thrown it in the wastebasket. He splits bulbs. Splits them! — Archie. We shall meet Mr. Frost at the McNair place tomorrow morning at ten minutes past eleven."

He turned and went, disregarding the client's protest at the delay. Through the open office door I heard, from the hall, the grunt of the elevator as he stepped in it, and the bang of its door.

Llewellyn Frost turned to me, and the color in his face may have been from gratification at his success, or from indignation at its postponement. I looked him over as a client — his wavy light brown hair brushed back, his wide-open brown eyes that left the matter of intelligence to a guess, his big nose and broad jaw which made his face too heavy even for his six feet.

"Anyhow, I'm much obliged to you, Mr. Goodwin." He sat down. "You were clever about it, too, keeping that Martin out of it. It was a big favor you did me, and I assure you I won't forget —"

"Wrong number." I waved him off. "I told you at the time, I keep all my favors for myself. I suggested that round robin only to try to drum up some business, and for a scientific experiment to find out how many ergs it would take to jostle him loose. We haven't had a case that was worth anything for nearly three months." I got hold of a notebook and pencil, and swiveled around and pulled my desk-leaf out. "And by the way, Mr. Frost, don't you forget that you thought of that round robin yourself. I'm not supposed to think."

"Certainly," he nodded. "Strictly confidential. I'll never mention it."

"Okay." I flipped the notebook open to the next blank page. "Now for this murder you want to buy a piece of. Spill it."

2

So the next morning I had Nero Wolfe braving the elements — the chief element for that day being bright warm March sunshine. I say I had him, because I had conceived the persuasion which was making him bust all precedents. What pulled him out of his front door, enraged and grim, with overcoat, scarf, gloves, stick, something he called gaiters, and a black felt pirate's hat size 8 pulled down to his ears, was the name of Winold Glueckner heading the signatures on that letter — Glueckner, who had recently received from an agent in Sarawak four bulbs of a pink Coelogyne pandurata, never seen before, and had scorned Wolfe's offer of three thousand bucks for two of them. Knowing what a tough old heinie

Glueckner was, I had my doubts whether he would turn loose of the bulbs no matter how many murders Wolfe solved at his request, but anyhow I had lit the fuse.

Driving from the house on 35th Street near the Hudson River — where Wolfe had lived for over twenty years and I had lived with him for nearly half of them — to the address on 52nd Street, I handled the sedan so as to keep it as smooth as a dip's fingers. Except for one I couldn't resist; on Fifth Avenue near Forty-third there was an ideal little hole about two feet across where I suppose someone had been prospecting for the twenty-six dollars they paid the Indians, and I maneuvered to hit it square at a good clip. I glanced in the mirror for a glimpse of Wolfe in the back seat and saw he was looking bitter and infuriated.

I said, "Sorry, sir, they're tearing up the streets."

He didn't answer.

From what Llewellyn Frost had told me the day before about the place of business of Boyden McNair Incorporated — all of which had gone into my notebook and been read to Nero Wolfe Monday evening — I hadn't realized the extent of its aspirations in the way of class. We met Llewellyn Frost downstairs, just inside the entrance. One of the first things I saw and heard, as Frost led us to the elevator to take us to the second floor, where the offices and private showrooms were, was a saleswoman who looked like a cross between a countess and Texas Guinan, telling a customer that in spite of the fact that the little green sport suit on the model was of High Meadow Loom hand-woven material and designed by Mr. McNair himself, it could be had for a paltry three hundred. I thought of the husband and shivered and crossed my fingers as I stepped into the elevator. And I remarked to myself, "I'll say it's a sinister joint."

The floor above was just as elegant, but quieter. There was no merchandise at all in sight, no saleswomen and no customers. A long wide corridor had doors on both sides at intervals, with etchings and hunting prints here and there on the wood paneling, and in the large room where we emerged from the elevator there were silk chairs and gold smoking stands and thick deep-colored rugs. I took that in at a glance and then centered my attention on the side of the room opposite the corridor, where a couple of goddesses were sitting on a settee. One of them, a blonde with dark blue eyes, was such a pronounced pippin that I had to stare so as not to blink, and the other one, slender and medium-dark, while not as remarkable, was a cinch in a contest for Miss Fifty-second Street.

The blonde nodded at us. The slender one said, "Hello, Lew."

Llewellyn Frost nodded back. " 'Lo, Helen. See you later."

As we went down the corridor I said to Wolfe, "See that? I mean, them? You ought to get around more. What are orchids to a pair of blossoms like that?"

He only grunted at me.

Frost knocked at the last door on the right, opened it, and stood aside for us to precede him. It was a large room, fairly narrow but long, and there was only enough let-up on the elegance to allow for the necessities of an office. The rugs were just as thick as up front, and the furniture was Decorators' Delight. The windows were covered with heavy yellow silk curtains, sweeping in folds to the floor, and the light came from glass chandeliers as big as barrels.

Frost said, "Mr. Nero Wolfe. Mr. Goodwin. Mr. McNair."

The man at the desk with carved legs got up and stuck out a paw, without enthusiasm. "How do you do, gentlemen. Be seated. Another chair, Lew?"

Wolfe looked grim. I glanced around at the chairs, and saw I'd have to act quick, for I knew that Wolfe was absolutely capable of running out on us for less than that, and having got him this far I was going to hold on to him if possible. I stepped around to the other side of the desk and put a hand on Boyden McNair's chair. He was still standing up.

"If you don't mind, sir. Mr. Wolfe prefers a roomy seat, just one of his whims. The other chairs are pretty damn narrow. If you don't mind?"

By that time I had it shoved around where Wolfe could take it. McNair stared. I brought one of the Decorators' Delights around for him, tossed him a grin, and went around and sat down by Llewellyn Frost.

McNair said to Frost, "Well, Lew, you know I'm busy. Did you tell these gentlemen I agreed to give them fifteen minutes?"

Frost glanced at Wolfe and then looked back at McNair. I could see his hands, with the fingers twined, resting on his thigh; the fingers were pressed tight. He said, "I told them I had persuaded you to see them. I don't believe fifteen minutes will be enough —"

"It'll have to be enough. I'm busy. This is a busy season." McNair had a thin tight voice and he kept shifting in his chair — that is, temporarily his chair. He went on, "Anyway, what's the use? What can I do?'' He spread out his hands, glanced at his wrist watch, and looked at Wolfe. ''I promised Lew fifteen minutes. I am at your service until 11:20.''

Wolfe shook his head. ''Judging from Mr. Frost's story, I shall need more. Two hours or more, I should say.''

''Impossible,'' McNair snapped. ''I'm busy. Now, fourteen minutes.''

''This is preposterous.'' Wolfe braced his hands on the arms of the borrowed chair and raised himself to his feet. He stopped Frost's ejaculation by showing him a palm, looked down at McNair and said quietly, ''I didn't need to come here to see you, sir. I did so in acknowledgement of an idiotic but charming gesture conceived and executed by Mr. Frost. I understand that Mr. Cramer of the police has had several conversations with you, and that he is violently dissatisfied with the lack of progress in his investigation of the murder of one of your employees on your premises. Mr. Cramer has a high opinion of my abilities. I shall telephone him within an hour and suggest that he bring you — and other persons — to my office." Wolfe wiggled a finger. "For much longer than fifteen minutes."

He moved. I got up. Frost started after him.

"Wait!" McNair called out. "Wait a minute, you don't understand!" Wolfe turned and stood. McNair continued, "In the first place, why try to browbeat me? That's ridiculous. Cramer couldn't take me to your office, or any place, if I didn't care to go, you know that. Of course Molly — of course the murder was terrible. Good God, don't I know it? And naturally I'll do anything I can to help clear it up. But what's the use? I've told Cramer everything I know, we've been over it a dozen times. Sit down." He pulled a handkerchief from his pocket and wiped his forehead and nose, started to return it to his pocket and then threw it on the desk. "I'm going to have a breakdown. Sit down. I worked fourteen hours a day getting the spring line ready, enough to kill a man, and then this comes on top of it. You've been dragged into this by Lew Frost. What the devil does he know about it?'' He glared at Frost. ''I've told it over and over to the police until I'm sick of it. Sit down, won't you? Ten minutes is all you'll need for what I know, anyhow. That's what makes it worse, as I've told Cramer, nobody knows anything. And Lew Frost knows less than that.'' He glared at the young man. ''You know damn well you're just trying to use it as a lever to pry Helen out of here.'' He transferred the glare to Wolfe. ''Do you expect me to have anything better than the barest courtesy for you? Why should I?''

Wolfe had returned to his chair and got himself lowered into it, without taking his eyes off McNair's face. Frost started to speak, but I silenced him with a shake of the head. McNair picked up the handkerchief and passed it across his forehead and threw it down again. He pulled open the top right drawer of his desk and looked in it, muttered, ''Where the devil's that aspirin?'' tried the drawer on the left, reached in and brought out a small bottle, shook a couple of tablets onto his palm, poured half a glass of water from a thermos carafe, tossed the tablets into his mouth, and washed them down.

He looked at Wolfe and complained resentfully, "I've had a hell of a headache for two weeks. I've taken a ton of aspirin and it doesn't help any. I'm going to have a breakdown. That's the truth —"

There was a knock, and the door opened. The intruder was a tall handsome woman in a black dress with rows of white buttons. She came on in, glanced politely around, and said in a voice full of culture:

"Excuse me, please." She looked at McNair: "That 1241 resort, the cashmere plain tabby with the medium oxford twill stripe — can that be done in two shades of natural shetland with basket instead of tabby?"

McNair frowned at her and demanded, "What?"

She took a breath. "That 1241 resort —"

"Oh. I heard you. It cannot. The line stands, Mrs. Lamont. You know that."

"I know. Mrs. Frost wants it."

McNair straightened up. "Mrs. Frost? Is she here?"

The woman nodded. "She's ordering. I told her you were engaged. She's taking two of the Portsmouth ensembles."

"Oh. She is." McNair had suddenly stopped fidgeting, and his voice, though still thin, sounded more under command. "I want to see her. Ask if it will suit her convenience to wait till I'm through here."

"And the 1241 in two shades of shetland —"

"Yes. Of course. Add fifty dollars."

The woman nodded, excused herself again, and departed.

McNair glanced at his wrist watch, shot a sharp one at young Frost, and looked at Wolfe. "You can still have ten minutes."

Wolfe shook his head. "I won't need them. You're nervous, Mr. McNair. You're upset."

"What? You won't need them?"

"No. You probably lead too active a life, running around getting women dressed." Wolfe shuddered. "Horrible. I would like to ask you two questions. First, regarding the death of Molly Lauck, have you anything to add to what you have told Mr. Cramer and Mr. Frost? I know pretty well what that is. Anything new?"

"No." McNair was frowning. He picked up his handkerchief and wiped his forehead. "No. Nothing whatever."

"Very well. Then it would be futile to take up more of your time. The other question: may I be shown a room where some of your employees may be sent to me for conversation? I shall make it as brief as possible. Particularly Miss Helen Frost, Miss Thelma Mitchell, and Mrs. Lamont. I don't suppose Mr. Perren Gebert happens to be here?"

McNair snapped, "Gebert? Why the devil should he be?"

"I don't know." Wolfe lifted his shoulders half an inch, and dropped them. "I ask. I understand he was here one week ago yesterday, the day Miss Lauck died, when you were having your show. I believe you call it a show?''

''I had a show, yes. Gebert dropped in. Scores of people were here. About talking with the girls and Mrs. Lamont — if you make it short you can do it here. I have to go down to the floor.''

''I would prefer something less — more humble. If you please.''

''Suit yourself.'' McNair got up. ''Take them to one of the booths, Lew. I'll tell Mrs. Lamont. Do you want her first?''

''I'd like to start with Miss Frost and Miss Mitchell. Together.''

''You may be interrupted, if they're needed.''

''I shall be patient.''

''All right. You tell them, Lew?''

He looked around, grabbed his handkerchief from the desk and stuffed it in his pocket, and bustled out.

Llewellyn Frost, rising, began to protest, ''I don't see why you didn't —''

Wolfe stopped him. ''Mr. Frost. I

endure only to my limit. Obviously, Mr. McNair is sick, but you cannot make that claim to tolerance. Don't forget that you are responsible for this grotesque expedition. Where is this booth?''

''Well, I'm paying for it.''

''Not adequately. You couldn't. Come, sir!''

Frost led us out and back down the corridor, and opened the door at the end on the left. He switched on lights, said he would be back soon, and disappeared. I moved my eyes. It was a small paneled room with a table, a smoking stand, full-length mirrors, and three dainty silk chairs. Wolfe stood and looked at the mess, and his lips tightened.

He said, ''Revolting. I will not — I will not.''

I grinned at him. ''I know damn well you won't, and for once I don't blame you. I'll get it.''

I went out and strode down the corridor to McNair's office, entered, heaved his chair to my shoulder, and proceeded back to the booth with it. Frost and the two goddesses were going in as I got there. Frost went for another chair, and I planked my prize down behind the table and observed to Wolfe, "If you get so you like it we'll take it home with us." Frost returned with his contribution, and I told him, "Go and get three bottles of cold light beer and a glass and an opener. We've got to keep him alive."

He lifted his brows at me. "You're crazy."

I murmured, "Was I crazy when I suggested that letter from the orchid guys? Get the beer."

He went. I negotiated myself into a chair with the blonde pippin on one side and the sylph on the other. Wolfe was sniffing the air. He suddenly demanded:

"Are all of these booths perfumed like this?"

"Yes, they are." The blonde smiled at him. "It's not us."

"No. It was here before you came in. Pfui. And you girls work here. They call you models?"

"That's what they call us. I'm Thelma Mitchell." The blonde waved an expert graceful hand. "This is Helen Frost."

Wolfe nodded, and turned to the sylph. "Why do you work here, Miss Frost? You don't have to. Do you?"

Helen Frost put level eyes on him, with a little crease in her brow between them. She said quietly, "My cousin told us you wished to ask us about — about Molly Lauck."

"Indeed." Wolfe leaned back, warily, to see if the chair would take it. There was no creak, and he settled. "Understand this, Miss Frost: I am a detective. Therefore, while I may be accused of incompetence or stupidity, I may not be charged with impertinence. However nonsensical or irrelevant my questions may seem to you, they may be filled with the deepest significance and the most sinister implications. That is the tradition of my profession. As a matter of fact, I was merely making an effort to get acquainted with you."

Her eyes stayed level. "I am doing this as a favor to my cousin Lew. He didn't ask me to get acquainted." She swallowed. "He asked me to answer questions about last Monday.''

Wolfe leaned forward and snapped, ''Only as a favor to your cousin? Wasn't Molly Lauck your friend? Wasn't she murdered? You aren't interested in helping with that?''

It didn't jolt her much. She swallowed again, but stayed steady. ''Interested — yes. Of course. But I've told the police — I don't see what Lew — I don't see why you —'' She stopped herself and jerked her head up and demanded, ''Haven't I said I'll answer your questions? It's awful — it's an awful thing —''

''So it is.'' Wolfe turned abruptly to the blonde. ''Miss Mitchell. I understand that at twenty minutes past four last Monday afternoon, a week ago yesterday, you and Miss Frost took the elevator together, downstairs, and got out at this floor. Right?''

She nodded.

''And there was no one up here; that is, you saw no one. You walked down the corridor to the fifth door on the left, across the corridor from Mr. McNair's office, and entered that room, which is an apartment used as a rest room for the four models who work here. Molly Lauck was in there. Right?''

She nodded again. Wolfe said, ''Tell me what happened.''

The blonde took a breath. ''Well, we started to talk about the show and the customers and so on. Nothing special. We did that about three minutes, and then suddenly Molly said she forgot, and she reached under a coat and pulled out a box —''

''Permit me. What were Miss Lauck's words?''

''She just said she forgot, she had some loot —''

''No. Please. What did she say? Her exact words.''

The blonde stared at him. ''Well, if I can. She said, let's see: 'Oh, I forgot, girls, I've got some loot. Swiped it as clean as a whistle.' While she was saying that she was pulling the box from under the coat —''

''Where was the coat?''

''It was her coat, lying on the table.''

"Where were you?"

"Me? I was right there, standing there. She was sitting on the table."

"Where was Miss Frost?"

"She was — she was across by the mirror, fixing her hair. Weren't you, Helen?"

The sylph merely nodded. Wolfe said:

"And then? Exactly. Exact words."

"Well, she handed me the box and I took it and opened it, and I said —"

"Had it been opened before?"

"I don't know. It didn't have any wrapping or ribbon or anything on it. I opened it and I said, 'Gee, it's two pounds and never been touched. Where'd you get it, Molly?' She said, 'I told you, I swiped it. Is it any good?' She asked Helen to have some —"

"Her words."

Miss Mitchell frowned. "I don't know. Just 'Have some, Helen,' or 'Join the party, Helen' — something like that. Anyway, Helen didn't take any —"

"What did she say?"

"I don't know. What did you say, Helen?"

Miss Frost spoke without swallowing. "I don't remember. I just had had cocktails, and I didn't want any."

The blonde nodded. "Something like that. Then Molly took a piece and I took a piece —"

"Please." Wolfe wiggled a finger at her. "You were holding the box?"

"Yes. Molly had handed it to me."

"Miss Frost didn't have it in her hands at all?"

"No, I told you, she said she didn't want any. She didn't even look at it."

"And you and Miss Lauck each took a piece —"

"Yes. I took candied pineapple. It was a mixture; chocolates, bonbons, nuts, candied fruits, everything. I ate it. Molly put her piece in her mouth, all of it, and after she bit into it she said — she said it was strong —"

"Words, please."

"Well, she said, let's see: 'My God, it's 200 proof, but not so bad, I can take it.' She made a face, but she chewed it and swallowed it. Then . . . well . . . you wouldn't believe how quick it was —"

"I'll try to. Tell me."

"Not more than half a minute, I'm sure it wasn't. I took another piece and was eating it, and Molly was looking into the box, saying something about taking the taste out of her mouth —"

She stopped because the door popped open. Llewellyn Frost appeared, carrying a paper bag. I got up and took it from him, and extracted from it the opener and glass and bottles and arranged them in front of Wolfe. Wolfe picked up the opener and felt of a bottle.

"Umph. Schreirer's. It's too cold."

I sat down again. "It'll make a bead. Try it." He poured. Helen Frost was saying to her cousin:

"So that's what you went for. Your detective wants to know exactly what I said, my exact words, and he asks Thelma if I handled the box of candy. . ."

Frost patted her on the shoulder. "Now, Helen. Take it easy. He knows what he's doing. . ."

One bottle was empty, and the glass.

35

Frost sat down. Wolfe wiped his lips.

"You were saying, Miss Mitchell, Miss Lauck spoke of taking the taste out of her mouth."

The blonde nodded. "Yes. And then — well — all of a sudden she straightened up and made a noise. She didn't scream, it was just a noise, a horrible noise. She got off the table and then leaned back against it and her face was all twisted . . . it was . . . twisted. She looked at me with her eyes staring, and her mouth went open and shut but she couldn't say anything, and suddenly she shook all over and grabbed for me and got hold of my hair . . . and . . . and . . ."

"Yes, Miss Mitchell."

The blonde gulped. "Well, when she went down she took me with her because she had hold of my hair. Then of course I was scared. I jerked away. Later, when the doctor . . . when people came, she had a bunch of my hair gripped in her fingers."

Wolfe eyed her. "You have good nerves, Miss Mitchell."

"I'm not a softy. I had a good cry after I got home that night, I cried it out. But I didn't cry then. Helen stood against the wall and trembled and stared and couldn't move, she'll tell you that herself. I ran to the elevator and yelled for help, and then I ran back and put the lid on the box of candy and held onto it until Mr. McNair came and then I gave it to him. Molly was dead, I could see that. She was crumpled up. She fell down dead." She gulped again. "Maybe you could tell me. The doctor said it was some kind of acid, and it said in the paper potassium cyanide."

Lew Frost put in, "Hydrocyanic. The police say — it's the same thing. I told you that. Didn't I?"

Wolfe wiggled a finger at him. "Please, Mr. Frost. It is I who am to earn the fee, you to pay it. — Then Miss Mitchell, you felt no discomfort from your two pieces, and Miss Lauck ate only one."

"That's all." The blonde shivered. "It's terrible, to think there's something that can kill you that quick. She couldn't even speak. You could see it go right through her, when she shook all over. I held onto the box, but I got rid of it as soon as I saw Mr. McNair.''

''Then, I understand, you ran away.''

She nodded. ''I ran to the washroom.'' She made a face. ''I had to throw up. I had eaten two pieces.''

''Indeed. Most efficient.'' Wolfe had opened another bottle, and was pouring. ''To go back a little. You had not seen that box of candy before Miss Lauck took it from under the coat?''

''No. I hadn't.''

''What do you suppose she meant when she said she had swiped it?''

''Why — she meant — she saw it somewhere and took it.''

Wolfe turned. ''Miss Frost. What do you suppose Miss Lauck meant by that?''

''I suppose she meant what she said, that she swiped it. Stole it.''

''Was that customary with her? Was she a thief?''

''Of course not. She only took a box of candy. She did it for a joke, I suppose. She liked to play jokes — to do things like that.''

"Had you seen the box before she produced it in that room?''

"No.''

Wolfe emptied his glass in five gulps, which was par, and wiped his lips. His half-shut eyes were on the blonde. "I believe you went to lunch that day with Miss Lauck. Tell us about that.''

"Well — Molly and I went together about one o'clock. We were hungry because we had been working hard — the show had been going on since eleven o'clock — but we only went to the drug store around the corner because we had to be back in twenty minutes to give Helen and the extras a chance. The show was supposed to be from eleven to two, but we knew they'd keep dropping in. We ate sandwiches and custard and came straight back.''

"Did you see Miss Lauck swipe the box of candy at the drug store?''

"Of course I didn't. She wouldn't do that.''

"Did you get it at the drug store

yourself and bring it back with you?"

Miss Mitchell stared at him. She said, disgusted, "For the Lord's sake. No."

"You're sure Miss Lauck didn't get it somewhere while out for lunch?"

"Of course I'm sure. I was right with her."

"And she didn't go out again during the afternoon?"

"No. We were working together until half past three, when there was a let-up and she left to go upstairs, and a little later Helen and I came up and found her here. There in the restroom."

"And she ate a piece of candy and died, and you ate two and didn't." Wolfe sighed. "There is of course the possibility that she had brought the box with her when she came to work that morning."

The blonde shook her head. "I've thought of that. We've all talked about it. She didn't have any package. Anyway, where could it have been all morning? It wasn't in the restroom, and there wasn't any place else . . ."

Wolfe nodded. "That's the devil of it.

It's recorded history. You aren't really telling me your fresh and direct memory of what happened last Monday, you're merely repeating the talk it has been resolved into. — I beg you, no offense; you can't help it. I should have been here last Monday afternoon — or rather, I shouldn't have been here at all. I shouldn't be here now." He glared at Llewellyn Frost, then remembered the beer, filled his glass, and drank.

He looked from one girl to the other. "You know, of course, what the problem is. Last Monday there were more than a hundred people here, mostly women but a few men, for that show. It was a cold March day and they all wore coats. Who brought that box of candy? The police have questioned everyone connected with this establishment. They have found no one who ever saw the box or will admit to any knowledge of it. No one who saw Miss Lauck with it or has any idea where she got it. An impossible situation!"

He wiggled a finger at Frost. "I told you, sir, this case is not within my province. I can use a dart or a rapier, but

I cannot set traps throughout the territory of the metropolitan district. Who brought the poison here? Whom was it intended for? God knows, but I am not prepared to make a call on Him, no matter how many orchid-growers are coerced into signing idiotic letters. I doubt if it is worthwhile for me to try even for the second half of your fee, since your cousin — your ortho-cousin — refuses to become acquainted with me. As for the first half, the solution of Miss Lauck's death, I could undertake that only through interviews with all of the persons who were in this place last Monday; and I doubt if you could persuade even the innocent ones to call at my office."

Lew Frost muttered, "It's your job. You took it. If you're not up to it —"

"Nonsense. Does a bridge engineer dig ditches?" Wolfe opened the third bottle. "I believe I have not thanked you for this beer. I do thank you. I assure you, sir, this problem is well within my abilities in so far as it is possible to apply them. In so far — for instance, take Miss Mitchell here. Is she telling

42

the truth? Did she murder Molly Lauck? Let us find out.'' He turned and got sharp. ''Miss Mitchell. Do you eat much candy?''

She said, ''You're being smart.''

''I'm begging your indulgence. It won't hurt you, with nerves like yours. Do you eat much candy?''

She drew her shoulders together, and released them. ''Once in a while. I have to be careful. I'm a model, and I watch myself.

''What is your favorite kind?''

''Candied fruits. I like nuts too.''

''You removed the lid from that box last Monday. What color was it?''

''Brown. A kind of gold-brown.''

''What kind was it? What did it say on the lid?''

''It said . . . it said, *Medley*. Some kind of a medley.''

Wolfe snapped, '' 'Some kind?' Do you mean to say you don't remember what name was on the lid?''

She frowned at him. ''No . . . I don't. That's funny. I would have thought —''

"So would I. You looked at it and took the lid off, and later replaced the lid and held onto the box, knowing there was deadly poison in it, and you weren't even curious enough —"

"Now wait a minute. You're not so smart. Molly was dead on the floor, and everybody was crowding into the room, and I was looking for Mr. McNair to give him the box, I didn't want the damn thing, and certainly I wasn't trying to think of things to be curious about." She frowned again. "At that, it *is* funny I didn't really see the name."

Wolfe nodded. He turned abruptly to Lew Frost. "You see, sir, how it is done. What is to be deduced from Miss Mitchell's performance? Is she cleverly pretending that she does not know what was on that lid, or is it credible that she really failed to notice it? I am merely demonstrating. For another example, take your cousin." He switched his eyes and shot at her, "You, Miss Frost. Do you eat candy?"

She looked at her cousin. "Is this necessary, Lew?"

Frost flushed. He opened his mouth, but Wolfe was in ahead:

"Miss Mitchell didn't beg off. Of course, she has good nerves."

The sylph leveled her eyes at him. "There's nothing wrong with my nerves. But this cheap — oh, well. I eat candy. I much prefer caramels, and since I work as a model and have to be careful too, I confine myself to them."

"Chocolate caramels? Nut caramels?"

"Any kind. Caramels. I like to chew them."

"How often do you eat them?"

"Maybe once a week."

"Do you buy them yourself?"

"No. I don't get a chance to. My cousin knows my preference, and he sends me boxes of Carlatti's. Too often. I have to give most of them away."

"You are very fond of them?"

She nodded. "Very."

"You find it hard to resist them when offered?"

"Sometimes, yes."

"Monday afternoon you had been

working hard? You were tired? You had had a short and unsatisfactory lunch?''

She was tolerating it. ''Yes.''

''Then, when Miss Lauck offered you caramels, why didn't you take one?''

''She didn't offer me caramels. There weren't any in that —'' She stopped. She glanced aside, at her cousin, and then put her eyes at Wolfe again. ''That is, I didn't suppose —''

''Suppose?'' Wolfe's voice suddenly softened. ''Miss Mitchell couldn't remember what was on the lid of that box. Can you, Miss Frost?''

''No. I don't know.''

''Miss Mitchell has said that you didn't handle the box. You were at the mirror, fixing your hair; you didn't even look at it. Is that correct?''

She was staring at him. ''Yes.''

''Miss Mitchell has also said that she replaced the lid on the box and kept it under her arm until she handed it to Mr. McNair. Is that correct?''

''I don't know. I . . . I didn't notice.''

''No. Naturally, under the

circumstances. But after the box was given to Mr. McNair, from that time until he turned it over to the police, did you see it at all? Did you have an opportunity to inspect it?''

''I didn't see it. No.''

''Just one more, Miss Frost — this finishes the demonstration: you are sure you don't know what was on that lid? It was not a brand you were familiar with?''

She shook her head. ''I have no idea.''

Wolfe leaned back and sighed. He picked up the third bottle and filled his glass and watched the foam work. No one spoke; we just looked at him, while he drank. He put the glass down and wiped his lips, and opened his eyes on his client.

''There you are, Mr. Frost,'' he said quietly. ''Even in a brief demonstration, where no results were expected, something is upturned. By her own testimony, your cousin never saw the contents of that box after Miss Lauck swiped it. She doesn't know what brand it was, so she could not have been familiar with its contents. And yet, she knew, quite positively, that there were no caramels in it. Therefore: she saw the contents of the box, somewhere, sometime, *before* Miss Lauck swiped it. That, sir, is deduction. That is what I meant when I spoke of interviews with all of the persons who were at this place last Monday.''

Lew Frost, glaring at him, blurted, ''You call this — what the hell do you call this? My cousin —''

''I told you, deduction.''

The sylph sat, pale, and stared at him. She opened her mouth a couple of times, but closed it without speaking. Thelma Mitchell horned in:

''She didn't say she knew positively there were no caramels in it. She only said —''

Wolfe put up a palm at her. ''You being loyal, Miss Mitchell? For shame. The first loyalty here is to the dead. Mr. Frost dragged me here because Molly Lauck died. He hired me to find out how and why. — Well, sir?

Didn't you?''

Frost sputtered, ''I didn't hire you to play damn fool tricks with a couple of nervous girls. You damn fat imbecile — listen! I already know more about this business than you'd ever find out in a hundred years! If you think I'm paying you — now what? Where you going? What's the game now? You get back in that chair I say —''

Wolfe had arisen, without haste, and moved around the table, going sideways past Thelma Mitchell's feet, and Frost had jumped up and started the motions of a stiff arm at him.

I got upright and stepped across. ''Don't shove, mister.'' I would just as soon have plugged him, but he would have had to drop on a lady. ''Subside, please. Come on, back up.''

He gave me a bad eye, but let that do. Wolfe had sidled by, towards the door, and at that moment there was a knock on it and it opened, and the handsome woman in the black dress with white buttons appeared. She moved in.

''Excuse me, please.'' She glanced

around, composed, and settled on me. "Can you spare Miss Frost? She is needed downstairs. And Mr. McNair says you wish to speak with me. I can give you a few minutes now."

I looked at Wolfe. He bowed to the woman, his head moving two inches. "Thank you, Mrs. Lamont. It won't be necessary. We have made excellent progress; more than could reasonably have been expected. — Archie. Did you pay for the beer? Give Mr. Frost a dollar. That should cover it."

I took out my wallet and extracted a buck and laid it on the table. A swift glance showed me that Helen Frost looked pale, Thelma Mitchell looked interested, and Llewellyn looked set for murder. Wolfe had left. I did likewise, and joined him outside where he was pushing the button for the elevator.

I said, "That beer couldn't have been more than two bits a throw, seventy-five cents for three."

He nodded. "Put the difference on his bill."

Downstairs we marched through the

activity without halting. McNair was over at one side talking with a dark medium-sized woman with a straight back and a proud mouth, and I let my head turn for a second look, surmising it was Helen Frost's mother. A goddess I hadn't seen before was parading in a brown topcoat in front of a horsey jane with a dog, and three or four other people were scattered around. Just before we got to the street door it opened and a man entered, a big broad guy with a scar on his cheek. I knew all about that scar. I tossed him a nod.

"Hi, Purley."

He stopped and stared, not at me, at Wolfe. "In the name of God! Did you shoot him out of a cannon?"

I grinned and went on.

On the way home I made attempts at friendly conversation over my shoulder, but without success. I tried:

"Those models are pretty creatures. Huh?"

No sale. I tried:

"Did you recognize that gentleman we met coming out? Our old friend Purley

51

Stebbins of the Homicide Squad. One of Cramer's hirelings.''

No response. I started looking ahead for a good hole.

3

The first telephone call from Llewellyn Frost came around half-past one, while Wolfe and I were doing the right thing by some sausage with ten kinds of herbs in it, which he got several times every spring from a Swiss up near Chappaqua who prepared it himself from home-made pigs. Fritz Brenner, the chef and household pride, was instructed to tell Llewellyn that Mr. Wolfe was at table and might not be disturbed. I wanted to go and take it, but Wolfe nailed me down with a finger. The second call came a little after two, while Wolfe was leisurely sipping coffee, and I went to the office for it.

Frost sounded concerned and aggravated. He wanted to know if he could expect to find Wolfe in at two-thirty, and I said yes, he would probably be in forevermore. After we hung up I stayed at my desk and fiddled around with some things, and in a few minutes Wolfe entered, peaceful and benign but ready to resent any attempt at turbulence, as he always was after a proper and unhurried meal.

He sat down at his desk, sighed happily, and looked around at the walls — the bookshelves, maps, Holbeins, more bookshelves, the engraving of Brilliat-Savarin. After a moment he opened the middle drawer and began taking out beer-bottle caps and piling them on the desk. He remarked:

"A little less tarragon, and add a pinch of chervil. Fritz might try that next time. I must suggest it to him."

"Yeah," I agreed, not wanting to argue about that. He knew damn well I loved tarragon. "But if you want to get those caps counted you'd better get a move on. Our client's on his way down here."

"Indeed." He began separating the caps into piles of five. "Confound it, in

54

spite of those three outside bottles, I think I'm already four ahead on the week."

"Well, that's normal." I swirled. "Listen, enlighten me before Frost gets here. What got you started on the Frost girl?"

His shoulders lifted a quarter of an inch and dropped again. "Rage. That was a cornered rat squealing. There I was, cornered in that insufferable scented hole, dragooned into a case where there was nothing to start on. Or rather, too much. Also, I dislike murder by inadvertence. Whoever poisoned that candy is a bungling ass. I merely began squealing." He frowned at the piles of caps. "Twenty-five, thirty, thirty-three. But the result was remarkable. And quite conclusive. It would be sardonic if we should earn the second half of our fee by having Miss Frost removed to prison. Not that I regard that as likely. I trust, Archie, you don't mind my babbling."

"No, it's okay right after a meal. Go right ahead. No jury would ever convict Miss Frost of anything anyhow."

"I suppose not. Why should they? Even a juror must be permitted his tribute to beauty. But if Miss Frost is in for an ordeal, I suspect it will not be that. Did you notice the large diamond on her finger? And the one set in her vanity case?"

I nodded. "So what? Is she engaged?"

"I couldn't say. I remarked the diamonds because they don't suit her. You have heard me observe that I have a feeling for phenomena. Her personality, her reserve — even allowing for the unusual circumstances — it is not natural for Miss Frost to wear diamonds. Then there was Mr. McNair's savage hostility, surely as unnatural as it was disagreeable, however he may hate Mr. Llewellyn Frost — and why does he hate him? More transparent was the reason for Mr. Frost's familiarity with so strange a term as 'ortho-cousin,' strictly a word for an anthropologist, though it leaves room for various speculations. . . . Ortho-cousins are those whose parents are of the same sex — the children of two brothers or of two sisters; whereas cross-cousins are those whose parents are brother and sister. In some tribes cross-cousins may marry, but not ortho-cousins. Obviously Mr. Frost has investigated the question thoroughly . . . Certainly it is possible that none of these oddities has any relation to the death of Molly Lauck, but they are to be noted, along with many others. I hope I am not boring you, Archie. As you are aware, this is the routine of my genius, though I do not ordinarily vocalize it. I sat in this chair one evening for five hours, thus considering the phenomena of Paul Chapin, his wife, and the members of that incredible League of Atonement. I talk chiefly because if I do not you will begin to rustle papers to annoy me, and I do not feel like being irritated. That sausage — but there's the bell. Our client. Ha! Still our client, though he may not think so."

Footsteps sounded from the hall, and soon again, returning. The office door opened and Fritz appeared. He

57

announced Mr. Frost, and Wolfe nodded and requested beer. Fritz went.

Llewellyn came bouncing in. He came bouncing, but you could tell by his eyes it was a case of dual personality. Back behind his eyes he was scared stiff. He bounced up to Wolfe's desk and began talking like a man who was already late for nine appointments.

"I could have told you on the phone, Mr. Wolfe, but I like to do business face to face. I like to see a man and let him see me. Especially for a thing like this. I owe you an apology. I flew off the handle and made a damn fool of myself. I want to apologize." He put out a hand. Wolfe looked at it, and then up at his face. He took his hand back, flushed, and went on, "You shouldn't be sore at me, I just flew off the handle. And anyway, you must understand this, I've got to insist on this, that that was nothing up there. Helen — my cousin was just flustered. I've had a talk with her. That didn't mean a thing. But naturally she's all cut up — she already was, anyhow — and we've talked it over, and I agree with her that I've got no right to be butting in up there. Maybe I shouldn't have butted in at all, but I thought — well — it doesn't matter what I thought. So I appreciate what you've done, and it was swell of you to go up there when it was against your rule . . . so we'll just call it a flop and if you'll just tell me how much I owe you . . .''

He stopped, smiling from Wolfe to me and back again like a haberdasher's clerk trying to sell an old number with a big spiff on it.

Wolfe surveyed him. ''Sit down, Mr. Frost.''

''Well . . . just to write a check. . .'' He backed into a chair and got onto his sitter, pulling a check folder from one pocket and a fountain pen from another. ''How much?''

''Ten thousand dollars.''

He gasped and looked up. ''What!''

Wolfe nodded. ''Ten thousand. That would be about right for completing your commission; half for solving the murder of Molly Lauck and half for getting your cousin away from that hell-hole.''

''But, my dear man, you did neither. You're loony.'' His eyes narrowed. ''Don't think you're going to hold me up. Don't think —''

Wolfe snapped, ''Ten thousand dollars. And you will wait here while the check is being certified.''

''You're crazy.'' Frost was sputtering again. ''I haven't got ten thousand dollars. My show's going big, but I had a lot of debts and still have. And even if I had it — what's the idea? Blackmail? If you're that kind —''

''Please, Mr. Frost. I beg you. May I speak?''

Llewellyn glared at him.

Wolfe settled back in his chair. ''There are three things I like about you, sir, but you have several bad habits. One is your assumption that words are brickbats to be hurled at people in an effort to stun them. You must learn to stop that. Another is your childish readiness to rush into action without stopping to consider the consequences.

Before you definitely hired me to undertake an investigation you should have scrutinized the possibilities. But the point is that you hired me; and let me tell you, you burned all bridges when you goaded me into that mad sortie to Fifty-second Street. That will have to be paid for. You and I are bound by contract; I am bound to pursue a certain inquiry, and you are bound to pay my reasonable and commensurate charge. And when, for personal and peculiar reasons, you grow to dislike the contract, what do you do? You come to my office and try to knock me out of my chair by propelling words like 'blackmail' at me! Pfui! The insolence of a spoiled child!''

He poured beer, and drank. Llewellyn Frost watched him. I, after getting it into my notebook, nodded my head at him in encouraging approval of one of his better efforts.

The client finally spoke. ''But look here, Mr. Wolfe. I didn't agree to let you go up there and . . . that is . . . I didn't have any idea you were going. . ." He stopped on that, and gave it up. "I'm not denying the contract. I didn't come here and start throwing brickbats. I just asked, if we call it off now, how much do I owe you?"

"And I told you."

"But I haven't got ten thousand dollars, not this minute. I think I could have it in a week. But even if I did, my God, just for a couple of hours' work —"

"It is not the work." Wolfe wiggled a finger at him. "It is simply that I will not permit my self-conceit to be bruised by the sort of handling you are trying to give it. It is true that I hire out my abilities for money, but I assure you that I am not to be regarded as a mere peddler of gewgaws or tricks. I am an artist or nothing. Would you commission Matisse to do a painting, and, when he had scribbled his first rough sketch, snatch it from him and crumple it up and tell him, 'That's enough, how much do I owe you?' No, you wouldn't do that. You think the comparison is fanciful? I don't. Every artist has his own conceit. I have mine. I know you are young, and your training has left vacant lots in your brain; you don't realize how offensively you have acted.''

''For God's sake.'' The client sat back. ''Well.'' He looked at me as if I might suggest something, and then back at Wolfe. He spread out his hands, palms up. ''All right, you're an artist. You're it. I've told you, I haven't got ten thousand dollars. How about a check dated a week from today?''

Wolfe shook his head. ''You could stop payment. I don't trust you; you are incensed; the flame of fear and resentment is burning in you. Besides, you should get more for your money, and I should do more to earn it. The only sensible course —''

The ring of the telephone interrupted him. I swung around to my desk and got it. I acknowedged my identity to a gruff male inquiry, waited a minute, and heard the familiar tones of another male voice. What it said induced a grin.

I turned to Wolfe: ''Inspector Cramer

says that one of his men saw you up at McNair's place this morning, and nearly died of the shock. So did he when he heard it. He says it would be a pleasure to discuss the case with you a while on the telephone."

"Not for me. I am engaged."

I returned to the wire and had more talk. Cramer was as amiable as a guy stopping you on a lonely hill because he's out of gas. I turned to Wolfe again:

"He'd like to stop in at six o'clock to smoke a cigar. He says, to compare notes. He means S O S."

Wolfe nodded.

I told Cramer sure, come ahead, and rang off.

The client had stood up. He looked back and forth from me to Wolfe, and said with no belligerence at all, "Was that Inspector Cramer? He — he's coming here?"

"Yeah, a little later." I answered because Wolfe had leaned back and closed his eyes. "He often drops around for a friendly chat when he has a case so easy it bores him."

"But he . . . I . . ." Llewellyn was groggy. He straightened up. "Listen, goddam it. I want to use that phone."

"Help yourself. Take my chair."

I vacated and he moved in. He started dialing without having to look up the number. He was jerky about it, but seemed to know what he was doing. I stood and listened.

"Hello, hello! That you, Styce? This is Lew Frost. Is my father still there? Try Mr. McNair's office. Yes, please. . . . Hello, Dad? Lew . . . No. . . . No, wait a minute. Is Aunt Callie still there? Waiting for me? Yeah, I know . . . No, listen, I'm talking from Nero Wolfe's office, 918 West 35th Street. I want you and Aunt Callie to come down here right away. . . . There's no use explaining on the phone, you'll have to come. . . . I can't explain that . . . Well, bring her anyway . . . Now, Dad, I'm doing the best I can. . . . Right. You can make it in ten minutes . . . No, it's a private house. . . ."

Wolfe's eyes were closed.

4

That conference was a lulu. On several occasions I have run through pages of my notebook where I took it down, just for the entertainment. Dudley Frost was one of the very few people who have sat in that office and talked Nero Wolfe to a frazzle. Of course, he did it more by volume than by vigor, but he did it.

It was after three when they got there. Fritz ushered them in. Calida Frost, Helen's mother, Lew's Aunt Callie — though I suppose it would be more genteel to introduce her as Mrs. Edwin Frost, since I never got to be cronies with her — she came first, and sure enough, she was the medium-sized woman with the straight back and proud mouth. She was good-looking and well made, with deep but direct eyes of an off color, something like the reddish brown of dark beer, and you wouldn't have thought she was old enough to be the mother of a grownup goddess. Dudley Frost, Lew's father, weighed two hundred pounds, from size rather than fat. He had gray hair and a trimmed gray moustache. Some rude collision had pushed his nose slightly off center, but only a close observer like me would have noticed it. He had on a beautiful gray pin-stripe suit and sported a red flower in his lapel.

Llewellyn went to the office door and brought them across and introduced them. Dudley Frost rumbled at Wolfe, "How do you do." He gave me one too. "How do you do." I was getting chairs under them. He turned to our client: "What's all this, now? What's the trouble, son? Look out, Calida, your bag's going to fall. What's up here, Mr. Wolfe? I was hoping to get in some bridge this afternoon. What's the difficulty? My son has explained to me — and to Mrs. Frost — my sister-in-law — we thought it best for him to come straight down here —"

Llewellyn blurted at him, "Mr. Wolfe wants ten thousand dollars."

He cackled. "God bless me, so do I. Though I've seen the time — but that's past." He gazed at Wolfe and in a change of pace ran all his words together: "What do you want ten thousand dollars for, Mr. Wolfe?"

Wolfe looked grim, seeing already that he was up against it. He said in one of his deeper tones, "To deposit in my bank account."

"Ha! Good. Damn good and I asked for it. Strictly speaking, that was the only proper reply to my question. I should have said, let me see, for what reason do you expect to get ten thousand dollars from anyone, and from whom do you expect it? I hope not from me, for I haven't got it. My son has explained to us that he engaged you tenta — tentatively for a certain kind of job in a fit of foolishness. My son is a donkey, but surely you don't expect him to give you ten thousand dollars merely because he's a donkey? I hope not, for he hasn't

got it either. Nor has my sister-in-law —
have you, Calida? What do you think,
Calida? Shall I go on with this? Do you
think I'm getting anywhere?''

Mrs. Edwin Frost was looking at
Wolfe, and didn't bother to turn to her
brother-in-law. She said in a low
pleasant tone, ''I think the most
important thing is to explain to Mr.
Wolfe that he jumped to a wrong
conclusion about what Helen said.'' She
smiled at Wolfe. ''My daughter Helen.
But first, since Lew thought it necessary
for us to come down here, perhaps we
should hear what Mr. Wolfe has to
say.''

Wolfe aimed his half-shut eyes at her.
''Very little, madam. Your nephew
commissioned me to perform an inquiry,
and persuaded me to take an
unprecedented step which was highly
distasteful to me. I no sooner began it
than he informed me it was a flop and
asked me how much he owed me. I told
him, and on account of the unusual
circumstances demanded immediate cash
payment. In a panic, he telephoned

his father."

Her brow was wrinkled. "You asked for ten thousand dollars?"

Wolfe inclined his head, and raised it.

"But, Mr. Wolfe." She hesitated. "Of course I am not familiar with your business" — she smiled at him — "or is it a profession? But surely that is a remarkable sum. Is that your usual rate?"

"Now see here." Dudley Frost had been squirming in his chair. "After all, this thing is simple. There are just certain points. In the first place, the thing was purely tentative. It must have been tentative, because how could Mr. Wolfe tell what he might or might not be able to find out until he had gone up there and looked things over? In the second place, figure Mr. Wolfe's time at twenty dollars an hour, and Lew owes him forty dollars. I've paid good lawyers less than that. In the third place, there's no sense in talking about ten thousand dollars, because we haven't got it." He leaned forward and put a paw on the desk. "That's being frank with you, Mr.

70

Wolfe. My sister-in-law hasn't got a cent, no one knows that better than I do. Her daughter — my niece — has got all that's left of my father's fortune. We're a pauper family, except for Helen. My son here seems to think he has got something started, but he has thought that before. I doubt if you could collect, but of course the only way to settle that is a lawsuit. Then it would drag along, and eventually you'd compromise on it —"

Our client had called at him several times — "Dad! . . . Dad!" in an effort to stop him, but with no success. Now Llewellyn reached across and gripped his father's knee. "Listen to me a minute, will you? If you'd give me a chance — Mr. Wolfe isn't letting it drag along! Inspector Cramer is coming here at six o'clock to compare notes with him. About this."

"Well? You don't need to crush my leg to a pulp. Who the deuce is Inspector Cramer?"

"You know very well who he is. Head of the Homicide Bureau."

"Oh, that chap. How do you know he's coming here? Who said he was?"

"He telephoned. Just before I phoned you. That's why I asked you and Aunt Callie to come down here."

I saw the glint in Dudley Frost's eye, as swift as it was, and wondered if Wolfe caught it too. It disappeared as fast as it came. He asked his son, "Who talked to Inspector Cramer? You?"

I put in, brusque, "No. Me."

"Ah." Dudley Frost smiled at me broadly, with understanding; he transferred it to Wolfe, and then back to me again. "You seem to have gone to a good deal of trouble around here. Of course I can see that that was the best way to get your threat in, to arrange for a call with my son in your office. But the point is —"

Wolfe snapped, "Put him out, Archie."

I laid the pencil and notebook on the desk and got up. Llewellyn arose and stood like a pigeon. I noticed that all his aunt did was lift one brow a little.

Dudley Frost laughed. "Now, Mr.

Wolfe. Sit down boys." He goggled at Wolfe. "God bless me, I don't blame you for trying to make an impression. Quite a natural —"

"Mr. Frost." Wolfe wiggled a finger. "Your suggestion that I need to fake a phone call to impress your son is highly offensive. Retract it, or go."

Frost laughed again. "Well, let's say you did it to impress me."

"That, sir, is worse."

"Then my sister-in-law. Are you impressed, Calida? I must admit I am. That is what it looks like. Mr. Wolfe wants ten thousand dollars. If he doesn't get it he intends to see Inspector Cramer — where and when doesn't matter — and tell him that Helen has said she saw that box of candy before Molly Lauck did. Of course Helen didn't tell him that, but that won't keep the police from tormenting her, and possibly the rest of us, and it might even get into the papers. In my position as the trustee of Helen's property, my responsibility is as great as yours, Calida, though she is your daughter." He turned to goggle at

73

his son. "It's your fault, Lew. Absolutely. You offered this man Wolfe his opportunity. Haven't you time and time again —"

Wolfe leaned far forward in his chair and reached until the tip of his finger hovered delicately within an inch of the brown tweed of Mrs. Frost's coat. He appealed to her: "Please. Stop him."

She shrugged her shoulders. Her brother-in-law was going right on. Then abruptly she rose from her chair, stepped around behind the others, and approached me. She came close enough to ask quietly, "Have you any good Irish whiskey?"

"Sure," I said. "Is that it?"

She nodded. "Straight. Double. With plain water."

I went to the cabinet and found the bottle of Old Corcoran. I made it plenty double, got a glass of water, put them on a tray stand, and took it over and deposited it beside the orator's chair. He looked at it and then at me.

"What the deuce is it? What? Where's the bottle?" He lifted it to his off-center nose and sniffed. ''Oh! Well.'' His eyes circled the group. ''Won't anyone join me? Calida? Lew?'' He sniffed the Irish again. ''No? To the Frosts, dead and alive, God bless 'em!'' He neither sipped it nor tossed it off, but drank it like milk. He lifted the glass of water and took a dainty sip, about half a teaspoonful, put it down again, leaned back in his chair and thoughtfully caressed his moustache with the tip of his finger. Wolfe was watching him like a hawk.

Mrs. Frost asked quietly, ''What is that about Inspector Cramer?''

Wolfe shifted to her. ''Nothing, madam, beyond what your nephew has told you.''

''He is coming here to consult with you?''

''So he said.''

''Regarding the . . . the death of Miss Lauck?''

''So he said.''

''Isn't that . . .'' She hesitated. ''Is it usual for you to confer with the police about the affairs of your clients?''

"It is usual for me to confer with anyone who might have useful information." Wolfe glanced at the clock. "Let's see if we can't cut across, Mrs. Frost. It is ten minutes to four. I permit nothing to interfere with my custom of spending the hours from four to six with my plants upstairs. As your brother-in-law said with amazing coherence, this thing is simple. I do not deliver an ultimatum to Mr. Llewellyn Frost, I merely offer him an alternative. Either he can pay me at once the amount I would have charged him for completing his commission — he knew before he came here that I ask high fees for my services — and dismiss me, or he can expect me to pursue the investigation to a conclusion and send him a bill. Of course it will be much more difficult for me if his own family tries to obstruct —"

Mrs. Frost shook her head. "We have no wish to obstruct," she said gently. "But it is apparent that you have misconstrued a remark my daughter Helen made while you were questioning her, and we . . . naturally, we are concerned about that. And then . . . if you are about to confer with the police, surely it would be desirable for you to understand. . ."

"I understand, Mrs. Frost." Wolfe glanced at the clock. "You would like to be assured that I shall not inform Inspector Cramer of my misconstruction of your daughter's remark. I'm sorry, I can't commit myself on that, unless I am either dismissed from the case now with payment in full, or am assured by Mr. Llewellyn Frost — and, under the circumstances, by you and your brother-in-law also — that I am to continue the investigation for which I was engaged. I may add, you people are quite unreasonably alarmed, which is to be expected with persons of your station in society. It is highly unlikely that your daughter has any guilty connection with the murder of Miss Lauck; and if by chance she possesses an important bit of information which discretion has caused her to conceal, the sooner she discloses it the better, before the police do somehow get wind of it.''

Mrs. Frost was frowning. ''My daughter has no information whatever.''

''Without offense — I would need to ask her about that myself.''

''And you . . . wish to be permitted to continue. If you are not, you intend to tell Inspector Cramer —''

''I have not said what I intend.''

''But you wish to continue.''

Wolfe nodded. ''Either that, or my fee now.''

''Listen, Calida. I've been sitting here thinking.'' It was Dudley Frost. He sat up straight. I saw Wolfe get his hands on the arms of his chair. Frost was going on: ''Why don't we get Helen down here? This man Wolfe is throwing a bluff. If we're not careful we'll find ourselves coughing up ten thousand dollars of Helen's money, and since I'm responsible for it, it's up to me to prevent it. Lew says he'll have it next week, but I've heard that before. A trustee is under the most sacred obligation to preserve the property under his care, and it couldn't be paid out of surplus income because you don't leave any surplus. The only way is to call this fellow's bluff —''

I was about ready to go to the cabinet for some more Irish, since apparently the previous serving had all been assimilated, when I saw it wouldn't be necessary. Wolfe shoved back his chair and got up, moved around and stopped in front of Llewellyn, and spoke loud enough to penetrate the Dudley Frost noise:

''I must go. Thank God. You can tell Mr. Goodwin your decision.'' He started his progress to the door, and didn't halt when Dudley Frost called at him:

''Now here! You can't run away like that! All right, all right, sir! All right!'' His target gone, he turned to his sister-in-law: ''Didn't I say, Calida, we'd call his bluff? See that? All it needs in a case like this —''

Mrs. Frost hadn't bothered to turn in her chair to witness Wolfe's departure. Llewellyn had reached across for another grip on his father's knee and was expostulating: ''Now, Dad, cut it out —

now listen a minute —''

I stood up and said, ''If you folks want to talk this over, I'll leave you alone a while.''

Mrs. Frost shook her head. ''Thank you, I don't believe it will be necessary.'' She turned to her nephew and sounded crisp: ''Lew, you started this. It looks as if you'll have to continue it.''

Llewellyn answered her, and his father joined in, but I paid no attention as I got at my desk and stuck a sheet of paper in the typewriter. I dated it at the top and tapped it off.

TO NERO WOLFE:
Please continue until further notice the investigation into the murder of Molly Lauck for which I engaged you yesterday, Monday, March 30, 1936.

I whirled it out of the machine, laid it on a corner of Wolfe's desk, and handed Llewellyn my pen. He bent over the paper to read it. His father jumped up and pulled at him.

"Don't sign that! What is it? Let me see it! Don't sign anything at all —"

Llewellyn surrendered it to him, and he read it through twice, with a frown. Mrs. Frost stretched out a hand for it, and ran over it at a glance. She looked at me.

"I don't believe my nephew will have to sign anything. . ."

"I believe he will." I was about as fed up as Wolfe had been. "One thing you people don't seem to realize, if Mr. Wolfe should feel himself relieved of his obligation to his client and tells Inspector Cramer his angle on that break of Miss Frost's, there won't be any argument about it. When Cramer has been working on a popular murder case for a week without getting anywhere, he gets so tough he swallows cigars whole. Of course he won't use a piece of hose on Miss Frost, but he'll have her brought to headquarters and snarl at her all night. You wouldn't want —"

"All right." Dudley Frost had his frown on me. "My son is willing for

Wolfe to continue. I've thought all along that's the best way to handle it. But he won't sign this. He won't sign anything —"

"Yes, he will." I took the paper from Calida Frost and put it on the desk again. "What do you think?" I threw up my hands. "Holy heaven! You're three and I'm one. That's no good in case of bad memories. What is there to it, anyhow? It says 'until further notice.' Mr. Wolfe said you could tell me your decision. Well, I've got to have a record of it or so help me, I'll have a talk with Inspector Cramer myself."

Lew Frost looked at his aunt and his father, and then at me. "It certainly is one sweet mess." He grimaced in disgust. "If I had ten thousand dollars this minute, I swear to God. . ."

I said, "Look out, that pen drips sometimes. Go ahead and sign it."

While the other two frowned at him, he bent over the paper and scrawled his name.

5

"I had a notion to call in a notary and make Stebbins swear to an affidavit." Inspector Cramer chewed on his cigar some more. "Nero Wolfe a mile away from home in broad daylight and in his right mind? Then it must be a raid on the United States Treasury and we'll have to call out the army and declare martial law."

It was a quarter past six. Wolfe was back in the office again, fairly placid after two hours with Horstmann among the plants, and was on his second bottle of beer. I was comfortable, with my feet up on the edge of the bottom drawer pulled out, and my notebook on my knees.

Wolfe, leaning back in his chair with his fingers twined at the peak of his middle, nodded grimly. "I don't wonder, sir. Some day I'll explain it to you. Just now the memory of it is too vivid; I'd rather not discuss it."

"Okay. What I thought, maybe you're not eccentric any more."

"Certainly I'm eccentric. Who isn't?"

"God knows I'm not." Cramer took his cigar from his mouth and looked at it and put it back again. "I'm too damn dumb to be eccentric. Take this Molly Lauck business, for instance. In eight days of intense effort, what do you think I've found out? Ask me." He leaned forward. "I've found out Molly Lauck's dead! No doubt about it! I screwed that out of the Medical Examiner." He leaned back again and made a face of disgust at both of us. "By God, I'm a whirlwind. Now that I've emptied the bag for you, how about you doing the same for me? Then you'll have your fee, which is what you want, and I'll have an excuse for keeping my job, which is what I need."

Wolfe shook his head. "Nothing, Mr. Cramer. I am not even aware Miss

Lauck is dead, except by hearsay. I have not seen the Medical Examiner.''

''Oh, come on.'' Cramer removed his cigar. ''Who hired you?''

''Mr. Llewellyn Frost.''

''That one, eh?'' Cramer grunted. ''To keep somebody clear?''

''No. To solve the murder.''

''You don't say. How long did it take you?''

Wolfe got himself forward to pour beer, and drank. Cramer was going on: ''What got Lew Frost so worked up about it? I don't get it. It wasn't him that the Lauck girl was after, it was that Frenchman, Perren Gebert. Why is Lew Frost so anxious to spend good dough for a hunk of truth and justice?''

''I couldn't say.'' Wolfe wiped his lips. ''As a matter of fact, there is nothing whatever I can tell you. I haven't the faintest notion —''

''You mean to say you went clear to 52nd Street just for the exercise?''

''No. God forbid. But I have no scrap of information, or surmise, for you regarding Miss Lauck's death.''

"Well." Cramer rubbed a palm on his knee. "Of course I know that the fact you've got nothing for me doesn't prove you have nothing for yourself. You going on with it?"

"I am."

"You're not committed to Lew Frost to dig holes for anybody?"

"If I understand you — I think I do — I am not."

Cramer stared at his worn-out cigar for a minute, then reached out and put it in the ashtray and felt in his pocket for a new one. He bit off the end and got the shreds off his tongue, socked his teeth into it again, and lit it. He puffed a thick cloud around him, got a new grip with his teeth, and settled back.

He said, "As conceited as you are, Wolfe, you told me once that I am better equipped to handle nine murder cases out of ten than you are."

"Did I?"

"Yeah. So I've been keeping count, and this Lauck case is the tenth since that rubber band guy, old man Perry. It's your turn again, so I'm glad you're already in it without me having to shove you. I know; you don't like to tell people things, not even Goodwin here. But since you've been up there, you might be willing to admit that you know how it happened. I understand that you've talked with McNair and the two girls who saw her eat it."

Wolfe nodded. "I've heard the obvious details."

"Okay. Obvious is right. I've gone over it ten times with those two. I've had sessions with everybody in the place. I've had twenty men out chasing after everyone who was there at the fashion show that day, and I've seen a couple of dozen of them myself. I've had half the force checking up all over town on sales of two-pound boxes of Bailey's Royal Medley during the past month, and the other half trying to trace purchases of potassium cyanide. I've sent two men out to Darby, Ohio, where Molly Lauck's parents live. I've had shadows on ten or twelve people where it looked like there was a chance of a tie-up."

"You see," Wolfe murmured, "as I said, you are better equipped."

"Go to hell. I use what I've got, and you know damn well I'm a good cop. But after these eight days, I don't even know for sure whether Molly Lauck was killed by poison that was intended for someone else. What if the Frost girl and the Mitchell girl did it together? You couldn't beat it for a set-up, and maybe they're that clever. Knowing Molly Lauck liked to play jokes, maybe they planted it for her to swipe, or maybe they just gave it to her and then told their story. But why? That's another item, I can't find anyone who had any reason at all to want to kill her. It seems she was mellow in the pump about this Perren Gebert and he couldn't see her, but there's no evidence that she was making herself a nuisance to him."

Wolfe murmured, "Mellow where?"

I put in, "Okay, boss. Soft-hearted."

"Gebert was there that day, too," Cramer went on, "but I can't get anywhere with him on that. There hasn't been another single nibble on motive, *if* the stuff was intended for Molly Lauck. In my opinion, it wasn't. It looks like she really did swipe it. And the minute you take that theory, what have you got? You've got the ocean. There were over a hundred people there that day, and it might have been intended for any one of them, and any of them might have brought it. You can see what a swell lay-out that is. We've traced over three hundred sales of two-pound boxes of Bailey's Royal Medley, and among that bunch of humans that was there at the show we've uncovered enough grudges and jealousies and bad blood and billiousness to account for twenty murders. What do we do with it now? We file it.''

He stopped and chewed savagely on his cigar. I grinned at him: ''Did you come here to inspect our filing system, Inspector? It's a beaut.''

He growled at me, ''Who asked you anything? I came here because I'm licked. What do you think of that? Did you ever hear me say that before? And no one else.'' He turned to Wolfe.

"When I heard you were up there today, of course I didn't know for who or what, but I thought to myself, now the fur's going to fly. Then I thought I might as well drop in and you might give me a piece as a souvenir. I'll take anything I can get. This is one of those cases that can't cool off, because the damn newspapers keep the heat turned on indefinitely, and I don't mean only the tabloids. Molly Lauck was young and beautiful. Half of the dames that were there at the show that day are in the Social Register. H. R. Cragg was there himself, with his wife, and so on. The two girls that saw her die are also young and beautiful. They won't let it cool off, and every time I go into the Commissioner's office he beats the arm of his chair. You've seen him do that right here in your own office."

Wolfe nodded. "Mr. Hombert is a disagreeable noise. I'm sorry I have nothing for you, Mr. Cramer, I really am."

"Yeah, I am too. But you can do this, anyhow: give me a push. Even if it's in the wrong direction and you know it.''

''Well . . . let's see.'' Wolfe leaned back with his eyes half closed. ''You are blocked on motive. You can find none as to Miss Lauck, and too many in other directions. You can't trace the purchase either of the candy or the poison. In fact, you have traced or found nothing whatever, and you are without a starting-point. But you do really have one; have you used it?''

Cramer stared. ''Have I used what?''

''The one thing that is indubitably connected with the murder. The box of candy. What have you done about that?''

''I've had it analyzed, of course.''

''Tell me about it.''

Cramer tapped ashes into the tray. ''There's not much to tell. It was a two-pound box that's on sale pretty well all over town, at druggists and branch stores, put up by Bailey of Philadelphia, selling at a dollar sixty. They call it Royal Medley, and there's a mixture in it, fruits, nuts, chocolates and so on. Before I turned it over to the chemist I got Bailey's factory on the phone and asked if all Royal Medley boxes were uniform. They said yes, they were packed strictly to a list, and they read the list to me. Then for a check I sent out for a couple of boxes of Royal Medley and spread them out and compared them with the list. Okay. By doing the same with the box Molly Lauck ate from, I found that three pieces were gone from it: candied pineapple, a candied plum, and a Jordan almond. That agreed with the Mitchell girl's story.''

Wolfe nodded. ''Fruits, nuts, chocolates — were there any caramels?''

''Caramels?'' Cramer stared at him. ''Why caramels?''

''No reason. I used to like them.''

Cramer grunted. ''Don't try to kid me. Anyhow, there aren't any caramels in a Bailey's Royal Medley. That's too bad, huh?''

''Perhaps. It certainly decreases the interest, for me. By the way, these details regarding the candy — have they been published? Has anyone been told?''

"No. I'm telling you. I hope you can keep a secret. It's the only one we've got."

"Excellent. And the chemist?"

"Sure, excellent, and what has it got me? The chemist found that there was nothing wrong with any of the candy left in the box, except four Jordan almonds in the top layer. The top layer of a Royal Medley box has five Jordan almonds in it, and Molly Lauck had eaten one. Each of the four had more than six grains of potassium cyanide in it."

"Indeed. Only the almonds were poisoned."

"Yeah, it's easy to see why they were picked. Potassium cyanide smells and tastes like almonds, only more so. The chemist said they would taste strong, but not enough to scare you off if you liked almonds. You know Jordan almonds? They're covered with hard candy of different colors. Holes had been bored in them, or picked in, and filled with the cyanide, and then coated over again so that you'd hardly notice it unless you looked for it.'' Cramer hunched up his shoulders and dropped them again. ''You say the box of candy was a starting-point? Well, I started, and where am I? I'm sitting here in your office telling you I'm licked, with that damn Goodwin pup there grinning at me.''

''Don't mind Mr. Goodwin. Archie, don't badger him! But, Mr. Cramer, you didn't start; you merely made the preparations for starting. It may not be too late. If, for instance. . .''

Wolfe, leaning back, closed his eyes, and I saw the almost imperceptible movement of his lips — out and in, a pause, and out and in again. Then again. . .

Cramer looked at me and lifted his brows. I nodded and told him, ''Sure, it'll be a miracle, wait and see.''

Wolfe muttered, ''Shut up, Archie.''

Cramer glared at me and I winked at him. Then we just sat. If it had gone on long I would have had to leave the room for a bust, because Cramer was funny. He sat cramped, afraid to make a movement so as not to disturb Wolfe's genius working; he wouldn't even knock the ashes off his cigar. I'll say he was licked. He kept glaring at me to show he was doing something.

Finally Wolfe stirred, opened his eyes, and spoke. "Mr. Cramer. This is just an invitation to luck. Can you meet Mr. Goodwin at nine o'clock tomorrow morning at Mr. McNair's place, and have with you five boxes of that Royal Medley?"

"Sure. Then what?"

"Well . . . try this. Your notebook, Archie?"

I flipped to a fresh page.

Three hours later, after dinner, at ten o'clock that night, I went over to Broadway and hunted up a box of Bailey's Royal Medley, and sat in the office until midnight with my desk covered with pieces of candy, memorizing a code.

6

At three minutes to nine the following morning, Wednesday, as I rolled the roadster to a stop on 52nd Street, in a nice open space evidently kept free by special police orders, I was feeling a little sorry for Nero Wolfe. He loved to stage a good scene and get an audience sitting on the edge of their chairs, and here was this one, his own idea, taking place a good mile from his plant rooms and his oversized chair. But, stepping onto the sidewalk in front of Boyden McNair Incorporated, I merely shrugged my shoulders and thought to myself, Well-a-day, you fat son-of-a-gun, you can't be a homebody and see the world too.

I walked across to the entrance, where the uniformed McNair doorman was standing alongside a chunky guy with a round red face and a hat too small for him pushed back on his forehead. As I reached for the door this latter moved to block me.

He put an arm out. "Excuse me, sir. Are you here by request? Your name, please?" He brought into view a piece of paper with a typewritten list on it.

I gazed down my nose at him. "Look here, my man. It was I who made the requests."

He squinted at me. "Yeah? Sure. The inspector says, nothing for you boys here. Beat it."

Naturally I would have been sore anyhow at being taken for a reporter, but what made it worse was that I had taken the trouble to put on my suit of quiet brown with a faint tan stripe, a light tan shirt, a green challis four-in-hand and my dark green soft-brim hat. I said to him:

"You're blind in one eye and can't see out of the other. Did you ever hear that one before? I'm Archie Goodwin of Nero Wolfe's office." I took out a card and stuck it at him.

He looked at it. ''Okay. They're expecting you upstairs.''

Inside was another dick, standing over by the elevator, and no one else around. This one I knew: Slim Foltz. We exchanged polite greetings, and I got in the elevator and went up.

Cramer had done pretty well. Chairs had been gathered from all over, and about fifty people, mostly women but a few men, were sitting there in the big room up front. There was a lot of buzz and chatter. Four or five dicks, city fellers, were in a group in a corner where the booths began. Across the room Inspector Cramer stood talking to Boyden McNair, and I walked over there.

Cramer nodded. ''Just a minute, Goodwin.'' He went on with McNair, and pretty soon turned to me. ''We got a pretty good crowd, huh? Sixty-two promised to come, and there's forty-one here. Not so bad.''

''All the employees here?''

''All but the doorman. Do we want

him?"

"Yeah, make it unanimous. Which booth?"

"Third on the left. Do you know Captain Dixon? I picked him for it."

"I used to know him." I walked down the corridor, counting three, and opened the door and went in. The room was a little bigger than the one we had used the day before. Sitting behind the table was a little squirt with a bald head and big ears and eyes like an eagle. There were pads of paper and pencils arranged neatly in front of him, and at one side was a stack of five boxes of Bailey's Royal Medley. I told him he was Captain Dixon and I was Archie Goodwin, and it was a nice morning. He looked at me by moving his eyes without disturbing his head, known as conservation of energy, and made a noise something between a hoot-owl and a bullfrog. I left him and went back to the front room.

McNair had gone around back of the crowd and found a chair. Cramer met me and said, "I don't think we'll wait for any more. They're going to get restless as it is."

"Okay, shoot." I went over and propped myself against the wall, facing the audience. They were all ages and sizes and shapes, and were about what you might expect. There are very few women who can afford to pay 300 bucks for a spring suit, and why do they have to be the kind you might as well wrap in an old piece of burlap for all the good it does? Nearly always. Among the exceptions present that morning was Mrs. Edwin Frost, who was sitting with her straight back in the front row, and with her were the two goddesses, one on each side. Llewellyn Frost and his father were directly behind them. I also noted a red-haired woman with creamy skin and eyes like stars, but later, during the test, I learned that her name was Countess von Rantz-Deichen of Prague, so I never tried to follow it up.

Cramer had faced the bunch and was telling them about it:

". . . .First I want to thank Mr.

McNair for closing his store this morning and permitting it to be used for this purpose. We appreciate his cooperation, and we realize that he is as anxious as we are to get to the bottom of this . . . this sad affair. Next I want to thank all of you for coming. It is a real pleasure and encouragement to know that there are so many good citizens ready to do their share in a . . . a sad affair like this. None of you had to come, of course. You are merely doing your duty — that is, you are helping out when it is needed. I thank you in the name of the Police Commissioner, Mr. Hombert, and the District Attorney, Mr. Skinner.''

I wanted to tell him, ''Don't stop there, what about the Mayor and the Borough Presidents and the Board of Aldermen and the Department of Plant and Structures. . .''

He was going on: ''I hope that none of you will be offended or irritated at the simple experiment we are going to try. It wasn't possible for us to explain it to each of you on the telephone, and I won't make a general explanation now. I suppose some of you will regard it as absurd, and in the case of most of you, and possibly all of you, it will be, but I hope you'll just take it and let it go at that. Then you can tell your friends how dumb the police are, and we'll all be satisfied. But I can assure you we're not doing this just for fun or to try to annoy somebody, but as a serious part of our effort to get to the bottom of this sad affair.

"Now this is all there is to it. I'm going to ask you to go one at a time down that corridor to the third door on the left. I've organized it to take as little time as possible; that's why we asked you to write your name twice, on two different pieces of paper, when you came in. Captain Dixon and Mr. Goodwin will be in that room, and I'll be there with them. We'll ask you a question, and that's all. When you come out you are requested to leave the building, or stay here by the corridor if you want to wait for someone, without speaking to those who have not yet been in the booth. Some of you, those who go in last, will have to be patient. I want to thank you again for your cooperation in this . . . this sad affair.''

Cramer took a breath of relief, wheeled, and called out toward the bunch of dicks: ''All right, Rowcliff, we might as well start with the front row.''

''Mr. Inspector!'' Cramer turned again. A woman with a big head and no shoulders had arisen in the middle of the audience and stuck her chin forward. ''I want to say, Mr. Inspector, that we are under no compulsion to answer any question you may think fit to ask. I am a member of the Better Citizens' League, and I came here to make sure that —''

Cramer put up a hand at her. ''Okay, madam. No compulsion at all —''

''Very well. It should be understood by all that citizenship has it privileges as well as its duties —''

Two or three snickered. Cramer tossed me a glance, and I joined him and followed him down the corridor and into the room. Captain Dixon didn't bother to move even his eyes this time, probably having enough of us already in his line of vision to make a good guess at our identity. Cramer grunted and sat down on one of the silk affairs against the partition.

"Now that we're ready to start," he growled, "I think it's the bunk."

Captain Dixon made a noise something between a pigeon and a sow with young. I had decided to wear out the ankles so as to see better. I removed the four top Royal Medleys from the stack and put them on the floor under the table, out of sight, and picked up the other one.

"As arranged?" I asked Cramer. "Am I to say it?"

He nodded. The door opened, and one of the dicks ushered in a middle-aged woman with a streamlined hat on the side of her head, and lips and fingernails the color of the first coat of paint they put on an iron bridge. She stopped and looked around without much curiosity. I put out a hand at her.

"The papers, please?"

She handed me the slips of paper, and I gave one to Captain Dixon and kept the other. ''Now, Mrs. Ballin, please do what I ask, naturally, as you would under ordinary circumstances, without any hesitation or nervousness —''

She smiled at me. ''I'm not nervous.''

''Good.'' I took the cover from the box and held it out to her. ''Take a piece of candy.''

Her shoulders lifted daintily, and fell. ''I very seldom eat candy.''

''We don't want you to eat it. Just take it. Please.''

She reached in without looking and snared a chocolate cream and held it up in her fingers and looked at me. I said, ''Okay. Put it back, please. That's all. Thank you. Good day, Mrs. Ballin.''

She glanced around at us, said, ''Dear me,'' in a tone of mild and friendly astonishment, and went.

I bent to the table and marked an X on a corner of her paper, and the figure 6 beneath her name. Cramer growled, ''Wolfe said three pieces.''

''Yeah. He said to use our judgment

too. In my judgment, if that dame was mixed up in anything, even Nero Wolfe would never find it out. What did you think of her, Captain?''

Dixon made a noise something between a hartebeest and a three-toed sloth. The door opened and in came a tall slender woman in a tight-fitting long black coat and a silver fox that must have had giantism. She kept her lips tight and gazed at us with deepest concentrated eyes. I took her slips and gave one to Dixon.

''Now, Miss Claymore, please do what I ask, naturally, as you would under ordinary circumstances, without any hesitation or nervousness. Will you?''

She shrank back a little, but nodded. I extended the box.

''Take a piece of candy.''

''Oh!'' she gasped. She goggled at the candy. ''That's the box. . .'' She shuddered, backed off, held her clenched fist against her mouth, and let out a fairly good shriek.

I said icily, ''Thank *you*. Good day,

madam. All right, officer.''

The dick touched her arm and turned her for the door. I observed, bending to mark her slip, ''That scream was just shop talk. That's Beth Claymore, and she's as phony on the stage as she is off. Did you see her in *The Price of Folly?*''

Cramer said calmly, ''It's a goddam joke.'' Dixon made a noise. The door opened and another woman came in.

We went through with it, and it took nearly two hours. The employees were saved till the last. What with one thing and another, some of the customers took three pieces, some two or one, and a few none at all. When the first box began to show signs of wear I began with a fresh one from the reserve. Dixon made a few more noises, but confined himself mostly to making notations on his slips, and I went ahead with mine.

There were a few ructions, but nothing serious. Helen Frost came in pale and stayed pale, and wasn't having any candy. Thelma Mitchell glared at me and took three pieces of candied fruit, with her teeth clinched on her lower lip.

Dudley Frost said it was nonsense and started an argument with Cramer and had to be suggested out by the dick. Llewellyn said nothing and made three different selections. Helen's mother picked out a thin narrow chocolate, a Jordan almond, and a gum drop, and wiped her fingers delicately on her handkerchief after she put them back. One customer that interested me because I had heard a few things about him was a bird in a morning coat with the shoulders padded. He looked about forty but might have been a little older, and had a thin nose, slick hair, and dark eyes that never stopped moving. His slip said Perren Gebert. He hesitated a second about having refreshment, then smiled to show he didn't mind humoring us, and took at random.

The employees came last, and last of all was Boyden McNair himself. After I had finished with him, Inspector Cramer stood up.

"Thank you, Mr. McNair. You've done us a big favor. We'll be out of here now in two minutes, and you can open up.''

''Did you . . . get anywhere?''
McNair was wiping his face with his
handkerchief. ''I don't know what all
this is going to do to my business. It's
terrible.'' He stuck his hand in his
pocket and pulled it out again. ''I've got
a headache. I'm going to the office and
get some aspirin. I ought to go home, or
go to a hospital. Did you . . . what kind
of a trick was this?''

''This in here?'' Cramer got out a
cigar. ''Oh, this was just psychology.
I'll let you know later if we got anything
out of it.''

''Yes. Now I've got to go out there
and see those women . . . well, let me
know.'' He turned and went.

I left with Cramer, and Captain Dixon
trailing behind. While we were leaving
the establishment, with his men to gather
up and straggling customers and the help
around, he kept himself calm and
dignified, but as soon as we were out on
the sidewalk he turned loose on me and
let me have it. I was surprised at how
bitter he was, and then, as he went on

getting warmer, I realized that he was just showing how high an opinion he had of Nero Wolfe. As soon as he gave me a chance I told him:

"Nuts, Inspector. You thought Wolfe was a magician, and just because he told us to do this someone was going to flop on their knees and claw at your pants and pull an I-done-it. Have patience. I'll go home and tell Wolfe about it, and you talk'em over with Captain Dixon — that is, if he can talk —"

Cramer grunted. "I should have had more sense. If that fat rhinoceros is kidding me, I'll make him eat his license and then he won't have any."

I had climbed in the roadster. "He's not kidding you. Wait and see. Give him a chance." I slipped in the gear and rolled away.

Little did I suspect what was waiting for me at West 35th Street. I got there about half past eleven, thinking that Wolfe would have been down from the plant rooms for half an hour and therefore I would catch him in good humor with his third bottle of beer, which was so much to the good, since I was not exactly the bearer of glad tidings. After parking in front and depositing my hat in the hall, I went to the office, and found to my surprise that it was empty. I sought the bathroom, but it was empty too. I proceeded to the kitchen to inquire of Fritz, and as soon as I crossed the threshold I stopped and my heart sank to my feet and kept on right through the floor.

Wolfe sat at the kitchen table with a pencil in his hand and sheets of paper scattered around. Fritz stood across from him, with the gleam in his eye that I knew only too well. Neither paid any attention to the noise I had made entering. Wolfe was saying:

". . . but we cannot get good peafowl. Archie could try that place on Long Island, but it is probably hopeless. A peafowl's breast flesh will not be sweet and tender and properly developed unless it is well protected from all alarms, especially from the air, to prevent nervousness, and Long Island is full of airplanes. The goose for this evening, with the stuffing as arranged, will be quite satisfactory. The kid will be ideal for tomorrow. We can phone Mr. Salzenback at once to butcher one, and Archie can drive to Garfield for it in the morning. You can proceed with the preliminaries for the sauce. Friday is a problem. If we try the peafowl we shall merely be inviting catastrophe. Squabs will do for tidbits, but the chief difficulty remains. Fritz, I'll tell you. Let us try a new tack entirely. Do you know shish-kabob? I have had it in Turkey. Marinate thin slices of tender lamb for several hours in red wine and spices. Here, I'll put it down: thyme, mace, peppercorns, garlic —''

I stood and took it in. It looked hopeless. There was no question but that it was the beginning of a major relapse. He hadn't had one for a long while, and it might last a week or more, and while that spell was on him you might as well try to talk business to a lamp post as to Nero Wolfe. When we were engaged on a case, I never liked to go out and leave him alone with Fritz, for this very reason. If only I had got home an hour earlier! It looked now as if it had gone too far to stop it. And this was one of the times when it seemed easy to guess what had brought it on: he hadn't really expected anything from the mess he had cooked up for Cramer and me, and he was covering up.

I gritted my teeth and walked over to the table. Wolfe went on talking, and Fritz didn't look at me. I said, "What's this, you going to start a restaurant?" No attention. I said, "I've got a report to make. Forty-five people ate candy out of those boxes, and they all died in agony. Cramer is dead. H. R. Cragg is dead. The goddesses are dead. I'm sick."

"Shut up, Archie. Is the car in front? Fritz will need a few things right away."

I knew if the delivery of supplies once started there wouldn't be a chance. I also knew that coaxing wouldn't do it, and bullying wouldn't do it. I was desperate, and I ran over Wolfe's weaknesses in my mind and picked one.

I butted in. "Listen. This cockeyed feast you're headed for, I know I can't stop it. I've tried that before. Okay —"

Wolfe said to Fritz, "But not the pimento. If you can find any of those yellow anguino peppers down on Sullivan Street —"

I didn't dare touch him, but I leaned down close to him. I bawled at him, "And what am I to tell Miss Frost when she comes here at two o'clock? I am empowered to make appointments, am I not? She is a lady, is she not? Of course, if common courtesy is overboard too —"

Wolfe stopped himself, pressed his lips together, and turned his head. He looked me in the eye. After a moment he asked quietly, "Who? What Miss Frost?"

"Miss Helen Frost. Daughter of Mrs. Edwin Frost, cousin of our client, Mr. Llewellyn Frost, niece of Mr. Dudley Frost. Remember?"

"I don't believe it. This is trickery. Birdlime."

"Sure." I straightened up. "This is

close to the limit. Very well. When she comes I'll tell her I exceeded my authority in venturing to make an appointment. — I won't be in for lunch, Fritz.'' I wheeled and strode out, to the office, and sat down at my desk and pulled the slips of paper from my pocket, wondering if it would work, and trying to decide what I would do if it did. I fooled with the slips pretending to arrange them, not breathing much so I could listen.

It was at least two minutes before I heard anything from the kitchen, and then it was Wolfe sliding back his chair. Next his footsteps approaching. I kept busy with the papers, and so didn't actually see him as he entered the office, crossed to his desk, and got lowered into his seat. I continued with my work.

Finally he said, in the sweet tone that made me want to kick him, ''So I am to change all my plans at the whim of a young woman who, to begin with, is a liar. Or at the least, postpone them.'' He suddenly exploded ferociously, ''Mr.

Goodwin! Are you conscious?''

I said without looking up, ''No.''

Silence. After a while I heard him sigh. ''All right, Archie.'' He had controlled himself back to his normal tone. ''Tell me about it.''

It was up to me. It was the first time I had ever stopped a relapse after it had got as far as the menu stage, but it looked as if it might turn out to be something like curing a headache by chopping off my head. I had to go through with it, and the only way that occurred to me was to take a slender thread that had dangled in front of me up at McNair's that morning, and try to sell it to Wolfe for a steel cable.

''Well,'' I said, and swiveled. ''We went and did it.''

''Go on.''

He had half-shut eyes on me. I knew he suspected me, and I wouldn't be surprised if he had my number right then. But he wasn't starting back for the kitchen.

''It was pretty close to a washout.'' I picked up the slips. ''Cramer's as sore

116

as a boil on your nose. Of course, he didn't know I was keeping track of the kind of candy they picked; he thought we were just looking for a giveaway in their actions, and naturally that was a flop. A third of them were scared and half of them were nervous and some got mad and a few were just casual. That's all there was to that. According to instructions, I watched their fingers while Cramer and Dixon looked at their faces, and put down symbols for their selections." I flipped the slips. "Seven of them took Jordan almonds. One of them took two."

Wolfe reached out and rang for beer. "And?"

"And so I put it down that way. I'll tell you. I'm not slick enough for that sort of thing. You know it and I know it. Who is? It's a waste of time to say you are, on account of inertia. Nevertheless, I am slicker than glue. Six of those people who took Jordan almonds, on account of their expressions and who they are and the way they did it — I don't think it meant anything. But the seventh one — I don't know. It's true he's going to have a nervous breakdown, he told you that himself. He was taken by surprise at the request to have a piece of candy, just as all the rest were. Cramer handled it right; he had men there to see that no one knew what was going on before they got inside the room. And Mr. Boyden McNair acted funny. When I stuck the box at him and asked him to take a piece he drew back a little, but lots of others did that. Then he pulled himself up and reached and looked in, and his fingers went straight to a Jordan almond and then jerked away, and he took a chocolate. I asked him quick to take another without giving him a chance to get it decided, and this time he touched two other pieces first and then took a Jordan almond, a white one. The third try he went straight to a gum drop and took it."

Fritz had come with beer for Wolfe and a scowl for me, and Wolfe had opened a bottle and was pouring. He murmured, "It was you who saw it, Archie. Your conclusion?"

I tossed the slips onto my desk. "My conclusion is that McNair was Jordan almond-conscious. You know, the way a workingman like me is class-conscious or a guzzler like you is beer-conscious. I'll admit it's vague, but you sent me up there to see if any of that bunch would betray an idea that Jordan almonds are different from any other candy, and either Boyden McNair did just that or I've got the soul of a male stenographer. And I don't even use all my fingers."

"Mr. McNair. Indeed." Wolfe had emptied one and was leaning back. "Miss Helen Frost, according to her cousin, our client, calls him Uncle Boyd. Did you know that I am an uncle, Archie?"

He knew perfectly well that I knew it, since I typed the monthly letters to Belgrade for him, but of course he wasn't expecting an answer. He had shut his eyes and became motionless. His brain may have been working, but so was mine; I had to figure out some plausible way of getting out of there to hop in the roadster and run up to 52nd

Street and kidnap Helen Frost. I wasn't worrying about the McNair thing. It was the one nibble I had got uptown, and I really thought there was a good chance that we might hook a fish from it; besides, I had given it to Wolfe straight and now it was up to him. But the two o'clock appointment I had mentioned, God help me. . .

I got an idea. I knew that with Wolfe's eyes shut for his genius to work, he was often beyond the reach of external stimuli. Several times I had even kicked over my wastebasket without getting a flicker from him. I sat and watched him a while, saw him breathing and that was all, and finally decided to risk it. I drew my feet in under me and lifted myself out of my chair without making it creak. I kept my eyes on Wolfe. Three short steps on the rubber tile took me to the first rug, and on that silence was a cinch. I tiptoed it, holding my breath, accelerating gradually as I approached the door. I made the threshold — a step in the hall — another —

Thunder rolled from the office behind me: "Mr. Goodwin!"

I had a notion to dash on out, snaring my hat on the fly, but an instant's reflection showed that would have been disastrous. He would have relapsed again during my absence, out of pure damn meanness. I turned and went back in.

He roared, "Where were you going?"

I tried to grin at him. "Nowhere. Just upstairs a minute."

"And why the furtive stealth?"

"I . . . why . . . egad, sir, I didn't want to disturb you."

"Indeed. You egad me, do you?" He straighted up in his chair. "Not disturb me? Ha! What else have you done but that during the past eight years? Who is it that violently disrupts any private plans which I may venture, on rare occasions, to undertake?" He wiggled a whole hand at me. "You were not going upstairs. You were going to sneak out of this house and rush through the city streets in a desperate endeavor to conceal the chicanery you practiced on

121

me. You were going to try to get Helen Frost and bring her here. Did you think I was not aware of your mendacity, there in the kitchen? Have I not told you that your powers of dissimulation are wretched? Very well. I have three things to say to you. The first is a reminder: we are to have rice fritters with black currant jam, and endive with tarragon, for lunch. The second is a piece of information: you will not have time to lunch here. The third is an instruction: you are to proceed to the McNair establishment, get Miss Frost, and have her at this office by two o'clock. Doubtless you will find opportunity to get a greasy sandwich somewhere. By the time you arrive here with Miss Frost I shall have finished with the fritters and endive.''

I said, ''Okay. I heard every word. The Frost girl has a stubborn eye. Have I got a free hand? Strangle her? Wrap her up?''

''But, Mr. Goodwin.'' It was a tone he seldom used; I would call it a sarcastic whine. ''She has an appointment here for two o'clock. Surely there should be no difficulty. If only common courtesy —''

I beat it to the hall for my hat.

7

On the way uptown in the roadster I
reflected that there was one obvious
lever to use on Helen Frost to pry her in
the direction I wanted her; and I'm a
great one for the obvious, because it
saves a lot of fiddling around. I decided
to use it.

The only parking space I could find
was a block away, and I walked from
there to the McNair entrance. The
uniformed doorman stood grinning at a
woman across the street who was trying
to feed sugar to a mounted cop's horse. I
went up to him:

''Remember me? I was here this
morning.''

Being accosted by a gentleman, he
started to straighten up to be genteel,
then recollected that I was connected

with the police, so he relaxed.

"Sure I remember. You're the one that passed out the candy."

"Right. Attention, please. I want to speak to Miss Helen Frost privately, but I don't want to make any more fuss in there. Has she gone to lunch yet?"

"No. She doesn't go until one o'clock."

"Is she inside?"

"Sure." He glanced at his watch. "She won't go for nearly half an hour."

"Okay." I nodded thanks and moseyed off. I had a notion to hunt up some oats for a gobble, but decided it would be better to stick around. I lit a cigarette and strolled to the corner of Fifth Avenue, and across the street, and back toward Madison a ways. Apparently the public was still interested in the place where the beautiful model was poisoned, for I noticed people slowing up and looking at the McNair entrance as they passed by, and now and then some stopped. The mounted cop was hanging around. I went on sauntering in the neighborhood, not getting far away.

At five minutes after one she came out, alone, and headed east. I tripped along, and crossed the street, and got behind her. A little before she got to Madison I snapped out:

"Miss Frost!"

She whirled on a dime. I took off my hat.

"Remember me? My name's Archie Goodwin. I'd like to have a few words —"

"This is outrageous!" She turned and started off.

She was quite a sketch. As independent as a hog on ice. I took a hop, skip and jump, and planted the frame square in front of her. "Listen. You're more childish even than your cousin Lew. I merely need, in performance of my duty, to ask you a couple of questions. You're on your way to get something to eat. I'm hungry and have to eat myself sooner or later. I can't invite you to lunch, because I wouldn't be allowed to put it on my expense account, but I can sit at a table with you for four minutes and then go elsewhere to eat if that is your desire. I am a self-made man, and am a roughneck but not rowdy. I graduated from high school at the age of seventeen and only a few months ago I gave two dollars to the Red Cross.''

On account of my firm aggressive talk people were looking at us, and she knew it. She said, ''I eat at Moreland's, around the corner on Madison. You can ask your questions there.''

One trick in. Moreland's was one of those dumps where they slice roast beef as thin as paper and specialize on vegetable plates. I let Helen Frost find a table, and trailed along and slid into a chair opposite her after she had sat down.

She looked at me and said, ''Well?''

I said, ''The waitress will hover. Order your lunch.''

''I can order later. What do you want?''

A sketch all right. But I stayed pleasant. ''I want to take you to 918 West 35th Street for a conversation with Nero Wolfe."

She stared at me. "That's ridiculous. What for?"

I said mildly, "We have to be there at two o'clock, so we haven't much time. Really, Miss Frost, it would be much more human if you'd get something to eat and let me do the same, while I explain. I'm not something revolting, like a radio crooner or an agent for the Liberty League."

"I . . . I'm not hungry. I can see you're funny. A month ago I would have thought you were a scream."

I nodded. "I'm a knockout." I beckoned to a waitress and consulted the card. "What will you have, Miss Frost?"

She ordered some kind of goo, and hot tea, and I favored the pork and beans, with a glass of milk.

With the waitress gone, I said, "There are lots of ways I could do this. I could scare you. Don't think I couldn't. Or I could try to persuade you that since your cousin is our client, and since Nero Wolfe is as square with a client as you would be with your twin if you had one, it's to your own interest to go and see him. But there's a better reason for your going than either of those. Ordinary decency. Whether Wolfe was right or wrong about what you said yesterday at McNair's doesn't matter. The point is that we've kept it to ourselves. You saw this morning what terms we're on with the police; they had me handling that test for them. But have they been ragging you on what you said yesterday? They have not. On the other hand, are you going to have to discuss it with someone — sooner or later? You're darned tooting you are, there's no way out of it. Who do you want to discuss it with? If you take my advice, Nero Wolfe, and the sooner the better. Don't forget that Miss Mitchell heard you say it too, and although she may be a good friend of yours —''

''Please don't talk any more.'' She was looking at her fork, which she was sliding back and forth on the tablecloth, and I saw how tight her fingers gripped it. I sat back and looked somewhere else.

The waitress came and began depositing food in front of us. Helen Frost waited until she was through, and gone, and then said more to herself than to me, "I can't eat."

"You ought to." I didn't pick up my tools. "You always ought to eat. Try it, anyhow. I've already eaten, I was only keeping you company." I fished for a dime and a nickel and laid them on the table. "My car is parked on 52nd, halfway to Park Avenue, on the downtown side. I'll expect you there at a quarter to two."

She didn't say anything. I beat it and found the waitress and got my check from her, paid at the desk, and went out. Across the street and down a little I found a drug store with a lunch counter, entered, and consumed two ham sandwiches and a couple of glasses of milk. I wondered what they would do with the beans, whether they would put them back in the pot, and thought it would be a crime to waste them. I didn't wonder much about Helen Frost, because it looked to me like a pipe, all sealed up. There wasn't anything else for her to do.

There wasn't. She came up to me at ten minutes to two, as I stood on the sidewalk alongside the roadster. I opened the door and she got in, and I climbed in and stepped on the starter.

As we rolled off I asked her, "Did you eat anything?"

She nodded. "A little. I telephoned Mrs. Lamont and told her where I'm going and said I'd be back at three o'clock."

"Uh-huh. You may make it."

I drove cocky because I felt cocky. I had her on the way and the sandwiches hadn't been greasy and it wasn't two o'clock yet; and even down in the mouth and with rings under her eyes, she was the kind of riding companion that makes it reasonable to put the top down so the public can see what you've got with you. Being a lover of beauty, I permitted myself occasional glances at her profile, and observed that her chin was even better from that angle than from the front. Of course there was an off chance that she was a murderess, but you can't have everything.

We made it at one minute past two. When I ushered her into the office there was no one there, and I left her there in a chair, fearing the worst. But it was okay. Wolfe was in the dining-room with his coffee cup emptied, doing his post-prandial beaming at space. I stood on the threshold and said:

"I trust the fritters were terrible. Miss Frost regrets being one minute late for her appointment. We got to chatting over a delicious lunch, and the time just flew."

"She's here? The devil." The beam changed to a frown as he made preparations to arise. "Don't suppose for a moment that I am beguiled. I don't really like this."

I preceded him to open the office door. He moved across to his desk more deliberately even than usual, circled around Miss Frost in her chair, and, before he lowered himself, inclined his head toward her without saying anything. She leveled her brown eyes at him, and I could see that by gum she was holding the fort and she was going to go on holding it. I got at ease in my chair with my notebook, not trying to camouflage it.

Wolfe asked her politely, ''You wished to see me, Miss Frost?''

Her eyes bulged a little. She said indignantly, ''I? You sent that man to bring me here.''

''Ah, so I did.'' Wolfe sighed. ''Now that you are here, have you anything in particular to say to me?''

She opened her mouth and shut it again, and then said simply, ''No.''

Wolfe heaved another sigh. He leaned back in his chair and made a movement to clasp his hands on his front middle, then remembered that it was too soon after lunch and let them drop on the arms of his chair. With half-shut eyes he sat comfortable, motionless.

At length he murmured at her, ''How old are you?''

''I'll be twenty-one in May.''

''Indeed. What day in May?''

"The seventh."

"I understand that you call Mr. McNair 'Uncle Boyd.' Your cousin told me that. Is he your uncle?"

"Why, no. Of course not. I just call him that."

"Have you known him a long while?"

"All my life. He is an old friend of my mother's."

"You would know his preferences then. In candy, for instance. What kind does he prefer?"

She lost color, but she was pretty good with her eyes and voice. She didn't bat a lash. "I . . . I don't know. Really. I couldn't say. . ."

"Come, Miss Frost." Wolfe kept his tone easy. "I am not asking you to divulge some esoteric secret guarded by you alone. On this sort of detail many people may be consulted — any of Mr. McNair's intimates, many of his acquaintances, the servants at his home, the shops where he buys candy if he does buy it. If, for example, he happens to prefer Jordan almonds, those persons could tell me. I happen at the moment to be consulting you. Is there any reason why you should try to conceal this point?''

''Of course not.'' She hadn't got her color back. ''I don't need to conceal anything.'' She swallowed. ''Mr. McNair does like Jordan almonds, that's perfectly true.'' Suddenly the color did appear, a spot on her cheek that showed how quick her blood was. ''But I didn't come here to talk about the kinds of candy that people like. I came here to tell you that you were entirely wrong about what I said yesterday.''

''Then you do have something in particular to say to me.''

''Certainly I have.'' She was warming up. ''That was just a trick and you know it. I didn't want my mother and my uncle to come down here, but my cousin Lew lost his head as usual, he's always getting scared about me anyhow, as if I didn't have brains enough to take care of myself. You merely tricked me into saying something — I don't know what — that gave you a chance to pretend —''

"But, Miss Frost." Wolfe had a palm up at her. "Your cousin Lew is perfectly correct. I mean, about your brains. — No, permit me! Let me save time. I won't repeat verbatim what was said yesterday; you know as well as I do. I shall merely assert that the words you said, and the way you said them, make it apodictical that you knew the contents of that particular box of candy before Miss Mitchell removed the lid."

"That isn't true! I didn't say —"

"Oh, but you did." Wolfe's tone sharpened. "Understand me. Confound it, do you think I'll squabble with a chit like you? Or do you expect your loveliness to paralyze my intelligence? — Archie. Take this on the typewriter, please. One carbon. Letter-size, headed at the top, Alternative Statements for Helen Frost."

I swiveled around and swung the machine up and got the paper in. "Shoot."

Wolfe dictated:

"1. I admit that I knew the

contents of the box of candy, and am ready to explain to Nero Wolfe how I knew, truthfully and in detail.

"2. I admit that I knew the contents. I refuse for the present to explain, but am ready to submit to questioning by Nero Wolfe on any other matters, reserving the right to withhold replies at my discretion.

"3. I admit that I knew the contents, but refuse to continue the conversation.

"4. I deny that I knew the contents."

Wolfe sat up. "Thank you, Archie. No, I'll take the carbon; the original to Miss Frost." He turned to her. "Read them over, please. — You observe the distinctions? Here's a pen; I would like you to initial one of them. One moment. First I should tell you, I am willing to accept either number one or number two. I will not accept either of the others. If you choose number three or number four, I shall have to resign the commission I have undertaken for your

cousin, and take certain steps at once.''

She wasn't a goddess any more; she was too flustered for a goddess. But it took her only a few seconds to collect enough sense to see that she was only gumming the works by fiddling with the paper. She looked level at Wolfe: ''I . . . I don't have to initial anything. Why should I initial anything?'' The spots of color appeared again. ''It's all a trick and you know it! Anybody that's clever enough can ask people questions and trick them around to some kind of an answer that sounds like —''

''Miss Frost! Please. Do you mean to stick to your absurd denial?''

''Certainly I stick to it, and there's nothing absurd about it. I can warn you, too, when my cousin Lew —''

Wolfe's head pivoted and he snapped, ''Archie. Get Mr. Cramer.''

I pulled my phone across and dialed the number. They switched me to the extension and I got the clerk and asked for Inspector Cramer. For the sake of Wolfe's cake that had to have a hot griddle right then, I was hoping he

wouldn't be out, and he wasn't. His voice boomed at me in the receiver:

"Hello! Hello, Goodwin! You got something?"

"Inspector Cramer? Hold the wire. Mr. Wolfe wants to speak to you."

I gave Wolfe a nod and he reached for his instrument. But the chit was on her feet, looking mad enought to eat nettle salad. Before lifting his receiver Wolfe said to her:

"As a courtesy, you may have a choice. Do you wish Mr. Goodwin to take you to police headquarters, or shall Mr. Cramer send for you?"

Her voice at him was a croak: "Don't . . . don't . . ." She grabbed up the pen and wrote her name under statement number two on the paper. She was so mad her hand trembled. Wolfe spoke into the phone:

"Mr. Cramer? How do you do. I was wondering if you have arrived at any conclusions from this morning . . . Indeed . . . I wouldn't say that . . . No, I haven't, but I've started a line of inquiry which may develop into something later . . . No, nothing for you now; as you know, I fancy my own discretion in these matters . . . You must leave that to me, sir . . .''

When he hung up, Helen Frost was sitting down again, looking at him with her chin up and her lips pushed together. Wolfe picked up the paper and glanced at it, handed it across to me, and settled back in his chair. He reached forward to ring for beer, and settled back again.

''So. Miss Frost, you have acknowledged that you possess information regarding an implement of murder which you refuse to disclose. I wish to remind you that I have not engaged to keep that acknowledgment confidential. For the present I shall do so; I am not committing myself beyond that. Do you know the police mind? One of its first and most constant assumptions is that any withheld knowledge regarding a crime is guilty knowledge. It is a preposterous assumption, but they hug it to their bosoms. For instance, if they knew what you have just signed, they would

proceed on the theory that you either put the poison in the candy or know who did. I shall not do that. But as a matter of form I shall ask the question: did you poison that candy?''

She was pretty good, at that. She answered in a calm voice that was only pinched a little, ''No. I didn't.''

''Do you know who did?''

''No.''

''Are you engaged to be married?''

She compressed her lips. ''That is none of your business.''

Wolfe said patiently, ''I shall have to ask you about many things which you will regard as none of my business. Really, Miss Frost, it is foolish of you to irritate me unnecessarily. The question I just asked is completely innocuous; any of your friends could probably answer it; why shouldn't you? Do you imagine this is a friendly chat we are having? By no means. It is a very one-sided affair. I am forcing you to reply to questions by threatening to turn you over to the police if you don't. Are you engaged to be married?''

She was cracking a little. Her fists were clenched in her lap, and she looked smaller, as if she had shrunk, and her eyes got so damp that finally a tear formed in the corner of each one and dripped out. Without paying any attention to them, she said to Wolfe, looking at him, ''You're a dirty fat beast. You . . . you . . .''

He nodded. ''I know. I ask questions of women only when it is unavoidable, because I abominate hysterics. Wipe your eyes.''

She didn't move. He sighed. ''Are you engaged to be married?''

Tears of rage were also in her voice. ''I am not.''

''Did you buy that diamond on your finger?''

She glanced at it involuntarily. ''No.''

''Who gave it to you?''

''Mr. McNair.''

''And the one set in your vanity case — who gave you that one?''

''Mr. McNair.''

''Astonishing. I wouldn't have supposed you cared for diamonds.''

Wolfe opened a bottle of beer and filled his glass. "You mustn't mind me, Miss Frost. I mean, my seeming inconsequence. A servant girl named Anna Fiore sat in that chair once and conversed with me for five hours. The Duchess of Rathkyn did so for most of a night. I am apt to poke into almost any corner, and I beg you to bear with me." He lifted the glass and emptied it in par. "For instance, this diamond business is curious. Do you like them?"

"I don't . . . not ordinarily."

"Is Mr. McNair fond of them? Does he make gifts of them more or less at random?"

"Not that I know of."

"And although you don't like them, you wear these out of . . . respect for Mr. McNair? Affection for an old friend?"

"I wear them because I happen to feel like it."

"Just so. You see, I know very little about Mr. McNair. Is he married?"

"As I told you, he is an old friend of my mother's. A lifelong friend. He had a daughter about my age, a month or so older, but she died when she was two years old. His wife had died before, when the baby was born. Mr. McNair is the finest man I have ever known. He is . . . he is my best friend.''

''And yet he puts diamonds on you. You must forgive my harping on the diamonds; I happen to dislike them. — Oh, yes, I meant to ask, do you know anyone else who is fond of Jordan almonds?''

''Anybody else?''

''Besides Mr. McNair.''

''No, I don't.''

Wolfe poured more beer and, leaving the foam to settle, leaned back and frowned at his victim. ''You know, Miss Frost, it is time something was said to you. In your conceit, you are assuming, for your youth and inexperience, a terrific responsibility. Molly Lauck died nine days ago, probably through bungling of someone's effort to kill another person. During all that time you have possessed knowledge which, handled with competence and dispatch, might do something much more important than wreak vengeance; it might save a life, and it is even possible that the life would be one worth saving. What do you think; isn't that responsibility pretty heavy for you? I have too much sense to try coercion. There's too much egotism and too much mule in you. But you really should consider it." He picked up his glass and drank.

She sat and watched him. Finally she said, "I have considered it. I'm not an egotist. I . . . I've considered."

Wolfe lifted his shoulders an inch and dropped them. "Very well. I understand that your father is dead. I gathered that from the statement of your uncle, Mr. Dudley Frost, that he is the trustee of your property."

She nodded. "My father died when I was only a few months old. So I've never had a father." She frowned. "That is . . ."

"Yes? That is?"

"Nothing." She shook her head. "Nothing at all."

"And what does your property consist of?"

"I inherited it from my father."

"To be sure. How much is it?"

She lifted her brows. "It is what my father left me."

"Oh, come, Miss Frost. Sizes of estates in trust are no secrets nowadays. How much are you worth?"

She shrugged. "I understand that it is something over two million dollars."

"Indeed. Is it intact?"

"Intact? Why shouldn't it be?"

"I have no idea. But don't think I am prying into affairs which your family considers too intimate for discussion with outsiders. Your uncle told me yesterday that your mother hasn't got a cent. His expression. Then your father's fortune was all left to you?"

She flushed a little. "Yes. It was. I have no brother or sister."

"And it will be turned over to you — excuse me. If you please, Archie."

It was the phone. I wheeled to my desk and got it. I recognized the quiet controlled voice before she gave her

146

name, and made my own tones restrained and dignified as she deserved. I don't like hysterics any better than Wolfe does.

I turned to Helen Frost: "Your mother would like to speak to you." I got up and held my chair for her, and she moved over to it.

"Yes, mother . . . Yes . . . No, I didn't . . . I know you said that, but under the circumstances — I can't very well tell you now . . . I couldn't ask Uncle Boyd about it because he wasn't back from lunch yet, so I just told Mrs. Lamont where I was going . . . No, mother, that's ridiculous, don't you think I'm old enough to know what I'm doing? . . . I can't do that, and I can't explain till I see you, and when I leave here I'll come straight home but I can't tell now when that will be . . . Don't worry about that, and for heaven's sake give me credit for having a little sense . . . No . . . Good-bye . . ."

She had color in her face again as she arose and returned to her seat. Wolfe had narrow eyes on her. He murmured sympathetically: "You don't like people fussing about you, do you, Miss Frost? Even your mother. I know. But you must tolerate it. Remember that physically and financially you are well worth some fuss. Mentally you are — well — in the pupa stage. I hope you don't mind my discussing you."

"It would do me no good to mind it."

"I didn't say it would. I only said I hoped you didn't. About your inheritance; I presume it will be turned over to you when you come of age on May seventh."

"I presume it will."

"That is only five weeks off. Twenty-nine, thirty-six — five weeks from tomorrow. Two million dollars. Another responsibility for you. Will you continue to work?"

"I don't know."

"Why have you been working? Not for income surely."

"Of course not. I work because I enjoy it. I felt silly not doing anything. And Uncle Boyd — Mr. McNair — it happened that there was work there I could do.''

''How long — confound it. Excuse me.''

It was the telephone again. I swiveled and picked it up and started my usual salutation, ''Hello, this is the office —''

''Hello! Hello there! I want to speak to Nero Wolfe!''

I made a face at my desk calendar; this was a voice I knew too. I turned on the aggressiveness: ''Don't bark like that. Mr. Wolfe is engaged. This is Goodwin, his confidential assistant. Who —''

''This is Mr. Dudley Frost! I don't care if he is engaged, I want to speak to him at once! Is my niece there? Let me speak to her! Let me speak to Wolfe first! He's going to be sorry —''

I roughened up: ''Listen, mister, if you don't turn off that valve a little I'll hang up on you. I mean it. Mr. Wolfe and Miss Frost are having a conversation, and I refuse to disturb them. If you want to leave a message —''

''I insist on speaking to Wolfe!''

"You C, A, N, apostrophe, T, can't. Don't be childish."

"I'll show you who's childish! You tell Wolfe — tell him that I am my niece's trustee. She is under my protection. I will not have her annoyed. I'll have Wolfe and you too arrested as nuisances! She is a minor! I'll have you prosecuted —"

"Listen, Mr. Frost. *Will* you listen? What you say is okay. Let me suggest that you have Inspector Cramer do the arresting, because he's been here often and knows the way. Furthermore, I'm going to hang up now, and if you aggravate me by keeping this phone ringing, I'll hunt you up and straighten your nose for you. I mean that with all my heart."

I cradled the instrument, picked up my notebook and turned and said curtly, "More fuss."

Helen Frost said in a strained voice, because she didn't like to have to ask, "My cousin?"

"No. Your uncle. Your cousin comes next."

Which was truer and more imminent than I knew. Her mouth opened at me as if for another question, but she decided against it. Wolfe resumed:

"I was about to ask, how long have you been working?"

"Nearly two years." She leaned forward at him. "I'd like to ask . . . is this . . . going on indefinitely? You're just trying to provoke me . . . "

Wolfe shook his head. "I'm trying not to provoke you. I'm collecting information, possibly none of it germane, but that's my affair." He glanced at the clock. "It's a quarter past three. At four o'clock I shall ask you to accompany me to my plant rooms on the roof; you'll find the orchids diverting. I should guess we shall be finished by six. I assure you, I'm going through with this. I intend to invite Mr. McNair to call on me this evening. If he finds that inconvenient, then tomorrow. If he refuses, Mr. Goodwin will go to his place in the morning and see what can be done. By the way, I need to be sure that you will be there tomorrow. You will?"

"Of course. I'm there every — Oh! No. I won't be there. The place will be closed."

"Closed? A Thursday? April second?"

She nodded. "Yes, April second. That's why. That's the date Mr. McNair's wife died."

"Indeed. And his daughter born?"

She nodded again. "He . . . he always closes up."

"And visits the cemetery?"

"Oh, no. His wife died in Europe, in Paris. Mr. McNair is a Scotsman. He only came to this country about twelve years ago, a little after mother and I came."

"Then you spent part of your childhood in Europe?"

"Most of it. The first eight years. I was born in Paris, but my father and mother were both Americans." She tilted up her chin. "I'm an American girl."

"You look it." Fritz brought more beer, and Wolfe poured some. "And after twenty years Mr. McNair still shuts up shop on April second in memory of his wife. A steadfast man. Of course, he lost his daughter also — when she was two, I believe you said — which completed his loss. Still he goes on dressing women . . . well. Then you won't be there tomorrow.''

''No, but I'll be with Mr. McNair. I . . . do that for him. He asked it a long time ago, and mother let me, and I always do it. I'm almost exactly the same age his daughter was. Of course I don't remember her, I was too young.''

''So you spend that day with him as a vicar for his daughter.'' Wolfe shivered. ''His mourning day. Ghoulish. And he puts diamonds on you. However . . . you are aware, of course, that your cousin, Mr. Llewellyn Frost, wants you to quit your job. Aren't you?''

''Perhaps I am. But that isn't even any of my business, is it? It's his.''

''Certainly. Hence mine, since he is my client. Do you forget that he hired me?''

''I do not.'' She sounded scornful.

"But I can assure you that I am not going to discuss my cousin Lew with you. He means well. I know that."

"But you don't like the fuss." Wolfe sighed. The foam had gone from his beer, and he tipped a little more in the glass, lifted it, and drank. I sat and tapped with my pencil on my notebook and looked at Miss Frost's ankles and the hint of shapeliness ascending therefrom. I wasn't exactly bored, but I was beginning to get anxious, wondering if the relapse germ was still working on Wolfe's nerve centers. Not only was he not getting anywhere with this hard-working heiress, it didn't sound to me as if he was half trying. Remembering the exhibitions I had seen him put on with others — for instance, Nyura Pronn in the Diplomacy Club business —, I was beginning to harbor a suspicion that he was only killing time. At anything like his top form, he should have had this poor little rich girl herded into a corner long ago. But here he was . . .

I was diverted by the doorbell buzz and the sound of Fritz's footsteps in the hall going to answer it. The idea popped into my head that Mr. Dudley Frost, not liking the way I had hung up on him, might be dropping around to get his nose straightened, and in a sort of negligent way I got solider in my chair, because I knew Wolfe was in no mood to be wafted away again by that verbal cyclone, and I damn well wasn't going to pass out any more of the Old Corcoran.

But it wasn't the cyclone, it was only the breeze, his son. Our client. Fritz came in and announced him, and at Wolfe's nod went back and brought him in. He wasn't alone. He ushered in ahead of him a plump little duck about his own age, with a round pink face and quick smart eyes. Lew Frost escorted this specimen forward, then dropped it and went to his cousin.

"Helen! You shouldn't have done this —"

"Now, Lew, for heaven's sake, why did you come here? Anyway, it's your fault that I had to come." She saw the plump one. "You too, Bennie?" She looked mad and grim. "Are you armed?"

Lew Frost turned to Wolfe, looking every inch a football player. "What the hell are you trying to pull? Do you think you can get away with this kind of stuff? How would you like it if I pulled you out of that chair —"

His plump friend grasped his arm, with authority. He was snappy: "None of that, Lew. Calm down. Introduce me."

Our client controlled himself with an effort. "But, Ben . . . all right. That's Nero Wolfe." He glared at Wolfe. "This is Mr. Benjamin Leach, my attorney. Try some tricks on him."

Wolfe inclined his head. "How do you do, Mr. Leach. I don't know any tricks, Mr. Frost. Anyway, aren't you getting things a little complicated? First you hire me to do a job for you, and now, judging from your attitude, you have hired Mr. Leach to circumvent me. If you keep on with that —"

"Not to circumvent you." The lawyer sounded friendly and smooth. "You see,

Mr. Wolfe, I'm an old friend of Lew's. He's a little hot-headed. He has told me something about this business . . . the, er, unusual circumstances, and I just thought it would be all right if he and I were present at any conversations you may have with Miss Frost. In fact, it would have been quite proper if you had arranged for us to be here from the beginning.'' He smiled pleasantly. ''Isn't that so? Two of you and two of us?''

Wolfe had on a grimace. ''You speak, sir, as if we were hostile armies drawn up for battle. Of course that's natural, since bad blood is for lawyers what a bad tooth is for a dentist. I mean nothing invidious; detectives live on trouble too. But they don't stir it up where there is none — at least, I don't. I don't ask you to sit down, because I don't want you here. I fancy that on that point we shall have to consult — yes, Fritz?''

Fritz had knocked and entered, and now walked across to the desk with his company gait, bearing the pewter tray. He bent at the waist and extended it.

Wolfe picked up the card and looked at it. "Still not the right one. Tell him . . . no. Show him in."

Fritz bowed and departed. The lawyer wheeled to face the door and Llewellyn turned his head, but Miss Frost just sat. The newcomer entered, and at sight of his thin nose and slick hair and dark darting eyes I squelched a grin and muttered to myself, "Still more fuss."

I stood up. "Over here, Mr. Gebert."

Lew Frost took a step and busted out at him, "You? What the hell do you want here?"

Wolfe spoke sharply, "Mr. Frost! This is my office!"

The lawyer took hold of our client — his too, of course — and held on. Perren Gebert paid no attention to either of them. He went past them before he stopped to incline his torso in Wolfe's direction. "Mr. Wolfe? How do you do? Permit me." He turned and bowed again, at Helen Frost, with a different technique. "So there you are! How are you? You're been crying! Forgive me, I have no tact, I shouldn't have mentioned that. How are you? All right?''

''Certainly I'm all right! For heaven's sake, Perren, why did *you* come?''

''I came to take you home.'' Gebert turned and shot the dark eyes at Wolfe. ''Permit me, sir. I came to escort Miss Frost home.''

''Indeed,'' Wolfe murmured. ''Officially? Forcibly? In spite of anything?''

''Well . . .'' Gebert smiled. ''Semi-officially. How shall I say it . . . Miss Frost is almost my fiancee.''

''Perren! That isn't true! I've told you not to say that!''

''I said 'almost,' Helen.'' He raised his palms to deprecate himself. ''I put in the 'almost,' and I permit myself to say it only in hope —''

''Well, don't say it again. Why did you come?''

Gebert got in another bow. ''The truth is, your mother suggested it.''

''Oh. She did.'' Miss Frost glanced around at all her protectors. She looked plenty exasperated. ''I suppose she suggested it to you too, Lew. And

159

you, Bennie?"

"Now, Helen." The lawyer sounded persuasive. "Don't start on me. I came here because when Lew told me about it, it seemed the best thing to do. — Be quiet, Lew! It seems to me that if we just discuss this thing quietly . . ."

The telephone rang, and I got back in my chair for it. Leach went on talking, spreading oil. As soon as I learned who it was on the phone I got discreet. I pronounced no names and kept my words down. It appeared to me likely that this time it was the right one. I asked him to hold the wire a minute, and choked the transmitter, and wrote on a piece of paper, *McN wants to pay us a call,* and handed it across to Wolfe.

Wolfe glanced at it and stuck it in his pocket and said softly, "Thank you, Archie. That's more like it. Tell Mr. Brown to telephone again in fifteen minutes."

I had trouble with that. McNair was urgent and wasn't going to be put off. The others had stopped talking. I made it reasurring but firm, and finally managed it. I hung up and told Wolfe:

"Okay."

He was making preparations to arise. He shoved his chair back, got his hands on its arms for levers, and up came the mountain. He stood and distributed a glance and put on his crispest tone:

"Gentlemen. It is nearly four o'clock and I must leave you. — No, permit me. Miss Frost has kindly accepted my invitation to come to my plant rooms and see my orchids. She is . . . she and I have concluded a little agreement. I may say that I am not an ogre and I resent your silly invasion of my premises. You gentlemen are leaving now, and certainly she is free to accompany you if she chooses to do that. — Miss Frost?"

She stood up. Her lips were compressed, but she opened them to say, "I'll look at the orchids."

They all began yapping at once. I got up and prepared for traffic duty in case of a jam. Llewellyn broke loose from his lawyer and started toward her, ready to throw her behind his saddle and gallop off. She gave them a good brave stare:

"For heaven's sake, shut up! Don't you think I'm old enough to take care of myself? Lew, stop that!"

She started off with Wolfe. All they could do was take it and look foolish. The lawyer friend pulled at his little pink nose. Perren Gebert stuck his hands in his pockets and stood straight. Llewellyn strode to the door, after the orchid lovers had passed through, and all we could see was his fine strong back. The sound of the elevator door closing came from the hall, and the whirr of its ascending.

I announced, "That'll be all for the present, and I don't like scenes. They get on my nerves."

Lew Frost whirled and told me, "Go to hell."

I grinned at him. "I can't plug you, because you're our client. But you might as well beat it. I've got work to do."

The plump one said, "Come on, Lew, we'll go to my office."

Perren Gebert was already on the move. Llewellyn stood aside and glared him full of holes as he passed. Then

Leach went and nudged his friend along. I tripped by to open the front door for them; Llewellyn was continuing with remarks, but I disdained them. He and his attorney went down the stoop to the sidewalk and headed east; Gebert had climbed into a neat little convertible which he had parked back of the roadster and was stepping on the starter. I shut the door and went back in.

I switched on the house phone for the plant room and pressed the button. In about twenty seconds Wolfe answered, and I told him:

''It's quiet and peaceful down here now. No fuss at all.''

His murmur came at me. ''Good. Miss Frost is in the middle room, enjoying the orchids . . . reasonably well. When Mr. McNair phones, tell him six o'clock. If he insists on coming earlier, let him, and keep him. Let me know when he is there, and have the office door closed. She left her vanity case on my desk. Send Fritz up with it.''

''Okay.''

I switched off and settled to wait for

McNair's call, reflecting on the relative pulling power of beauty in distress and two million iron men and how it probably depended on whether you were the romantic type or not.

8

Two hours later, at six o'clock, I sat at my desk pounding the typewriter with emphasis and a burst of speed, copying off the opening pages of one of Hoehn's catalogues. The radio was turned on, loud, for the band of the Hotel Portland Surf Room. Together the radio and I made quite a din. Boyden McNair, with his right elbow on his knee and his bent head resting on the hand which covered his eyes, sat near Wolfe's desk in the dunce's chair, yclept that by me on the day that District Attorney Anderson of Westchester sat in it while Wolfe made a dunce of him.

McNair had been there nearly an hour. He had done a lot of sputtering on the phone and had refused to wait until six o'clock, and had finally appeared a little after five, done some sputtering, and then settled down because there wasn't anything else to do. He had his bottle of aspirin along in his pocket and had already washed a couple of them down, me furnishing the water and also offering phenacetin tablets as an improvement, without any sale. He wouldn't take a drink, though he certainly looked as if he needed one.

The six o'clock radio and typewriter din was for the purpose of covering any sound of voices that might come from the hall as Nero Wolfe escorted his guest, Miss Frost, from the elevator to the front door and let her out to the taxi which Fritz had ordered from the kitchen phone. Of course I couldn't hear anything either, so I kept glancing at the office door without letting my fingers stop, and at length it opened and Wolfe entered. Observing the *mise en scène,* he winked at me with his right eye and steered for his desk. He got across and desposited in his chair before the visitor knew he was there. I arose and turned off the radio and quiet descended on us.

McNair's head jerked up. He saw Wolfe, blinked, stood up and looked around.

"Where's Miss Frost?" he demanded.

Wolfe said, "I'm sorry to have kept you waiting, Mr. McNair. Miss Frost has gone home."

"What?" McNair gaped at him. "Gone home? I don't believe it. Who took her? Gebert and Lew Frost were here . . ."

"They were indeed." Wolfe wiggled a finger at him. "I entreat you, sir. This room has been filled with idiots this afternoon, and I would enjoy some sanity for a change. I am not a liar. I put Miss Frost into a cab not ten minutes ago, and she was going straight home."

"Ten minutes . . . but I was here! Right here in this chair! You knew I wanted to see her! What kind of a trick —"

"I know you wanted to see her. But I didn't want you to, and she is perfectly safe if she gets through the traffic. I do not intend that you shall see Miss Frost until I've had a talk with you. It was a

trick, yes, but I've a right to play tricks.
What about your own tricks? What about
the outright lies you have been telling
the police since the day Molly Lauck
was murdered? Well, sir? Answer me!''

McNair started twice to speak, but
didn't. He looked at Wolfe. He sat
down. He pulled his handkerchief from
his pocket and then put it back again
without using it. Sweat showed on his
forehead.

Finally he said, in a thin cool voice,
''I don't know what you're talking
about.''

''Of course you know.'' Wolfe pinned
him down with his eyes. ''I'm talking
about the box of poisoned candy. I know
how Miss Frost became aware of its
contents. I know that you have known
from the beginning, and that you have
deliberately withheld vital information
from the police in a murder case. Don't
be an idiot, Mr. McNair. I have a
statement signed by Helen Frost; there
was nothing else for her to do. If I told
the police what I know you would be
locked up. For the present I don't tell

them, because I wish to earn a fee, and if you were locked up I couldn't get at you. I pay you the compliment of assuming that you have some brains. If you poisoned that candy, I advise you to say nothing, leave here at once, and beware of me; if you didn't, talk to the point, and there will be no dodging the truth.'' Wolfe leaned back and murmured, ''I dislike ultimatums, even my own. But this has gone far enough.''

MacNair sat motionless. Then I saw a shiver in his left shoulder, a quick little spasm, and the fingers of his left hand, on the arm of his chair, began twitching. He looked down at them, and reached over with his other hand and gripped and twisted them, and the shoulder had another spasm, and I saw the muscles jerking in the side of his neck. His nerves were certainly shot. His eyes moved around and fell on the empty glass standing on the edge of Wolfe's desk, and he turned to me and asked as if it were a big favor:

''Could I have a little more water?''

I took the glass and went and filled it

and brought it back, and when he didn't lift his hand to take it I put it down on the desk again. He paid no attention to it.

He muttered aloud, but to no one in particular, "I've got to make up my own mind. I thought I had, but I didn't expect this."

Wolfe said, "If you were a clever man you'd have done that before the unexpected forced you."

McNair took out his handkerchief and this time wiped off the sweat. He said quietly, "Good God, I'm not clever. I'm the most complete fool that was ever born. I've ruined my whole life." His shoulder twitched again. "It wouldn't do any good to tell the police what you know, Mr. Wolfe. I didn't poison that candy."

Wolfe said, "Go on."

McNair nodded. "I'll go on. I don't blame Helen for telling you about it, after the way you trapped her yesterday morning. I can imagine what she was up against here today, but I don't hold that against you either. I've got beyond all

170

the ordinary resentments, they don't mean anything. You notice I'm not even trying to find out what Helen told you. I know if she told you anything she told you the truth.''

He lifted his head to get Wolfe straighter in the eye. ''I didn't poison the candy. When I went upstairs to my office about twelve o'clock that day, to get away from the crowd for a few minutes, the box was there on my desk. I opened it and looked in it, but didn't take any because I had a devil of a headache. When Helen came in a little later I offered her some, but thank God she didn't take any either, because there were no caramels in it. When I went back downstairs I left it on my desk, and Molly must have seen it there later, and took it. She . . . liked to play pranks.''

He stopped and wiped his brow again. Wolfe asked:

''What did you do with the paper and twine the box was wrapped with?''

''There wasn't any. It wasn't wrapped.''

''Who put it on your desk?''

"I don't know. Twenty-five or thirty people had been in and out of there before 11:30, looking at some Crenuit models I didn't want to show publicly."

"Who do you think put it there?"

"I haven't any idea about it."

"Who do you think might want to kill you?"

"No one would want to kill me. That's why I'm sure it was meant for someone else and was left there by mistake. Anyway, there's no more reason to suppose —"

"I'm not supposing." Wolfe sounded disgusted. "You are certainly on solid ground when you say you're not clever. But surely you're not halfwitted. Consider what you're telling me: you found the box on your desk, you have no suspicion as to who put it there, you are convinced it was not intended for you and have no idea who it was meant for, and yet you have carefully concealed from the police the fact that you saw it there. I have never heard such nonsense; a babe in arms would laugh at you." Wolfe sighed deeply. "I shall have to have beer. I imagine this will require all my patience. Will you have some beer?''

McNair ignored the invitation. He said quietly, ''I'm a Scotsman, Mr. Wolfe. I've admitted I'm a fool. In some vital ways I'm weak. But maybe you know how stubborn a weak man can be sometimes? I can be stubborn.'' He leaned forward a little and his voice got thinner. ''What I've just told you about that box of candy is what I'm going to tell until I die.''

''Indeed.'' Wolfe surveyed him. ''So that's it. But you don't seem to realize that while nothing more formidable than my patience may confront you, something more disagreeable is sure to. If I do not clear this thing up reasonably soon I shall have to tell what I know to the police; I shall owe that to Mr. Cramer, since I have accepted his cooperation. If you stick to the absurd rigamarole you have told me, they will assume you are guilty; they will torment you, they will take you to their dungeon and harass you endlessly, they may even beat you with their fists, though that is not likely with a man of your standing, they will destroy your dignity, your business, and your digestion. In the end, with luck and perseverance, they might even electrocute you. I doubt if you're fool enough to be as stubbon as all that.''

''I'm stubborn enough,'' McNair asserted. He leaned forward again. ''But look here. I'm not fool enough not to know what I'm doing. I'm tired and I'm worn out and I'm all in, but I know what I'm doing. You think you've forced me to admit something by getting Helen here and bullying her, but I would just as soon have admitted that to you anyhow. Then here's another thing. I've just practically told you that part of my story about that box isn't true, but that I'm going to stick to it. I didn't need to do that, I could have told you the story and made you think I expected you to believe it. I did it because I didn't want you to think I'm a bigger fool than I am. I wanted you to have as good an opinion of me as possible under the circumstances, because I want to ask you to do me a very important favor. I came here to see Helen, that's true, and to see how . . . how she was, but I also came to ask this favor of you. I want you to accept a legacy in my will.''

Wolfe didn't surprise easily, but that got him. He stared. It got me too; it sounded offhand, as if McNair was actually going to try to bribe Nero Wolfe to turn off the heat, and that was such a novel idea that I began to admire him. I focused my lamps on him with renewed interest.

McNair went on, ''What I want to leave you is a responsibility. A . . . a small article, and a responsibility. It's astonishing that I have to ask this of you. I've lived in New York for twelve years, and I realized the other day, when I had occasion to consider it, that I have not one friend I can trust. Oh, trust ordinarily, sure, several of them, but not trust with something vital, something more important than my life. But today at my lawyer's I had to name such a person, and I named you. That's astonishing, because I've only met you once, for a few minutes yesterday morning. But you seemed to me to be the kind of man that . . . that will be needed if I die. Last night and this morning I made some inquiries, and I think you are. It has to be a man with nerve, and one that can't be made a fool of, and he has to be honest clear through. I don't know anyone as good as that, and it had to be done today, so I decided to take a chance and name you.''

McNair slid forward in his chair and put both hands on the edge of Wolfe's desk, gripping it, and I saw the muscles in his neck moving again. ''I made provision for you to get paid for it, and it will be a fair-sized estate, my business is in good shape, and I've been careful with investments. For you it will just be another job, but for me, if I'm dead, it will be of the most vital importance. If I could only be sure . . . sure . . . Mr. Wolfe, that would let my spirit rest. I went to my lawyer's office this afternoon and made my will over, and I named you. I left you . . . this job. I should have come to you first, but I didn't want to take any chance of not having it down in black and white and signed. Of course I can't leave it that way without your consent. You've got to give it, then I'll be all right.'' His shoulder began to jerk, and he gripped the edge of the desk tighter. ''Then let it come.''

Wolfe said, ''Sit back in your chair, Mr. McNair. No? You'll work yourself into a fit. Then let what come? Death?''

''Anything.''

Wolfe shook his head. ''A bad state of mind. But apparently your mind has practically ceased to function. You are incoherent. Of course you have now made completely untenable your position in regard to the poisoned candy. Obviously —''

McNair broke in, ''I've named you. Will you do it?''

''Permit me, please.'' Wolfe wiggled a finger at him. ''Obviously you know who poisoned the candy, and you know it was meant for you. You are obsessed with fear that this unfriendly person will proceed to kill you in spite of the fatal bungling of that effort. Possibly others are in danger also; yet, instead of permitting someone with a little wit to handle the affair by giving him your confidence, you sit there and drivel and boast to me of your stubbornness. More than that, you have the gall to request me to agree to undertake a commission although I am completely ignorant of its nature and have no idea how much I shall get for it. Pfui! — No, permit me. Either all this is true, or you are yourself a murderer and are attempting so elaborate a gullery that it is no wonder you have a headache. You ask, will I do it. If you mean, will I agree to do an unknown job for an unknown wage, certainly not.''

McNair still had his hold of the edge of the desk, and kept it there while Wolfe poured beer. He said, ''That's all right. I don't mind your talking like that. I expected it. I know that's the kind of a man you are, and that's all right. I don't expect you to agree to do an unknown job. I'm going to tell you about it, that's what I came here for. But I'd feel easier . . . if you'd just say . . . you'll do it if there's nothing wrong with it . . . if you'd just say that . . ."

"Why should I?" Wolfe was impatient. "There is no great urgency; you have plenty of time; I do not dine until eight o'clock. You need not fear your nemesis is in ambush for you in this room; death will not stalk you here. Go on and tell me about it. But let me advise you: it will be taken down, and will need your signature."

"No." McNair got energetic and positive. "I don't want it written down. And I don't want this man here."

"Then I don't want to hear it." Wolfe pointed a thumb at me. "This is Mr. Goodwin, my confidential assistant. Whatever opinion you have formed of me includes him of necessity. His discretion is the twin of his valor."

McNair looked at me. "He's young. I don't know him."

"As you please." Wolfe shrugged. "I shan't try to persuade you."

"I know. You know you don't have to. You know I can't help myself, I'm in a corner. But it must not be written down."

"On that I'll concede something." Wolfe had got himself patient again. "Mr. Goodwin can record it, and then, if it is so decided, it can be destroyed."

McNair had abandoned his clutch on the desk. He looked from Wolfe to me and back again and, seeing the look in his eyes, if it hadn't been during business hours — Nero Wolfe's business hours — I would have felt sorry for him. He certainly was in no condition to put over a bargain with Nero Wolfe. He slid back on his seat and clasped his hands together, then after a moment separated them and took hold of the arms of the chair. He looked back and forth at us again.

He said abruptly, "You'll have to know about me or you wouldn't believe what I did. I was born in 1885 in Camfirth, Scotland. My folks had a little money. I wasn't much in school and was never very healthy, nothing really wrong, just craichy. I thought I could draw, and when I was twenty-two I went to Paris to study art. I loved it and worked at it, but never really did anything, just enough to keep me in Paris wasting the little money my parents had. When they died a little later my sister and I had nothing, but I'll come to that." He stopped and put his hands up to his temples and pressed and rubbed. "My head's going to bust."

"Take it easy," Wolfe murmured. "You'll feel better pretty soon. You're probably telling me something you should have told somebody years ago."

"No," McNair said bitterly. "Something that should never have happened. And I can't tell it now, not all of it, but I can tell enough. Maybe I'm really crazy, maybe I've lost my balance, maybe I'm just destroying all that I've safeguarded for so many years of suffering, I don't know. Anyhow, I can't help it, I've got to leave you the red box, and you would know then.

"Of course I knew lots of people in Paris. One I knew was an American girl named Anne Crandall, and I married her in 1913 and we had a baby girl. I lost both of them. My wife died the day the baby was born, April second, 1915, and I lost my daughter two years later." McNair stopped, looking at Wolfe, and demanded fiercely, "Did you ever have a baby daughter?"

Wolfe merely shook his head. McNair went on, "Some other people I knew were two wealthy American brothers, the Frosts, Edwin and Dudley. They were around Paris most of the time. There was also a girl there I had known all my life, in Scotland, named Calida Buchan. She was after art too, and got about as much of it as I did. Edwin Frost married her a few months after I married Anne, though it looked for a while as if his older brother Dudley was going to get her. I think he would have, if he hadn't been off drinking one night."

McNair halted and pressed at his temples again. I asked him, "Phenacetin?"

He shook his head. "These help a

little." He got the aspirin bottle from his pocket, jiggled a couple of tablets onto his palm, tossed them in his mouth, took the glass of water and gulped. He said to Wolfe, "You're right. I'm going to feel better after this is over. I've been carrying too big a load of remorse and for too many years."

Wolfe nodded. "And Dudley Frost went off drinking . . ."

"Yes. But that wasn't important. Anyway, Edwin and Calida were married. Soon after that Dudley returned to America, where his son was. His wife had died like mine, in childbirth, some six years before. I don't think he went back to France until more than three years later, when America entered the war. Edwin was dead; he had entered the British aviation corps and got killed in 1916. By that time I wasn't in Paris any more. They wouldn't take me in the army on account of my health. I didn't have any money. I had gone down to Spain with my baby daughter —"

He stopped, and I looked up from my notebook. He was bending over a little, with both hands, the fingers spread out, pressed against his belly, and his face was enough to tell you that something had suddenly happened that was a lot worse than a headache.

I heard Wolfe's voice like a whip: "Archie! Get him!"

I jumped up and across and reached for him. But I missed him, because he suddenly went into a spasm, a convulsion all over his body, and shot up out of his chair and stood there swaying.

He let out a scream: "Christ Jesus!" He put his hands, the fists doubled up, on Wolfe's desk, and tried to push himself back up straight. He screamed again, "Oh, Christ!" Then another convulsion went over him and he gasped at Wolfe: "The red box — the number — God, let me tell him!" He let out a moan that came from his guts and went down.

I had hold of him, but I let him go to the floor because he was out. I knelt by him, and saw Wolfe's shoes appear beyond him. I said, "Still breathing.

No. I don't think so. I think he's gone.''

Wolfe said, "Get Doctor Vollmer. Get Mr. Cramer. First let me have that bottle from his pocket."

As I moved for the phone I heard a mutter behind me, "I was wrong. Death did stalk him here. I'm an imbecile."

9

Late the following morning, Thursday, April 2nd, I sat at my desk and folded checks and put them in envelopes as Wolfe signed them and passed them over to me. The March bills were being paid. He had come down from the plant rooms punctually at eleven, and we were improving our time as we awaited a promised visit from Inspector Cramer.

McNair had been dead when Doc Vollmer got there from his home only a block away, and still dead when Cramer and a couple of dicks arrived. An assistant medical examiner had come and done routine, and the remains had been carted away for a post mortem. Wolfe had told Cramer everything perfectly straight, without holding out on him, but had refused his request for a typed copy of my notes on the session with McNair. The aspirin bottle, which had orginally held 50 tablets and still contained fourteen, was turned over to the inspector. Toward the end with Cramer, after eight o'clock, Wolfe got a little short with him, because it was past dinnertime. I had formerly thought that his inclination to eat when the time came in spite of hell and homicide was just another detail of his build-up for eccentricity, but it wasn't; he was just hungry. Not to mention that it was Fritz Brenner's cuisine that was waiting for him.

I had made my usual diplomatic advances to Wolfe Wednesday evening after dinner, and again this morning when he got down from the plant rooms, but all I had got was a few assorted rebuffs. I hadn't pressed him much, because I saw it was a case where a little thoughtless enthusiasm might easily project me out of bounds. He was about as touchy as I had ever seen him. A neat and complete murder had had its finale right in his own office, in front of his eyes, less than ten minutes after he had grandly assured the victim that nemesis was verboten on those premises. So I wasn't surprised he wasn't inclined to talk, and I made no effort to sink the spurs in him. All right, I thought, go ahead and be taciturn, you're in it up to your neck now anyway, and you'll have to stop treading water and head for a shore sooner or later.

Inspector Cramer arrived as I inserted ·the last check in its envelope. Fritz ushered him in. He looked busy but not too harassed; in fact, he tipped me a wink as he sat down, knocked ashes from his cigar, returned it to the corner of his mouth and started off conversationally.

''You know, Wolfe, I was just thinking on the way up here, this time I've got a brand new excuse for coming to see you. I've been here for a lot of different reasons, to try to pry something loose from you, to find out if you were haboring a suspect, to charge you with obstructing justice, and so on and so on, but this is the first time I've ever had the excuse that it's the scene of the crime. In fact, I'm sitting right on it. Wasn't he in this chair? Huh?''

I told Wolfe consolingly, ''It's all right, boss. That's just humor. The light touch.''

''I hear it.'' Wolfe was grim. ''I have merited even Mr. Cramer's humor. You may exhaust your supply, sir.'' It had eaten into him even worse than I thought.

''Oh, I've got more.'' Cramer chuckled. ''You know Lanzetta of the D.A.'s office? Hates your epidermis ever since that Fairmount business three years ago? He phoned the Commissioner this morning to warn him there was a chance you were putting over a fast one. The Commissioner told me about it, and I told him you're rapid all right, but not faster than light.'' Cramer chuckled again, removed his cigar, and slipped his briefcase from the desk onto his knees and unclasped it. He grunted. ''Well. Here's this murder. I've got to get back before lunch. You had any inspiration?''

''No.'' Wolfe remained grim. ''I've

almost had indigestion.'' He wiggled a finger at the briefcase. ''Have you papers of Mr. McNair's?''

Cramer shook his head. ''This is just a lot of junk. There may be one or two items worth something. I've followed up your line, that it's sure to be hooked up with the Frosts, on account of the way McNair started his story to you. The Frosts and this fellow Gebert are being investigated from every angle, up, down and across. But there's two other bare possibilities I don't like to lose sight of. First, suicide. Second, this woman, this Countess von Rantz-Deichen, that's been after McNair lately. There's a chance —''

''Tommyrot!'' Wolfe was explosive. ''Excuse me, Mr. Cramer. I am in no mood for fantasy. Get on.''

''Okay.'' Cramer grunted. ''Sore, huh? Okay. Fantasy. Notwithstanding, I'll leave two men on the Countess.'' He was shuffling through papers from the briefcase. ''First for the bottle of aspirin. There were fourteen tablets in it. Twelve of them were perfectly all right.

The other two consisted of potassium cyanide tablets, approximately five grains each, with a thin coating of aspirin on the outside, apparently put on as a dry dust and carefully tapped down all over. The chemist says the coating was put on skillfully and thoroughly, so there would have been no cyanide taste for the few seconds before the tablet was swallowed. There was no cyanide smell, the bitter almond smell, in the bottle, but of course it was bone dry."

Wolfe muttered, "And vet you talk of suicide."

"I said bare possibility. Okay, forget it. The preliminary on the autopsy says cyanide of potassium, but they can't tell whether the tablets he took were loaded or not, because that stuff evaporates fast as soon as it's moist. I don't suppose he's worrying much about whether it was one or two tablets, so I'm not either. Next, who put the phonies in with the aspirins? Or anyway, who had a chance to? I've had three good men on that, and they're still on it. The answer so far is, most anyone. For the past week and more McNair has been taking aspirin the way a chicken takes corn. There has been a bottle either on his desk or in a drawer all the time. There's none there now, so when he went out yesterday he must have stuck it in his pocket. Thirty-six are gone from that fifty, and if you figure he took twelve a day that would mean that bottle has been in use three days, and in that time dozens of people have been in and out of his office where the bottle was kept. Of course all the Frosts have, and this Gebert. By the way —'' Cramer thumbed to find a paper and stopped at one — ''what's a camal . . . camallot doo something in French?''

Wolfe nodded. ''*Camelot du roi*. A member of a Parisian royalist political gang.''

''Oh. Gebert used to be one. I cabled Paris last night and had one back this morning. Gebert was one of those. He has been around New York now over three years, and we're after him. The preliminary reports I've had are vague. N.V.M.S. Paris says so too.''

Wolfe lifted a brow. "N.V.M.S."

I told him, "Police gibberish. No visible means of subsistence. Bonton for bum."

Wolfe sighed. Cramer went on, "We're doing all the routine. Fingerprints on the bottle, on the drawers of McNair's desk and so on. Purchases of potassium cyanide —"

Wolfe stopped him: "I know. Pfui. Not for this murderer, Mr. Cramer. You'll have to do better than routine."

"Sure I will. Or you will." Cramer discarded his cigar and got into his pocket for a new one. "But I'm just telling you. We've discovered one or two things. For instance, yesterday afternoon McNair asked his lawyer if there was any way of finding out whether Dudley Frost, as trustee of the property of his niece, had squandered any of it, and he told the lawyer to do that in a hurry. He said that when Edwin Frost died twenty years ago he cut off his wife without a cent and left everything to his daughter Helen, and made his brother Dudley the trustee under such condition that no one, not even Helen, could demand an accounting of Dudley, and Dudley has never made any accounting. According to McNair. We're on that too. Do you get anywhere with it? If Dudley Frost is short a million or so as trustee, what good does it do him to bump off McNair?''

''I couldn't say. Will you have some beer?''

''No thanks.'' Cramer got his cigar lit and his teeth sunk in it. He puffed it just short of a conflagration. ''Well, we may get somewhere on that.'' He thumbed at the papers again. ''Next is an item that you ought to find interesting. It happens that McNair's lawyer is a guy that can be approached, within reason, and after your tip last night I was after him early this morning. He gave me that dope on Dudley Frost, and he admitted McNair made a will yesterday. In fact, after I explained to him how serious murder is, he let me see it and copy it. McNair gave it to you straight. He named you all right.''

''Without my consent.'' Wolfe was

194

pouring beer. "Mr. McNair was not my client."

Cramer grunted. "He is now. You wouldn't turn down a dead man, would you? He left a few little bequests, and the residuary estate to a sister, Isabel McNair, living in Scotland in a place called Camfirth. There's a mention of private instructions which he had given his sister regarding the estate." Cramer turned a sheet over. "Then you begin to come in. Paragraph six names you as executor, without remuneration. The next paragraph reads:

7. To Nero Wolfe, of 918 West 35th Street, New York City, I bequeath my red leather box and its contents. I have informed him where it is to be found, and the contents are to be considered as his sole property, to be used by him at his will and his discretion. I direct that any bill he may render, for a reasonable amount, for services performed by him in this connection, shall be considered a just and proper debt of my estate, which

shall be promptly paid.

"Well." Cramer coughed up smoke. "He's your client now. Or he will be as soon as this is probated."

Wolfe shook his head. "I did not consent. I offer two comments: first, note the appalling caution of the Scotch. When Mr. McNair wrote that he was in a frenzy of desperation, he was engaging me for a job so vital to him that it had to be done right or his spirit could not rest, and yet he inserted, *for a reasonable amount*." Wolfe sighed. "Obviously, that too was necessary for the repose of his spirit. Second, he has left me a pig in a poke. Where is the red leather box?"

Cramer looked straight at him and said quietly, "I wonder."

Wolfe opened his eyes for suspicion. "What do you mean, sir, by that tone? You wonder what?"

"I wonder where the red box is." Cramer upturned a palm. "Why shouldn't I? It's a hundred to one that what's in it will solve this case." He looked around, and back at Wolfe. "I don't suppose there's any chance it could be right here in this office this minute, for instance in the safe or in one of the drawers of Goodwin's desk." He turned to me. "Mind looking, son?"

I grinned at him. "I don't have to. I've got it in my shoe."

Wolfe said, "Mr. Cramer. I told you last evening how far Mr. McNair got with his tale. Do you mean to say that you have the effrontery to suspect —"

"Now listen." Cramer got louder and firmer. "Don't dump that on me. If I had any effrontery I wouldn't bother to bring it here with me, I'd just borrow some. I've seen your indignant innocence too often. I remind you of the recent occasion when I ventured to suggest that that Fox woman might be hiding in your house. I also remind you that McNair said yesterday in his will — here, I'll read it — *I have informed him where it is to be found*. Get it? Past tense. Sure, I know, you've told me everything McNair said yesterday afternoon, but where did he get that past

197

tense idea before he saw you yesterday? You saw him Tuesday, too —"

"Nonsense. Tuesday was a brief first interview —"

"All right, I've known you to get further than that at a first interview. All right, I know I'm yelling and I'm going to keep on yelling. For once I'll be damned if I'm going to stand in line out on the sidewalk until you decide to open the doors and let us in to see the show. There's no reason in God's world why you shouldn't produce that red box right now and let me have a hand in it. I'm not trying to shove you off from a fee; go to it; I'm for you. But I'm the head of the Homicide Squad of the City of New York, and I'm sick and tired of you playing Godalmighty with any evidence and any clues and any facts and any witnesses — and anything you may happen to think you need for a while — nothing doing! Not this time! Not on your life!"

Wolfe murmured mildly, "Let me know when you're through."

"I'm not going to be through."

"Yes, you are. Sooner than you think. You're playing in bad luck, Mr. Cramer. In demanding that I produce Mr. McNair's red box, you have chosen the worst possible moment for bringing up your reserves and battering down the fort. I confess that I have on occasions quibbled with you and played with double meanings, but you have never known me to tell you a direct and categorical lie. Never, sir. I tell you now that I have never seen Mr. McNair's red box, I have no idea where it is or was, and I have no knowledge whatever of its contents. So please don't yell at me like that."

Cramer was staring, with his jaw loose. Being that he was usually so masterful, he looked so remarkable with his jaw hanging that I thought it wouldn't hurt him any for me to show him how sympathetic I felt, so with my pencil in one hand and the notebook in the other, I raised them both high above my head, opened my mouth and expanded my chest, and executed a major yawn. He saw me, but he didn't throw his cigar at me, because he actually was stunned. Finally he shaped words for Wolfe:

"You mean that straight? You haven't got it?"

"I have not."

"You don't know where it is? You don't know what's in it?"

"I do not."

"Then why did he say yesterday in his will he had told you where it was?"

"He intended to. He was anticipating."

"He never told you?"

Wolfe frowned. "Confound it, sir! Leave redundancy to music and cross-examinations. I am not playing you a tune, and I don't like to be badgered."

Ash fell from Cramer's cigar to the rug. He paid no attention to it. He muttered, "I'll be damned," and sank back in his chair. I considered it a good spot for another yawn, but almost got startled into lockjaw in the middle of it when Cramer suddenly exploded at me savagely: "For God's sake fall in it, you clown!"

I expostulated with him: "Good heavens, Inspector, a fellow can't help it if he has to —"

"Shut up!" He sat and looked silly. That was about to get monotonous when he went plaintive with Wolfe: "This is a healthy smack, all right. I didn't know you had me buffaloed as bad as that. I've got so used to you having rabbits in your hat that I was taking two things for granted as a sure bet. First, that the answer to this case is in that red box. Second, that you had it or knew where it was. Now you tell me number two is out. All right, I believe you. How about number one?"

Wolfe nodded. "I would agree. A sure bet, I think, that if we had the contents of the red box we would know who tried to kill Mr. McNair a week ago Monday, and who did kill him yesterday." Wolfe compressed his lips a moment and then added, "Killed him here. In my office. In my presence."

"Yeah. Sure." Cramer poked his cigar in the tray. "For you that's what makes it a crime instead of a case." He turned abruptly to me: "Would you get my office on the phone?"

I swiveled to my desk and pulled the instrument across and dialed. I got the number, and the extension, and asked them to hold it, and vacated my chair. Cramer went over and got in it.

"Burke? Cramer. Got a pad? Put this down: red leather box, don't know size or weight or old or new. Probably not very big, because the chances are it contains only papers, documents. It belonged to Boyden McNair. One: Give ten men copies of McNair's photograph and send them to all the safe deposit vaults in town. Find any safe deposit box he had, and as soon as it's found get a court order to open it. Send Haskins to that bird at the Midtown National that's so damn cocky. Two: Phone the men that are going through McNair's apartment and his place of business and tell them about the box and the one who finds it can have a day off. Three: Start all over again with McNair's friends and acquaintances and ask if they ever saw McNair have such a box and when and where and what does it look like. Ask Collinger, McNair's lawyer, too. I was so damn sure — I didn't ask him that. Four: Send another cable to Scotland and tell them to ask McNair's sister about the box. Did an answer come to the one you sent this morning? . . . No, hardly time. Got it? . . . Good. Start it quick. I'll be down pretty soon."

He rang off. Wolfe murmured, "Ten men . . . a hundred . . . a thousand . . . Really, Mr. Cramer, with such an outfit as that, you should catch at least ten culprits for every crime committed."

"Yeah. We do." Cramer looked around. "Oh, I guess I left my hat in the hall. I'll let you know when we find the box, since it's your property. I may look into it first, just to make sure there's no bombs in it. I'd hate like the devil to see Goodwin here get hurt. You going to do any exploring?"

Wolfe shook his head. "With your army of terriers scratching at every hole? There would be no room. I'm sorry, sir, for your disappointment here; if I knew where the red box was you would be the first to hear of it. I trust that we are still brothers-in-arms? That is to say, in this present affair?"

"Absolutely. Pals."

"Good. Then I'll make one little suggestion. See that the Frosts, all of them, are acquainted with the terms of Mr. McNair's will immediately. You needn't bother about Mr. Gebert; I surmise that if the Frosts know it he soon will. You are in a better position than I am to do this without trumpets."

"Right. Anything else?"

"That's all. Except that if you do find the box I wouldn't advise you to tack its contents to your bulletin board. I imagine they will need to be handled with restraint and delicacy. The person who put those coated poison tablets in the bottle of aspirin is fairly ingenious."

"Uh-huh. Anything else?"

"Just better luck elsewhere than you have had here."

"Thanks. I'll need *that* all right."

He departed.

Wolfe rang for beer. I went to the kitchen for a glass of milk and came back to the office with it and stood by the window and started sipping. A glance at Wolfe had showed me that things were at a standstill, because he was sitting up with his eyes open, turning the pages of a Richardt folder which had come in the morning mail. I shrugged negligently. After I had finished the milk I sat at my desk and sealed the envelopes containing checks, and stamped them, went to the hall for my hat and moseyed out and down to the corner to drop them in a mailbox. When I got back again Wolfe was still having recess; he had taken a *laeliocattleya luminosa aurea* from the vase on his desk and was lifting the anthers to look at the pollinia with his glass. But at least he hadn't started on the atlas. I sat down and observed:

"It's a nice balmy spring day outdoors. April second. McNair's mourning day. You said yesterday it was ghoulish. Now he's a ghoul himself."

Wolfe muttered indifferently, "He is not a ghoul."

"Then he's inert matter."

"He is not inert matter. Unless he has been embalmed with uncommon thoroughness. The activity of decomposition is tremendous."

"All right, then he's a banquet. Anything you say. Might I inquire, have you turned the case over to Inspector Cramer? Should I go down and ask him for instructions?"

No response. I waited a decent interval, then went on, "Take this red leather box, for instance. Say Cramer finds it and opens it and learns all the things it would be fun to know, and hitches up his horse and buggy and goes and gets the murderer, *with* evidence. There would go the first half of your fee from Llewellyn. The second half is already gone, since McNair is dead and of course that heiress won't work there any more. It begins to look as if you not only had the discomfort of seeing McNair die right in front of you, you're not even going to be able to send anyone a bill for it. You've taught me to be tough in money matters. Do you realize that Doc Vollmer will charge five bucks for the call he made here yesterday? You could have him send the bill to McNair's estate, but you'd have the trouble and expense of handling it anyhow, since you're the executor without remuneration. And by the way, what about that executor stuff? Aren't you supposed to bustle around and do something?''

No response.

I said, ''And besides, Cramer hasn't really got any right to the red box at all. Legally it's yours. But if he gets hold of it he'll plunder it, don't think he won't. Then of course you could have your lawyer write him a letter —''

''Shut up, Archie.'' Wolfe put down the glass. ''You are talking twaddle. Or perhaps you aren't; do you mean business? Would you go out with your pistol and shoot all the men in Mr. Cramer's army? I see no other way to stop their search. And then find the red box yourself?''

I grinned at him condescendingly. ''I wouldn't do that, because I wouldn't have to. If I was the kind of man you are, I would just sit calmly in my chair with my eyes shut, and use psychology on it. Like you did with Paul Chapin, remember? First I would decide what the psychology of McNair was like, covering every point. Then I would say to myself, if my psychology was like that, and if I had a very important article like a red box to hide, where would I hide it? Then I would say to someone else, Archie, please go at once to such and such a place and get the red box and bring it here. That way you would get hold of it before any of Cramer's men —''

''That will do.'' Wolfe was positive but unperturbed. ''I'll tolerate the goad, Archie, only when it is needed. In the present case I don't need that, I need facts; but I refuse to waste your energies and mine in assembling a collection of them which may be completely useless once the red box is found. As for finding it, we're obviously out of that, with Cramer's terriers at every hole.'' He got a little acid. ''I choose to remind you of what my program contemplated yesterday: supervising the cooking of a goose. Not watching a man die of poison. And yours for this morning: driving to Mr. Salzenbach's place at Garfield for a freshly butchered kid. Not pestering me with inanities. And for this afternoon — yes, Fritz?''

Fritz approached. ''Mr. Llewellyn Frost to see you.''

''The devil.'' Wolfe sighed. ''Nothing can be done now. Archie, if you — no. After all, he's our client. Show him in.''

10

Apparently Llewellyn hadn't come this time, as he had the day before, to pull fat men out of chairs. Nor did he have his lawyer along. He looked a little squashed, and amenable, and his necktie was crooked. He told both of us good morning as if he was counting on our agreeing with him and was in need of that support, and even thanked Wolfe for inviting him to sit down. Then he sat and glanced from one to the other of us as if it was an open question whether he could remember what it was he had come for.

Wolfe said, "You've had a shock, Mr. Frost. So have I: Mr. McNair sat in the chair you're in now when he swallowed the poison.

Lew Frost nodded. "I know. He died

right here."

"He did indeed. They say that three grains have been known to kill a man in thirty seconds. Mr. McNair took five, or ten. He had convulsions almost immediately, and died within a minute. I offer you condolence. Though you and he were not on the best of terms, still you had known him long. Hadn't you?"

Llewellyn nodded again. "I had known him about twelve years. We . . . we weren't exactly on bad terms . . ." He halted, and considered. "well, I suppose we were. Not personal, though. I mean, I don't think we disliked each other. The fact is, it was nothing but a misunderstanding. I've learned only this morning that I was wrong in the chief thing I had against him. I thought he wanted my cousin to marry that fellow Gebert, and now I've learned that he didn't at all. He was dead against it." Llewellyn considered again. "That . . . that made me think . . . I mean, I was all wrong about this. You see, when I came to see you Monday . . . and last week too . . . I thought I knew some things. I didn't say anything about it to you, or Mr. Goodwin here when I was telling him, because I knew I was prejudiced. I didn't want to accuse anyone. I just wanted you to find out. And I want to say . . . I want to apologize. My cousin has told me she did see that box of candy, and how and where. It would have been better if she had told you all about it, I can see that. She can too. But the hell of it was I had my mind on another . . . another . . . I mean to say, I thought I knew something . . ."

"I understand, sir." Wolfe sounded impatient. "You knew that Molly Lauck was enamored of Mr. Perren Gebert. You knew that Mr. Gebert wanted to marry your cousin Helen, and you thought that Mr. McNair favored that idea. You were more than ready to suspect that the genesis of the poisoned candy was that eroto-matrimonial tangle, since you were vitally concerned in it because you wished to marry your cousin yourself."

Llewellyn stared at him. "Where did

you get that idea?'' His face began to get red, and he sputtered, ''Me marry her? You're crazy! What kind of a damn fool —''

''Please don't do that.'' Wolfe wiggled a finger at him. ''You should know that detectives do sometimes detect — at least some of them do. I don't say that you intended to marry your cousin, merely that you wanted to. I knew that early in our conversation last Monday afternoon, when you told me that she is your ortho-cousin. There was no reason why so abstruse and unusual a term should have been in the forefront of your mind, as it obviously was, unless you had been so preoccupied with the idea of marrying your cousin, and so concerned as to the custom and propriety of marriage between first cousins, that you had gone into it exhaustively. It was evident that canon law and the Levitical degrees had not been enough for you; you had even ventured into anthropology. Or possibly that had not been enough for someone else — herself, her mother, your father . . .''

213

Lew Frost blurted, his face still red, "You didn't detect that. She told you. Yesterday . . . did she tell you?"

Wolfe shook his head. "No, sir. I did detect it. Among other things. It wouldn't surprise me to know that when you called here three days ago you were fairly well convinced that either Mr. McNair or Mr. Gebert had killed Molly Lauck. Certainly you were in no condition to discriminate between nonsense and likelihood."

"I know I wasn't. But I wasn't convinced of . . . anything." Llewellyn chewed at his lip. "Now, of course, I'm up a tree. This McNair business is terrible. The newspapers have started it up all over again. The police have been after us this morning — us Frosts — as if we . . . as if we knew something about it. And of course Helen is all cut up. She wanted to go to see McNair's body this morning, and had to be told that she couldn't because they were doing a post mortem, and that was pleasant. Then she wanted to come to see you, and finally I drove her down here. I came in first because I didn't know who might be in here. She's out front in my car. May I bring her in?''

Wolfe grimaced. ''There's nothing I can do for her, at this moment. I suspect she's in no condition —''

''She wants to see you.''

Wolfe lifted his shoulders an inch, and dropped them. ''Get her.''

Lew Frost arose and strode out. I went along to manipulate the door. Parked at the curb was a gray coupe, and from it emerged Helen Frost. Llewellyn escorted her up the stoop and into the hall, and I must say she didn't bear much resemblance to a goddess. Her eyes were puffed up and her nose was blotchy and she looked sick. Her ortho-cousin led her on to the office, and I followed them in. She gave Wolfe a nod and seated herself in the dunce's chair, then looked at Llewellyn, at me, and at Wolfe, as if she wasn't sure she knew us.

She looked at the floor, and up again. ''It was right here,'' she said in a dead tone. ''Wasn't it? Right here.''

Wolfe nodded. ''Yes, Miss Frost. But

if that is what you came here for, to shudder at the spot where your best friend died, that won't help us any." He straightened up a little. "This is a detective bureau, not a nursery for morbidity. Yes, he died here. He swallowed the poison sitting in that chair; he staggered to his feet and tried to keep himself upright by putting his fists on my desk; he collapsed to the floor in a convulsion and died; if he were still there you could reach down and touch him without moving from your chair."

Helen was staring at him and not breathing; Llewellyn protested: "For God's sake, Wolfe, do you think —"

Wolfe showed him a palm. "I think I had to sit here and watch Mr. McNair being murdered in my office. — Archie. Your notebook, please. Yesterday I told Miss Frost it was time something was said to her. What did I say then? Read it."

I got the book and flipped back the pages and found it and read it out:

. . . In your conceit, you are assuming, for your youth and inexperience, a terrific responsibility. Molly Lauck died nine days ago, probably through bungling of someone's effort to kill another person. During all that time you have possessed knowledge which, handled with competence and dispatch, might do something much more important than wreak vengeance; it might save a life, and it is even possible that the life would be one worth saving. What do you —

"That will do." Wolfe turned to her. "That, mademoiselle, was a courteous and reasonable appeal. I do not often appeal to anyone like that; I am too conceited. I did appeal to you, without success. If it is painful to you to be reminded that your best friend died yesterday, in agony, on the spot now occupied by your chair, do you think it was agreeable to me to sit here and watch him do it?" He shifted abruptly to Llewellyn. "And you, sir, who engaged me to solve a problem and then proceeded to hamper me as soon as I made the first step — now you are quick on the trigger to resent it if I do not show tenderness and consideration for your cousin's remorse and grief. I know none because I have none. If I offer anything for sale in this office that is worth buying, it certainly is not a warm heart and maudlin sympathy for the distress of spoiled obtuse children." He turned to Helen. "Yesterday, in your pride, you asked for nothing and offered nothing. What information you gave was forced from you by a threat. What did you come for today? What do you want?"

Llewellyn had arisen and moved to her chair. He was holding himself in. "Come on, Helen," he entreated her. "Come on, get out of here . . ."

She reached up and touched his sleeve, and shook her head without looking at him. "Sit down, Lew," she told him. "Please. I deserve it." There was a spot of color on the cheek I could see.

"No. Come on."

She shook her head again. "I'm going to stay."

"I'm not." He shot out his chin in Wolfe's direction. "Look here, I apologized to you. All right, I owed you that. But now I want to say . . . that thing I signed here Tuesday . . . I'm giving you notice I'm done with that. I'm not paying you ten thousand dollars, because I haven't got it and you haven't earned it. I can pay a reasonable amount whenever you send a bill. The deal's off."

Wolfe nodded and murmured, "I expected that, of course. The suspicions you hired me to substantiate have evaporated. The threat of molestation of your cousin, caused by her admission that she had seen the box of candy, no longer exists. Half of your purpose is accomplished, since your cousin will not work any more — at least, not at Mr. McNair's. As for the other half, to continue the investigation of the murder of Molly Lauck would mean of necessity an inquiry into Mr. McNair's death also, and that might easily result in something highly distasteful to a Frost. That's the logic of it, for you, perfectly correct; and if I expected to collect even a fair fraction of my fee I shall probably have to sue you for it.'' He sighed, and leaned back. ''And you stampeded me to 52nd Street with that confounded letter. Good day, sir. I don't blame you; but I shall certainly send you a bill for ten thousand dollars. I know what you are thinking: that you won't be sued because I won't go to a courtroom to testify. You are correct; but I shall certainly send you a bill.''

''Go ahead. Come on, Helen.''

She didn't budge. She said quietly, ''Sit down, Lew.''

''What for? Come on! Did you hear what he said about distasteful to a Frost? Don't you see it's him that has started the police after us as if we were all a bunch of murderers? And that he started it on account of something that McNair said to him yesterday before — before it happened? Just as Dad said, and Aunt Callie too? Do you wonder they wouldn't let you come down here unless I came along? I'm not saying McNair told him any lies, I'm just saying —"

"Lew! Stop it!" She wasn't loud, but determined. She put a hand on his sleeve again. "Listen, Lew. You know very well that all the misunderstandings we've ever had have been about Uncle Boyd. Don't you think we might stop having them, now that he's dead? I told Mr. Wolfe yesterday . . . he . . . he was the finest man I have ever known . . . I don't expect you to agree with that . . . but it's true. I know he didn't like you, and I honestly thought that was the only thing he was wrong about." She stood up and put a hand on each of his arms. "You're a fine man, too, Lew. You have lots of fine things in you. But I loved Uncle Boyd." She shut her lips tight and nodded her head up and down several times. Finally she swallowed, and went on, "He was a grand person . . . he was. He gave me what common sense I've got, and it was him that kept me from being just a complete silly fool . . . ." She tightened her lips again, and then again went on, "He always used to say . . . whenever I . . . I . . . ."

She turned away abruptly and sat down, lowered her face into her palms, and began to cry.

Llewellyn started at her. "Now, Helen, for God's sake, I know how you feel —"

I growled at him, "Sit down and shut up. Can it!"

He was going to keep on comforting her. I bounced up and grabbed his shoulder and whirled him. "You're not a client here any more. Don't argue. Didn't I tell you scenes make me nervous?" I left him glaring and went to the cabinet and got a shot of brandy and a glass of cold water, and went and stood alongside Helen Frost's chair. Pretty soon she got quieter, and then fished a handkerchief out of her bag and began dabbing. I waited until she could see to tell her:

"Brandy. 1890 Guarnier. Shall I put water in it?"

She shook her head and reached for it and gulped it down nicely. I offered her the water and she took a swallow of that. Then she looked at Nero Wolfe and said, "You'll have to excuse me. I'm not asking for any tenderness, but you'll have to excuse me." She looked at her cousin. "I'm not going to talk to you about Uncle Boyd any more. It doesn't do any good, does it? It's foolish." She dabbed at her eyes again, took in a long trembling breath and let it out, and turned back to Wolfe.

She said, "I don't care what Uncle Boyd told you about us Frosts. It couldn't have been anything very terrible, because he wouldn't tell lies. I don't care if you're working with the police, either. There couldn't be anything more . . . more distasteful to a Frost than what has happened. Anyway, the police never found out anything at all about Molly Lauck, and you did."

Her tears had dried. She went on, "I'm sorry I didn't tell you . . . of course I'm sorry. I thought I was keeping a secret for Uncle Boyd, but I'm sorry anyway. I only wish there was anything else I could tell you . . . but anyway . . . I can do this. This is the only time I've been truly glad I have lots of money. I'll pay you anything to find out who killed Uncle Boyd. Anything, and . . . and you won't have to sue me for it.''

I got her glass and went to the cabinet to get her some more brandy. I grinned at the bottle as I poured, reflecting that this case was turning out to be just one damned client after another.

11

Llewellyn was expostulating. "But, Helen, it's a police job. Not that he could be any more offensive than the police are, but it's a police job and let them do it. Anyway, Dad and Aunt Callie will be sore as the devil, you know they will, you know how they went after me when I . . . Tuesday."

Helen said, "I don't care if they're sore. It's not their money, it's mine. I'm doing this. Of course I won't be of age until next month — does that matter, Mr. Wolfe? Is that all right?"

"Quite all right."

"Will you do it?"

"Will I accept your commission? In spite of my experience with another Frost as a client, yes."

She turned to her ortho-cousin. "You

do as you please, Lew. Go on home and tell them if you want to. But I . . . I'd like to have you . . ."

He was frowning at her. "Are you set on this?"

"Yes. Good and set."

"Okay." He settled back in his chair. "I stick here. I'm for the Frosts, but you're the first one on the list. You're . . . Oh, nothing." He flushed a little. "Go to it."

"Thank you, Lew." She turned to Wolfe. "I suppose you want me to sign something?"

Wolfe shook his head. "That won't be necessary." He had leaned back and his eyes were half closed. "My charge will be adequate, but not exorbitant. I shan't attempt to make you pay for your cousin's volatility. But one thing must be clearly understood. You are engaging me for this job because of your affection and esteem for Mr. McNair and your desire that his murderer should be discovered and punished. You are at present under the spell of powerful emotions. Are you sure that tomorrow or next week you will still want this thing done? Do you want the murderer caught and tried and convicted and executed if it should happen to be, for instance, your cousin, your uncle, your mother — or Mr. Perren Gebert?''

''But that . . . that's ridiculous . . .''

''Maybe, but it remains a question to be answered. Do you want to pay me for catching the murderer, no matter who it is?''

She gazed at him, and said finally, ''Yes. Whoever killed Uncle Boyd — yes, I do.''

''You won't go back on that?''

''No.''

''Good for you. I believe you. I'll try the job for you. Now I want to ask you some questions, but it is possible that your reply to the first one will make the others unnecessary. When did you last see Mr. McNair's red leather box?''

''His what?'' She frowned. ''Red leather box?''

''That's it.''

''Never. I never did see it. I didn't

know he had one.''

''Indeed. — You, sir, are you answering questions?''

Lew Frost said, ''I guess I am. Sure. But not about a red leather box. I've never seen it.''

Wolfe sighed. ''Then I'm afraid we'll have to go on. I may as well tell you, Miss Frost, that Mr. McNair foresaw — at least, feared — what was waiting for him. While you were here yesterday he was at his lawyer's executing his will. He left his property to his sister Isabel, who lives in Scotland. He named me executor of his estate, and bequeathed me his red leather box and its contents. He called here to ask me to accept the trust and the legacy.''

''He named you executor?'' Llewellyn was gazing at him incredulously. ''Why, he didn't know you. Day before yesterday he didn't even want to talk to you . . .''

''Just so. That shows the extent of his desperation. But it is evident that the red box holds the secret of his death. As a matter of fact, Miss Frost, I was glad to see you here today. I hoped for something from you — a description of the box, if nothing more."

She shook her head. "I never saw it. I didn't know . . . but I don't understand . . . if he wanted you to have it, why didn't he tell you yesterday . . ."

"He intended to. He didn't get that far. His last words — his last futile struggle against his fate — were an effort to tell me where the red box is. I should inform you: Inspector Cramer has a copy of the will, and at this moment scores of police are searching for the box, so if you or your cousin can give me any hint there is no time to lose. It is desirable for me to get the box first. Not to protect the murderer, but I have my own way of doing things — and the police have no client but the electric chair."

Llewellyn said, "But you say he left it to you, it's your property . . ."

"Murder evidence is no one's property, once the law touches it. No, if Mr. Cramer finds it, the best we can hope for is the role of privileged spectator. So turn your minds back, both of you. Look back at the days, weeks, months, years. Resurrect, if you can, some remark of Mr. McNair's, some forgotten gesture, perhaps of irritation or embarrassment at being interrupted, perhaps the hurried closing of a drawer, or the unintentional disclosure of a hiding-place. A remark by someone else who may have had knowledge of it. Some action of Mr. McNair's, unique or habitual, at the time unexplained . . ."

Llewellyn was slowly shaking his head. Helen said, "Nothing. I'll try to think, but I'm sure there's nothing I can remember like that."

"That's too bad. Keep trying. Of course the police are ransacking his apartment and his place of business. Had he preempted any other spot of earth or water? A garage, a boat, a place in the country?"

Llewellyn was looking at his cousin with inquiring brows. She nodded. "Yes. Glennanne. A little cottage with a few acres of land up near Brewster."

"Glennanne?"

"Yes. His wife's name was Anne and his daughter's was Glenna."

"Did he own it?"

"Yes. He bought it about six years ago."

"What and where is Brewster?"

"It's a little village about fifty miles north of New York."

"Indeed." Wolfe sat up. "Archie. Get Saul, Orrie, Johnny and Fred here immediately. If they cannot all be prompt, send the first two to search Glennanne, and let the others join them when they come. The cottage, first, swiftly, and thoroughly, then the grounds. Is there a garden, Miss Frost? Tools?"

She nodded. "He . . . he grew some flowers."

"Good. They can take the sedan. Get extra things for digging if they need them, and they should have lights to continue after dark. The cottage is most likely — a hole in the wall, a loose floor-board. Get them. Wait. First your notebook; take this and type it on a letterhead:

I hearby authorize the bearer, Saul Panzer, to take complete charge of the house and ground of Glennanne, property of Boyden McNair, deceased, and to undertake certain activities there in accordance with my instructions.

"Leave room for my signature above the designation, 'Executor of the estate of Boyden McNair.' I have not yet qualified, but we can tie the red tape later." He nodded me off. "Now, Miss Frost, perhaps you can tell me —"

I moved to the phone and started dialing. I got Saul and Orrie right off the bat, and they said they would come pronto. Fred Durkin was out, but his wife said she knew where to get hold of him and would have him call in ten minutes. Johnny Keems, when he wasn't on a job for us, had formed the habit of phoning every day at nine to give me his program, and had told me that morning that he was still on a watchdog assignment for Del Pritchard, so I tried

that office. They had Johnny booked for the day, but before I finished typing the authorization for Saul, Fred called, so I had three anyhow.

Saul Panzer arrived first and Wolfe had Fritz show him into the office. He came in with his hat in his hand, shot me a wink, asked Wolfe how he did, got himself an everlasting blueprint of the two Frosts in one quick glance, and pointed his big nose inquiringly at Wolfe.

Wolfe gave him the dope and told him what he was supposed to find. Helen Frost told him how to get to Glennanne from the village of Brewster. I handed him the signed authorization and forty bucks for expenses, and he pulled out his old brown wallet and deposited them in it with care. Wolfe told him to get the car from the garage and wait in front to pick up Fred and Orrie as they arrived.

Saul nodded. "Yes, sir. If I find the box, do I leave Fred or Orrie at the place when I come away?"

"Yes. Until notified. Fred."

"If any strangers offer to help me

look, do I let them?''

Wolfe frowned. ''I was about to mention that. Surely there can be no objection if we show a preference for law and order. With all courtesy, you can ask to see a search warrant.''

''Is there something hot in the box?'' Saul blushed. ''I mean, stolen property?''

''No. It is legally mine. Defend it.''

''Right.'' Saul went. I reflected that if he ever got his mitts on the box I wouldn't like to be the guy to try to take it away from him, small as he was. He didn't think any more of Nero Wolfe than I do of my patrician nose and big brown intelligent eyes.

Wolfe had pushed the button for Fritz, the long push, not the two shorts for beer. Fritz came, and stood.

Wolfe frowned at him. ''Can you stretch lunch for us? Two guests?''

''No,'' Llewellyn broke in, ''really — we'll have to get back — I promised Dad and Aunt Callie —''

''You can phone them. I would advise Miss Frost to stay. At any moment we may hear that the box has been found,

234

and that would mean a crisis. And to provide against the possibility that it will not be found, I shall need a great deal of information. Miss Frost?''

She nodded. ''I'll stay. I'm not hungry. I'll stay. You'll stay with me, Lew?''

He grumbled something at her, but stayed put. Wolfe told Fritz:

''The fricandeau should be ample. Add lettuce to the salad if the endive is short, and of course increase the oil. Chill a bottle of the '28 Marcobrunner. As soon as you are ready.'' He wiggled Fritz away with a finger, and settled back in his chair. ''Now, Miss Frost. We are engaged in a joint enterprise. I need facts. I am going to ask you a lot of foolish questions. If one of them turns out to be wise or clever you will not know it, but let us hope that I will. Please do not waste time in expostulation. If I ask you whether your mother has recently sent you to the corner druggist for potassium cyanide tablets, just say no, and listen to the next one. I once solved a difficult case by learning from a young woman, after questioning her for five hours, that she had been handed a newspaper with a piece cut out. Your inalienable rights of privacy are temporarily suspended. Is that understood?''

''Yes.'' She looked straight at him. ''I don't care. Of course I know you're clever, I want you to be. I know how easily you caught me in a lie Tuesday morning. But you ought to know . . . you can't catch me in one now, because I haven't anything to lie about. I don't see how anything I know can help you . . .''

''Possibly it can't. We can only try. Let us first straighten out the present a little, and work back. I should inform you: Mr. McNair did tell me a few things yesterday before he was interrupted. I have a little background to start with. Now — for instance — what did Mr. Gebert mean yesterday when he said you were almost his fiancee?''

She compressed her lips, but then spoke right to it: ''He didn't mean anything, really. He has — several times he has asked me to marry him.''

''Have you encouraged him?''

''No.''

''Has anyone?''

''Why . . . who could?''

''Lots of people. Your maid, the pastor of his church, a member of your family — has anyone?''

She said, after a pause, ''No.''

''You said you had nothing to lie about.''

''But I —'' She stopped, and tried to smile at him. It was then that I began to think she was a pretty good kid, when I saw her try to smile to show that she wasn't meaning to cheat on him. She went on, ''This is so very personal . . . I don't see how . . .''

Wolfe wiggled a finger at her. ''We are proceeding on this theory, that in any event whatever, we wish to discover the murderer of Mr. McNair. Even — merely for instance — if it should mean dragging your mother into a courtroom to testify against someone she likes. If that is our aim, you must leave the method of pursuit to me; and I beg you, don't balk and shy at every little pebble. Who encouraged Mr. Gebert?''

''I won't do it again,'' she promised. ''No one really encouraged him. I've known him all my life, and mother knew him before I was born. Mother and father knew him. He has always been . . . attentive, and amusing, and in some ways he is interesting and I like him. In other ways I dislike him extremely. Mother has told me I should control my dislike on account of his good points, and she said that since he was such an old friend I shouldn't wound his feelings by cutting him off, that it wouldn't hurt to let him think he was still in the field as long as I hadn't decided.''

''You agreed to that?''

''Well, I . . . I didn't fight it. My mother is very persuasive.''

''What was the attitude of your uncle? Mr. Dudley Frost. The trustee of your property.''

''Oh, I never discussed things like that with him. But I know what it would have been. He didn't like Perren.''

"And Mr. McNair?"

"He disliked Perren more than I did. Outwardly they were friends, but . . . anyway, Uncle Boyd wasn't two-faced. Shall I tell you . . ."

"By all means."

"Well, one day about a year ago Uncle Boyd sent for me to go upstairs to his office, and when I went in Perren was there. Uncle Boyd was standing up and looking white and determined. I asked him what was the matter, and he said he only wanted to tell me, in Perren's presence, that any influence his friendship and affection might have on me was unalterably opposed to my marriage with Perren. He said it very . . . formally, and that wasn't like him. He didn't ask me to promise or anything. He just said that and then told me to go."

"And in spite of that, Mr. Gebert has persisted with his courtship."

"Of course he has. Why wouldn't he? Lots of men have. I'm so rich it's worth quite an effort."

"Dear me." Wolfe's eyes flickered

open at her and half shut again. "As cynical as that about it? But a brave cynicism which is of course proper. Nothing is more admirable than the fortitude with which millionaires tolerate the disadvantages of their wealth. What is Mr. Gebert's profession?"

"He hasn't any. That's one of the things I don't like about him. He doesn't do anything."

"Has he an income?"

"I don't know. Really, I don't know a thing about it. I suppose he has . . . I've heard him make vague remarks. He lives at the Chesebrough, and he drives a car."

"I know. Mr. Goodwin informed me he drove it here yesterday. At all events, a man of courage. You knew him in Europe; what did he do there?"

"No more than here, as far as I remember — of course I was young then. He was wounded in the war, and afterwards came to visit us in Spain — that is, my mother, I was only two years old — and he went to Egypt with us a little later, but when we went on to the

Orient he went back —''

''One moment, please.'' Wolfe was frowning. ''Let us tidy up the chronology. There seems to have been quite a party in Spain; almost Mr. McNair's last words were that he had gone to Spain with his baby daughter. We'll start when your life started. You were born, you told me yesterday, in Paris — on May 7th, 1915. Your father was already in the war, as a member of the British Aviation Corps, and he was killed when you were a few months old. When did your mother take you to Spain?''

''Early in 1916. She was afraid to stay in Paris, on account of the war. We went first to Barcelona and then to Cartagena. A little later Uncle Boyd and Glenna came down and joined us there. He had no money and his health was bad, and mother . . . helped him. I think Perren came, not long after, partly because Uncle Boyd was there — they had both been friends of my father's. Then in 1917 Glenna died, and soon after that Uncle Boyd went back to

Scotland, and mother took me to Egypt because they were afraid of a revolution or something in Spain, and Perren went with us."

"Good. I own a house in Egypt which I haven't seen for twenty years. It has Rhages and Veramine tiles on the doorway. How long were you in Egypt?"

"About two years. In 1919, when I was four years old — of course mother has told me all this — three English people were killed in a riot in Cairo, and mother decided to leave. Perren went back to France. Mother and I went to Bombay, and later to Bali and Japan and Hawaii. My uncle, who was the trustee of my property, kept insisting that I should have an American education, and finally, in 1924 — I was nine years old then — we left Hawaii and came to New York. It was from that time on, really, that I knew Uncle Boyd, because of course I didn't remember him from Spain, since I had been only two years old."

"He had his business in New York

when you got here?"

"No. He has told me — he started designing for Wilmerding in London and was very successful and became a partner, and then he decided New York was better and came over here in 1925 and went in for himself. Of course he looked mother up first thing, and she was a little help to him on account of the people she knew, but he would have gone to the top anyway because he had great ability. He was very talented. Paris and London were beginning to copy him. You would never have thought, just being with him, talking with him . . . you would never have thought . . ."

She faltered, and stopped. Wolfe began to murmur something at her to steady her, but an interruption saved him the trouble. Fritz appeared to announce lunch. Wolfe pushed back his chair:

"Your coat will be all right here, Miss Frost. Your hat? But permit me to insist, as a favor; to eat with a hat on, except in a railroad station, is barbarous. Thank you. Restaurant? I know nothing of restaurants; short of compulsion, I would not eat in one were Vatel himself the chef.''

Then, after we were seated at the table, when Fritz came to pass the relish platter, Wolfe performed the introduction according to his custom with guests who had not tasted that cooking before:

"Miss Frost, Mr. Frost, this is Mr. Brenner.''

Also according to custom, there was no shop talk during the meal. Llewellyn was fidgety, but he ate; and the fact appeared to be that our new client was hungry as the devil. Probably she had had no breakfast. Anyway, she gave the fricandeau a play which made Wolfe regard her with open approval. He carried the burden of the conversation, chiefly about Egypt, tiles, the uses of a camel's double lip, and the theory that England's colonizing genius was due to her repulsive climate, on account of which Britons with any sense and will power invariably decided to go somewhere else to work. It was two-thirty when the salad was finished, so we went back to the office and had Fritz serve coffee there.

Helen Frost telephoned her mother. Apparently there was considerable parental protest from the other end of the wire, for Helen sounded first persuasive, then irritated, and finally fairly sassy. During that performance Llewellyn sat and scowled at her, and I couldn't tell whether the scowl was for her or the opposition. It had no effect on our client either way, for she was sitting at my desk and didn't see it.

Wolfe started in on her again, resuming the Perren Gebert tune, but for the first half hour or so it was spotty because the telephone kept interrupting. Johnny Keems called to say that he could leave the Pritchard job if we needed him, and I told him that we'd manage to struggle along somehow. Dudley Frost phoned to give his son hell, and Llewellyn took it calmly and announced that his cousin Helen needed him where he was, whereupon she kept a straight face but I smothered a snicker. Next came a ring from Fred Durkin, to say that they had arrived and taken possession of Glennanne, finding no one there, and had begun operations; the phone at the cottage was out of order, so Saul had sent Fred to the village to make that report. A man named Collinger phoned and insisted on speaking to Wolfe, and I listened in and took it down as usual; he was Boyden McNair's lawyer, and wanted to know if Wolfe could call at his office right away for a conference regarding the will, and of course the bare idea set Wolfe's digestion back at least ten minutes. It was arranged that Collinger would come to 35th Street the following morning. Then, a little after three o'clock, Inspector Cramer got us, and reported that his army was making uniform progress on all fronts: namely, none. No red box and no information about it; no hide or hair of motive anywhere; nothing among McNair's papers that could be stretched to imply murder; no line on a buyer of potassium cyanide; no anything.

Cramer sounded a little weary.

"Here's a funny item, too," he said in a wounded tone, "we can't find the young Frosts anywhere. Your client, Lew, isn't at his home or his office in the Portland Theatre or anywhere else, and Helen, the daughter, isn't around either. Her mother says she went out around eleven o'clock, but she doesn't know where, and I've learned that Helen was closer to McNair than anyone else, very close friends, so she's our best chance on the red box. Then what's she doing running around town, with McNair just croaked? There's just a chance that something's got too hot for them and they've faded. Lew was up at the Frost apartment on 65th Street and they went out together. We're trying to trail —"

"Mr. Cramer. Please. I've mumbled at you twice. Miss Helen Frost and Mr. Llewellyn Frost are in my office; I'm conversing with them. They had lunch —"

"Huh? They're there now?"

"Yes. They got here this morning shortly after you left."

"I'll be damned." Cramer shrilled a

little. "What are you trying to do, lick off some cream for yourself? I want to see them. Ask them to come down — or wait, let me talk to her. Put her on."

"Now, Mr. Cramer." Wolfe cleared his throat. "I do not lick cream; and this man and woman came to see me unannounced and unexpected. I am perfectly willing that you should talk with her, but there is no point —"

"What do you mean, willing? What's that, humor? Why the devil shouldn't you be willing?"

"I should. But it is appropriate to mention it, since Miss Frost is my client, and is therefore under my —"

"Your client? Since when?" Cramer was boiling. "What kind of a shenanigan is this? You told me Lew Frost hired you!"

"So he did. But that — er — we have changed that. I have — speaking as a horse— I have changed riders in the middle of the stream. I am working for Miss Frost. I was about to say, there is no point in a duplication of effort. She has had a bad shock and is under a strain. You may question her if you wish, but I have done so and am not through with her, and there is little likelihood that her interests will conflict with yours in the end. She is as anxious to find Mr. McNair's murderer as you are; that is what she hired me for. I may tell you this: neither she nor her cousin has any knowledge of the red box. They have never seen it or heard of it.''

''The devil.'' There was a pause on the wire. ''I want to see her and have a talk with her.''

Wolfe sighed. ''In that infernal den? She is tired, she has nothing to say that can help you, she is worth two million dollars, and she will be old enough to vote before next fall. Why don't you call at her home after dinner this evening? Or send one of your lieutenants?''

''Because I — Oh, the hell with it. I ought to know better than to argue with you. And she doesn't know where the red box is?''

''She knows nothing whatever about it. Nor does her cousin. My word for that.''

"Okay. I'll get her later maybe. Let me know what you find, huh?"

"By all means."

Wolfe hung up and pushed the instrument away, leaned back and locked his fingers on his belly, and slowly shook his head as he murmured, "That man talks too much. — I'm sure, Miss Frost, that you won't be offended at missing a visit to police headquarters. It is one of my strongest prejudices, my disinclination to permit a client of mine to appear there. Let us hope that Mr. Cramer's search for the red box will keep him entertained."

Llewellyn put in, "In my opinion, that's the only thing to do anyway, wait till it's found. All this hash of ancient history — if you were as careful to protect your client from your own annoyance as you are —"

"I remind you, sir, you are here by sufferance. Your cousin has the sense, when she hires an expert, to permit him his hocus-pocus. — What were we saying, Miss Frost? Oh, yes. You were telling me that Mr. Gebert came to New

York in 1931. You were then sixteen years old. You say that he is forty-four, so he was then thirty-nine, not an advanced age. I presume he called upon your mother at once, as an old friend?"

She nodded. "Yes. We knew he was coming; he had written. Of course I didn't remember him; I hadn't seen him since I was four years old."

"Of course not. Did he perhaps come on a political mission? I understand that he was a member of the *camelots du roi*."

"I don't think so. I'm sure he didn't — but that's silly, certainly I can't be sure. But I think not."

"At any rate, as far as you know, he doesn't work, and you don't like that."

"I don't like that in anyone."

"Remarkable sentiment for an heiress. However. If Mr. Gebert should marry you, that would be a job for him. Let us abandon him to that slim hope for his redemption. It is getting on for four o'clock, when I must leave you. I need to ask you about a sentence you left unfinished yesterday, shortly after I made my unsuccessful appeal to you. You told me that your father died when you were only a few months old, and that therefore you had never had a father, and then you said, 'That is,' and stopped. I prodded you, but you said it was nothing, and we let it go at that. It may in fact be nothing, but I would like to have it — whatever was ready for your tongue. Do you remember?''

She nodded. ''It really was nothing. Just something foolish.''

''Let me have it. I've told you, we're combing a meadow for a mustard seed.''

''But this was nothing at all. Just a dream, a childish dream I had once. Then I had it several times after that, always the same. A dream about myself . . .''

''Tell me.''

''Well . . . the first time I had it I was about six years old, in Bali. I've wondered since if anything had happened that day to make me have such a dream, but I couldn't remember anything. I dreamed I was a baby, not an infant but big enough to walk and run, around two I imagine, and on a chair, on a napkin, there was an orange that had been peeled and divided into sections. I took a section of the orange and ate it, then took another one and turned to a man sitting there on a bench, and handed it to him, and I said plainly, 'For daddy.' It was my voice, only it was a baby talking. Then I ate another section, and then took another one and said 'For daddy' again, and kept on that way till it was all gone. I woke up from the dream trembling and began to cry. Mother was sleeping in another bed — it was on a screened veranda — and she came to me and asked what was the matter, and I said, 'I'm crying because I feel so good.' I never did tell her what the dream was. I had it quite a few times after that — I think the last time was when I was about eleven years old, here in New York. I always cried when I had it.''

Wolfe asked, ''What did the man look like?''

She shook her head. ''That's why it was just foolish. It wasn't a man, it just looked like a man. There was one photograph of my father which mother had kept, but I couldn't tell if it looked like him in the dream. It just . . . I just simply called it daddy.''

''Indeed.'' Wolfe's lips pushed out and in. At length he observed, ''Possibly remarkable, on account of the specific picture. Did you eat sections of orange when you were young?''

''I suppose so. I've always liked oranges.''

''Well. No telling. Possibly, as you say, nothing at all. You mentioned a photograph of your father. Your mother had kept only one?''

''Yes. She kept that for me.''

''None for herself?''

''No.'' A pause, then Helen said quietly, ''There's no secret about it. And it was perfectly natural. Mother was bitterly offended at the terms of father's will, and I think she had a right to be. They had a serious misunderstanding of some sort, I never knew what, about the time I was born, but no matter how serious it was . . . anyway, he left her nothing. Nothing whatever, not even a small income.''

Wolfe nodded. ''So I understand. It was left in trust for you, with your uncle — your father's brother Dudley — as trustee. Have you ever read the will?''

''Once, a long while ago. Not long after we came to New York my uncle had me read it.''

''At the age of nine. But you waded through it. Good for you. I also understand that your uncle was invested with sole power and authority, without any right of oversight by you or anyone else. I believe the usual legal phrase is 'absolute and uncontrolled discretion.' So that, as a matter of fact, you do not know how much you will be worth on your twenty-first birthday; it may be millions and it may be nothing. You may be in debt. If any —''

Lew Frost got in. ''What are you trying to insinuate? If you mean that my father —''

Wolfe snapped, ''Don't do that! I insinuate nothing; I merely state the fact of my client's ignorance regarding her property. It may be augmented; it may be depleted; she doesn't know. Do you, Miss Frost?"

"No." She was frowning. "I don't know. I know that for over twenty years the income has been paid in full, promptly every quarter. Really, Mr. Wolfe, I think we're getting —"

"We shall soon be through; I must leave you shortly. As for irrelevance, I warned you that we might wander anywhere. Indulge me in two more questions about your father's will: do you enter into complete possession and control on May seventh?"

"Yes, I do."

"And in case of your death before your twenty-first birthday, who inherits?"

"If I were married and had a child, the child. If not, half to my uncle and half to his son, my cousin Lew."

"Indeed. Nothing to your mother even then?"

"Nothing."

"So. Your father fancied his side of that controversy. Wolfe turned to

Llewellyn. "Take good care of your cousin for another five weeks. Should harm befall her in that time, you will have a million dollars and the devil will have his horns on your pillow. Wills are noxious things. Frequently. It is astonishing, the amount of mischief a man's choler may do long after the brain-cells which nourished the choler have rotted away." He wiggled a finger at our client. "Soon, of course, you yourself must make a will, to dispose of the pile in case you should die on — say — May eighth, or subsequently. I suppose you have a lawyer?"

"No. I've never needed one."

"You will now. That's what a fortune is for, to support the lawyers who defend it for you against depredation." Wolfe glanced at the clock. "I must leave you. I trust the afternoon has not been wasted; I suppose you feel that it has. I don't think so. May I leave it that way for the present? I thank you for your indulgence. And while we continue to mark time, waiting for that confounded box to be found, I have a little favor to ask. Could you take Mr. Goodwin home to tea with you?''

Llewellyn's scowl, which had been turned on for the past hour, deepend. Helen Frost glanced at me and then back at Wolfe.

''Why,'' she said, ''I suppose . . . if you want . . .''

''I do want. I presume it would be possible to have Mr. Gebert there?''

She nodded. ''He's there now. Or he was when I phoned mother. Of course . . . you know . . . mother doesn't approve . . .''

''I'm aware of that. She thinks you're poking a stick in a hornet's nest. But the fact is the police are the hornets; you've avoided them, and she hasn't. Mr. Goodwin is a discreet and wholesome man and not without acuity. I want him to talk with Mr. Gebert, and with your mother too if she will permit it. You will soon be of age, Miss Frost; you have chosen to attempt a difficult and possibly dangerous project; surely you can prevail on your family and close friends for some consideration. If they are ignorant of any circumstance regarding Mr. McNair's death, all the more should they be ready to establish that point and help us to stumble on a path that will lead us away from ignorance. So if you would invite Mr. Goodwin for a cup of tea . . .''

Llewellyn said sourly, ''I think Dad's there, too, he was going to stay till we got back. It'll just be a big stew — if it's Gebert you want, why can't we send him down here? He'll do anything Helen tells him to.''

''Because for two hours I shall be engaged with my plants.'' Wolfe looked at the clock again, and got up from his chair.

Our client was biting her lip. She quit that, and looked at me. ''Will you have tea with us, Mr. Goodwin?''

I nodded. ''Yeah. Much obliged.''

Wolfe, moving toward the door, said to her, ''It is a pleasure to earn a fee from a client like you. You can come to a yes or no without first encircling the globe. I hope and believe that when we are finished you will have nothing to regret.'' He moved on, and turned at the threshold. ''By the way, Archie, if you will just get that package from your room before you leave. Put it on my bed.''

He went on to the elevator. I arose and told my prospective hostess I would be back in a minute, left the office and hopped up the stairs. I didn't stop at the second floor, where my room was, but kept going to the top, and got there almost as soon as the elevator did with the load it had. At the door to the plant rooms Wolfe stood, awaiting me.

''One idea,'' he murmured, ''is to observe the reactions of the others upon the cousins' return from our office before there has been an opportunity for the exchange of information. Another is to get an accurate opinion as to whether any of them has ever seen the red box or has possession of it now. The third is a general assault on reticence.''

''Okay. How candid are we?''

''Reasonably so. Bear in mind that with all three there, the chances are many to one that you will be talking to the murderer, so the candor will be one-sided. You, of course, will be expecting cooperation.''

''Sure, I always do, because I'm wholesome.''

I ran back downstairs and found that our client had on her hat and coat and gloves and her cousin was standing beside her, looking grave but a little doubtful.

I grinned at them. ''Come on, children.''

12

Strictly speaking, that wasn't my job. I know pretty well what my field is. Aside from my primary function as the thorn in the seat of Wolfe's chair to keep him from going to sleep and waking up only for meals, I'm chiefly cut out for two things: to jump and grab something before the other guy can get his paws on it, and to collect pieces of the puzzle for Wolfe to work on. This expedition to 65th Street was neither of those. I don't pretend to be strong on nuances. Fundamentally I'm the direct type, and that's why I can never be a really fine detective. Although I keep it down as much as I can, so it won't interfere with my work, I always have an inclination in a case of murder to march up to all the possible suspects, one after the other, and look them in the eye and ask them, "Did you put that poison in the aspirin bottle?" and just keep that up until one of them says, "Yes." As I say, I keep it down, but I have to fight it.

The Frost apartment on 65th Street wasn't as gaudy as I had expected, in view of my intimate knowledge of the Frost finances. It was a bit shiny, with one side of the entrance hall solid with mirrors, even the door to the closet where I hung my hat, and, in the living room, chairs and little tables with chromium chassis, a lot of red stuff around in upholsteries and drapes, a metal grille in front of the fireplace, which apparently wasn't used, and oil paintings in modern silver frames.

Anyway, it certainly was cheerfuller than the people that were in it. Dudley Frost was in a big chair at one side, with a table at his elbow holding a whiskey bottle, a water carafe, and a couple of glasses. Perren Gebert stood near a window at the other end, with his back to the room and his hands in his pockets. As we entered he turned, and Helen's mother walked toward us, with a little lift to her brow as she saw me.

"Oh," she said. To her daughter: "You've brought . . ."

Helen nodded firmly. "Yes, mother." She was holding her chin a little higher than natural, to keep the spunk going. "You — all of you have met Mr. Goodwin. Yesterday morning at . . . that candy business with the police. I've engaged Nero Wolfe to investigate Uncle Boyd's death, and Mr. Goodwin works for him —"

Dudley Frost bawled from his chair, "Lew! Come here! Damn it, what kind of nonsense —"

Llewellyn hurried over there to stem it. Perren Gebert had approached us and was smiling at me:

"Ah! The fellow that doesn't like scenes. You remember I told you, Calida?" He transfered the smile to Miss Frost. "My dear Helen! You've engaged Mr. Wolfe? Are you one of the Erinyes? Alecto? Megaera? Tisiphone? Where's your snaky hair? So one can really buy anything with money, even vengeance?"

Mrs. Frost murmured at him, "Stop it, Perren."

"I'm not buying vengeance." Helen colored a little. "I told you this morning, Perren, you're being especially hateful. You'd better not make me cry again, or I'll . . . well, don't. Yes, I've engaged Mr. Wolfe, and Mr. Goodwin has come here and he wants to talk to you."

"To me?" Perren shrugged. "About Boyd? If you ask it, he may, but I warn him not to expect much. The police have been here most of the day, and I've realized how little I really knew about Boyd, though I've known him more than twenty years."

I said, "I stopped expecting long ago. Anything you tell me will be velvet. — I'm supposed to talk to you, too, Mrs. Frost. And your brother-in-law. I have to take notes, and it gives me a cramp to write standing up . . ."

She nodded at me, and turned. "Over here, I think." She started toward Dudley Frost's side of the room, and I joined her. Her straight back was graceful, and she was unquestionably streamlined for her age. Llewellyn started carrying chairs, and Gebert came up with one. As we got seated and I pulled out my notebook and pencil, I noticed that Helen still had to keep her chin up, but her mother didn't. Mrs. Frost was saying:

"I hope you understand this, Mr. Goodwin. This is a terrible thing, an awful thing, and we were all very old friends of Mr. McNair's, and we don't enjoy talking about it. I knew him all my life, from childhood."

I said, "Yeah. You're Scotch?"

She nodded. "My name was Buchan."

"So McNair told us." I jerked my eyes up quick from my notebook, which was my habit against the handicap of not being able to keep a steely gaze on the victim. But she wasn't recoiling in dismay; she was just nodding again.

"Yes. I gathered from what the policemen said that Boyden had told Mr. Wolfe a good deal of his early life. Of course you have the advantage of knowing what it was he had to say to Mr. Wolfe. I knew, naturally, that Boyden was not well . . . his nerves . . .''

Gebert put in, ''He was what you call a wreck. He was in a very bad condition. That is why I told the police, they will find it was suicide.''

''The man was crazy!'' This was a croak from Dudley Frost. ''I've told you what he did yesterday! He instructed his lawyer to demand an accounting on Edwin's estate! On what grounds? On the ground that he is Helen's godfather? Absolutely fantastic and illegal! I always thought he was crazy —''

That started a general rumpus. Mrs. Frost expostulated with some spirit, Llewellyn with respectful irritation, and Helen with a nervous outburst. Perren Gebert looked around at them, nodded at me as if he and I shared an entertaining secret, and got out a cigarette. I didn't try to put it all down, but just surveyed the scene and listened. Dudley Frost was surrendering no ground:

''. . . crazy as a loon! Why shouldn't

he commit suicide? Helen, my dear, I adore you, you know damned well I do, but I refuse to assume respect for your liking for that nincompoop merely because he is no longer alive! He had no use for me and I had none for him! So what's the use pretending about it? As far as your dragging this man in here is concerned —"

"Dad! Now, Dad! Cut it out —"

Perren Gebert said to no one, "And half a bottle gone." Mrs. Frost, sitting with her lips tight and patient, glanced at him. I leaned forward to get closer to Dudley Frost and practically yelled at him:

"What is it? Where does it hurt?"

He jerked back and glared at me. "Where does what hurt?"

I grinned. "Nothing. I just wanted to see if you could hear. I gather you would just as soon I'd go. The best way to manage that, for all of you, is to let me ask a few foolish questions, and you answer them briefly and maybe honestly."

"We've already answered them. All

the foolish questions there are. We've been doing that all day. All because that nincompoop McNair —''

''Okay. I've already got it down that he was a nincompoop. You've made remarks about suicide. What reason did McNair have for killing himself?''

''How the devil do I know?''

''Then you can't think one up offhand?''

''I don't have to think one up. The man was crazy. I've always said so. I said so over twenty years ago, in Paris, when he used to paint rows of eggs strung on wires and call it The Cosmos.''

Helen started to burst, ''Uncle Boyd was never —'' She was seated at my right, and I reached and tapped her sleeve with the tips of my fingers and told her, ''Swallow it. You can't crack every nut in the bag.'' I turned to Perren Gebert:

''You mentioned suicide first. What reason did McNair have for killing himself?''

Gebert shrugged. ''A specific reason?

I don't know. He was very bad in his nerves.''

''Yeah. He had a headache. How about you, Mrs. Frost? Have you got a reason?''

She looked at me. You couldn't take that woman's eyes casually; you had to make an effort. She said, ''You make your question a little provocative. Don't you? If you mean, do I know a concrete motive for Boyden to commit suicide, I don't.''

''Do you think he did?''

She frowned. ''I don't know what to think. If I think of suicide, it is only because I knew him quite intimately, and it is even more difficult to believe that there was anyone who . . . that someone killed him.''

I started to sigh, then realized that I was imitating Nero Wolfe, and choked it off. I looked around at them. ''Of course, you all know that McNair died in Nero Wolfe's office. You know that Wolfe and I were there, and naturally we know what he had been telling us about and how he was feeling. I don't know how careful the police are with their conclusions, but Mr. Wolfe is very snooty about his. He has already made one or two about this case, and the first one is that McNair didn't kill himself. Suicide is out. So if you have any idea that that theory will be found acceptable, either now or eventually, obliterate it. Guess again.''

Perren Gebert extended a long arm to crush his cigarette in a tray. ''For my part,'' he said, ''I don't feel compelled to guess. I made one to be chairitable. Suppose you tell us why it wasn't sucide.''

Mrs. Frost said quietly, ''I asked you to sit down in my house, Mr. Goodwin, because my daughter brought you. But I wonder if you know when you are being offensive? We . . . I have no theory to advance . . .''

Dudley Frost started to croak: ''Take no notice of him, Calida. Disregard him. I refuse to speak to him.'' He reached for the whiskey bottle.

I said, ''If you ask me, I could be even more offensive and still hope to make the grade to heaven.'' I got Mrs. Frost's eyes again. ''For instance, I might remark on your phony la-de-da about asking me to sit down in your house. It isn't your house, it's your daughter's, unless she gave it to you —'' There was a gasp at my right from the client, and Mrs. Frost's mouth opened, but I went on ahead of the rush:

''Just to show you how offensive I can be if I work at it. What kind of ninnies do you think we are? Even the cops aren't as thick as you seem to believe.It's time you folks pinched yourselves and woke up. Boyden McNair gets bumped off, and Helen Frost here happens to have enough regard for him to want to know who did it, and enough gumption to get the right man for the job, and enough jack to pay him. She's your daughter and niece and cousin and almost fiancee. She brings me here. I already know enough to be aware that you've got vital information which you don't intend to cough up, and you know I know it. And look at the kindergarten stuff you hand me! McNair had a headache, so he went to Nero Wolfe's office to poison himself! You might at least have the politeness to tell me straight that you refuse to discuss the matter because you don't intend to get involved if you can help it, then we can proceed with the involving.'' I pointed my pencil at Perren Gebert's long thin nose. ''For instance, you! Did you know that Dudley Frost might tell us where the red box is?''

I concentrated on Gebert, but Mrs. Frost was off line only a little to the left of him, so I was having a glimpse of her too. Gebert fell for it absolutely. His head jerked around to look at Dudley Frost and then back at me. Mrs. Frost jerked too, first at Gebert, then back into steadiness. Dudley Frost was sputtering at me:

''What's that? What red box? That idiotic thing in McNair's will? Damn you, are you crazy too? Do you dare —''

I grinned at him. ''Hold it. I just said you might. Yeah, the thing McNair left to Wolfe in his will. Have you got it?''

He turned to his son and growled, "I refuse to speak to him."

"Okay. But the truth is, I'm a friend of yours. I'm tipping you off. Did you know that there's a way for the District Attorney to force an accounting from you of your brother's estate? And did you ever hear of a search warrant? I suppose when the cops went with one to your apartment this afternoon to look for the red box, there was a maid there to let them in. Didn't she phone you? And of course in looking for the box they would have occasion to glance at anything that might be around. Or maybe they didn't get there yet; they may be on the way now. And don't go blaming your maid, she can't help it—"

Dudley Frost had scrambled to his feet. "They wouldn't — that would be an outrage —"

"Sure it would. I'm not saying they've done it, I'm just telling you, in a case of murder they'll do anything —"

Dudley Frost had started across the room. "Come on, Lew — by Gad, we'll see —"

"But, Dad, I don't —"

"Come on, I say! Are you my son?" He had turned at the far end of the room. "Thank you for the refreshment, Calida, let me know if there is anything I can do. Lew, damn it, come on! Helen, my dear, you are a fool, I've always said so. Lew!"

Llewellyn stopped to murmur something to Helen, nodded to his aunt, ignored Gebert, and hurried after his father to assist in the defense of their castle. There were rumblings from the entrance hall, and then the door opening and closing.

Mrs. Frost stood up and looked down at her daughter. She spoke to her quietly: "This is frightful, Helen. That this should come . . . and just now, just when you will soon be a woman and ready for your life as you want it. I know what Boyd was to you, and he was a great deal to me, too. Just now you're holding things against me that time will make you forget . . . you're remembering that I thought it wise to temper the affection you had for him. I thought it best; you were a girl, and girls should look to youth. Helen, my dear child . . ."

She bent down and touched her daughter's shoulder, touched her hair and straightened up again. "You have strong impulses, like your father, and sometimes you don't quite manage them. I don't agree with Perren when he sneers at you for trying to buy vengeance. Perren loves to sneer; it's his favorite pose; he would call it being sardonic . . . but you know him. I think the impulse that led you to hire this detective was a generous one. Certainly I have every reason to know that you are generous." Her voice stayed low, but it got more of a ring in it, a music of metal. "I'm your mother, and I don't believe you really want to bring people here who tell me that I refuse to discuss . . . this matter . . . because I don't intend to get involved. I'm sorry I was brusque with you today on the telephone, but my nerves were on edge. Policemen were here, and you were away, just making more trouble for us to no good purpose. Really . . . really, don't you see that? Cheap insults and bullying for your own family won't help any. I think you've learned, in twenty-one years, that you can depend on me, and I'd like to feel that I can depend on you too . . ."

Helen Frost stood up. Seeing her face, with no color in it and her mouth twisted, it looked shaky to me, and I considered butting in, but decided to keep my trap shut. She stood straight, with her hands, fists, hanging at her sides, and her eyes were dark with trouble but held level at Mrs. Frost, which was why I didn't speak. Gebert took a couple of steps toward her and stopped.

She said, "You can depend on me, mother. But so can Uncle Boyd. That's all right, isn't it? Oh, isn't it?" She looked at me and said in a funny tone like a child, "Don't insult my mother, Mr. Goodwin." Then she turned abruptly and run out on us, skipped the shebang. She left by a door on the right, not toward the hall, and closed it behind her.

Perren Gebert shrugged his shoulders and thrust his hands into his pockets, then pulled one out to rub the side of his thin nose with his forefinger. Mrs. Frost, with a couple of teeth clamped on her lower lip, looked at him and then back at the door where her daughter had gone.

I said brightly, "I don't think she fired me. I didn't understand it that way. What do you think?"

Gebert showed me a thin smile. "You leave now. No?"

"Maybe." I still had my notebook open in my hand. "But you folks might as well understand that we mean business. We're not just having fun, we do this for a living. I don't believe you can talk her out of it. This place belongs to her. I'm willing to have a showdown right now; say we go to her bedroom or wherever she went, and ask if I'm kicked out." I directed my gaze at Mrs. Frost. "Or have a little chat right here. You know, they might find that red box at Dudley Frost's, at that. How would that set with you?''

She said, ''Stupid senseless tricks.''

I nodded. ''Yeah, I guess so. Even Stephen. If you bounced me, Inspector Cramer would send me right back here with a man if Wolfe asked him to, and you've in no position to ritz the cops, because they're sensitive and they would only get suspicious. At present they're not actually suspicious, they just think you're hiding something because people like you don't want any publicity except in society columns and cigarette ads. For instance, they believe you know where the red box is. You know, of course, it's Nero Wolfe's property; McNair left it to him. We really would like to have it, just for curiosity.''

Gebert, after listening to me politely, cocked his head at Mrs. Frost. He smiled at her: ''You see, Calida, this fellow really believes we could tell him something. He's perfectly sincere about it. The police, too. The only way to get rid of them is to humor them. Why not tell them something?'' He waved a hand inclusively. "All sorts of things."

She looked at him without approval. "This is nothing to be playful about. Certainly not your kind of playfulness."

He lifted his brows. "I don't mean to be playful. They want information about Boyd, and unquestionably we have it, quantities of it." He looked at me. "You do shorthand in that book? Good. Put this down: McNair was an inveterate eater of snails, and he preferred calvados to cognac. His wife died in childbirth because he was insisting on being an artist and was too poor and incompetent to provide proper care for her. — What, Calida? But the fellow wants facts! — Edwin Frost once paid McNair two thousand francs — at that time four hundred dollars — for one of his pictures, and the next day traded it to a flower girl for a violet — not a bunch, a violet. McNair named his daughter Glenna because it means valley, and she came out of the valley of death, since her mother died at her birth — just a morsel of Calvinistic merriment. A lighthearted man, Boyd was! Mrs. Frost here was his oldest friend and she once rescued him from despair and penury; yet, when he became the foremost living designer and manufacturer of women's woolen garments, he invariably charged her top prices for everything she bought. And he never —''

''Perren! Stop it!''

''My dear Calida! Stop when I've just started? Give the fellow what he wants and he'll let us alone. It's a pity we can't give him his red box; Boyd really should have told us about that. But I realize that his chief interest is in Boyd's death, not his life. I can be helpful on that too. Knowing so well how Boyd lived, surely I should know how he died. As a matter of fact, when I heard of his death last evening, I was reminded of a quotation from Norboisin — the girl Denise gasps it as she expires: '*Au moins, je meurs ardemment!*' Might not Boyd have used those very words, Calida? Of course, with Denise the adverb applied to herself, whereas with Boyd it would have been meant for the agent —''

''Perren!'' It was not a protest this time, but a command. Mrs. Frost's tone and look together refrigerated him into silence. She surveyed him: ''You are a babbling fool. Would you make a jest of it? No one but a fool jests at death.''

Gebert made her a little bow. ''Except his own, perhaps, Calida. To keep up appearances.''

''You may. I am Scotch, too, like Boyd. It is no joke to me.'' She turned her head and let me have her eyes again. ''You may as well go. As you say, this is my daughter's house; we do not put you out. But my daughter is still a minor — and anyway, we cannot help you. I have nothing whatever to say, beyond what I have told the police. If you enjoy Mr. Gebert's vaudeville I can leave you with him.''

I shook my head. ''No, I don't like it much.'' I stuck my notebook in my pocket. ''Anyhow, I've got an appointment downtown, to squeeze blood out of a stone, which will be a cinch. It's just possible Mr. Wolfe will phone to invite you to his office for a chat. Have you anything on for this evening?''

She froze me. ''Mr. Wolfe's taking advantage of my daughter's emotional impulse is abominable. I don't wish to see him. If he should come here —''

''Don't let that worry you.'' I grinned at her. ''He's done all his traveling for this season and then some. But I expect I'll be seeing you again.'' I started off, and after a few steps turned. ''By the way, if I were you I wouldn't make much of a point of persuading your daughter to fire us. It would just make Mr. Wolfe suspicious, and that turns him into a fiend. I can't handle him when he's like that.''

It didn't look as if even that one was going to cause her to burst into sobs, so I beat it. In the entrance hall I tried to open up the wrong mirror, then found the right one and got my hat. The etiquette seemed to be turned off, so I let myself out and steered for the elevator.

I had to flag a taxi to take me home, because I had ridden up with our client and her cousin, not caring to leave them along together at that juncture.

It was after six o'clock when I got there. I went to the kitchen first and commandeered a glass of milk, took a couple of sniffs at the goulash steaming gently on the simmer plate, and told Fritz it didn't smell much like freshly butchered kid to me. I slid out when he brandished a skimming spoon.

Wolfe was at his desk with a book, *Seven Pillars of Wisdom*, by Lawrence, which he had already read twice, and I knew what mood he was in when I saw that the tray and glass were on his desk but no empty bottle. It was one of his most childish tricks, every now and then, especially when he was ahead of his quota more than usual, to drop the bottle into the wastebasket as soon as he emptied it, and if I was in the office he did it when I wasn't looking. It was that sort of thing that kept me skeptical about the fundamental condition of his brain, and that particular trick was all the more

284

foolish because he was unquestionably on the square with the bottle caps; he faithfully put every single one in the drawer; I know that, because I've checked up on him time and time again. When he was ahead on quota he made some belittling remark about statistics with each cap he dropped in, but he never tried to get away with one.

I tossed my notebook on my desk and sat down and sipped at the milk. There was no use trying to explode him off of that book. But after a while he picked up the thin strip of ebony he used for a bookmark, inserted it, closed the book, laid it down, and reached out and rang for beer. Then he leaned back and admitted I was alive.

"Pleasant afternoon, Archie?"

I grunted. "That was one hell of a tea. Dudley Frost was the only one who had any, and he wasn't inclined to divvy so I sent him home. I only got one real hot piece of news, that no one but a fool jests at death. How does that strike you?"

Wolfe grimaced. "Tell me about it."

I read it to him from the notebook, filling in the gaps from memory, though I didn't need much because I've condensed my symbols until I can take down the Constitution of the United States on the back of an old envelope, which might be a good place for it. Wolfe's beer arrived, and met its fate. Except for time out for swallowing, he listened, as usual, settled back comfortably with his eyes closed.

I tossed the notebook to the back of my desk, swiveled, and pulled the bottom drawer out and got my feet up. "That's the crop. That one's in the bag. What shall I start on now?"

Wolfe opened his eyes. "Your French is not even ludicrous. We'll return to that. Why did you frighten Mr. Frost away by talk of a search warrant? Is there a subtlety there too deep for me?"

"No, just momentum. I asked him that question about the red box to get a line on the other two, and as I went along it occurred to me it might be fun to find out if he had anything at home he didn't want anyone to see, and anyway what good was he? I got rid of him.''

''Oh. I was about to credit you with superior finesse. It would have been that, to get him away, on the chance that there might be a remark, a glance, a gesture, not to be expected in his presence. In fact, that is exactly what happened. I congratulate you anyhow. As for Mr. Frost — everyone has something at home they don't want anyone to see; that is one of the functions of a home, to provide a spot to keep such things. — And you say they haven't the red box and don't know where it is.''

''I offer that opinion. The look Gebert shot at Frost when I hinted Frost had it, and the look Mrs. Frost gave Gebert, as I told you. It's a cinch that what they think is in the box means something important to them. It's a good guess that they haven't got it and don't know where it is, or they wouldn't have been so quick on the trigger when I hinted that. As for Frost, God knows. That's the advantage a guy has that always explodes no matter what you say, there's no symptomatic nuances for an observer like me.''

''You? Ha! I am impressed. I confess I am surprised that Mrs. Frost didn't find a pretext as soon as you entered, to take her daughter to some other room. Is the woman immune to trepidation? Even common curiosity . . .''

I shook my head. ''If it's common, she hasn't got it. That dame has got a steel spine, a governor on her main artery that prevents acceleration, and a patent air-cooling system for her brain. If you wanted to prove she murdered anyone you'd have to see her do it and be sure to have a camera along.''

''Dear me.'' Wolfe came forward in his chair to pour beer. ''Then we must find another culprit, which may be a nuisance.'' He watched the foam subside. ''Take your book and look at your notes on Mr. Gebert's vaudeville. Where he quoted Norboisin; read that sentence.''

''You'd like some more fun with my French?''

''No, indeed; it isn't fun. Since your

shorthand is phonetic, do as well as you can with your symbols. I think I know the quotation, but I want to be sure. It has been years since I read Norboisin, and I haven't his books.''

I read the whole paragraph, beginning ''My dear Calida.'' I took the French on high and sailed right through it, ludicrous or not, having had three lessons in it altogether: one from Fritz in 1930, and two from a girl I met once when we were working on a forgery case.

''Want to hear it again?''

''No, thanks.'' Wolfe's lips were pushing in and out. ''And Mrs. Frost calls it babbling. It would have been instructive to be there, for the tone and the eyes. Mr. Gebert was indeed sardonic, to tell you in so many words who killed Mr. McNair. Was it a lie, to be provoking? Or the truth, to display his own alertness? Or a conjecture, for a little subtlety of his own? I think, the second. I do indeed. It runs with my surmises, but he could not know that. And granted that we know the murderer, what the devil is to be done about it? Probably no amount of patience would suffice. If Mr. Cramer gets his hands on the red box and decides to act without me, he is apt to lose the spark entirely and leave both of us with fuel that will not ignite." He drank his beer, put the glass down, and wiped his lips. "Archie. We need that confounded box."

"Yeah. I'll go get it in just a minute. First, just to humor me, exactly when did Gebert tell us who killed McNair? You wouldn't by any chance be talking just to hear yourself?"

"Of course not. Isn't it obvious? But I forget — you don't know French. *Ardemment* means ardently. The quotation translates, 'At least, I die ardently.' "

"Really?" I elevated the brows. "The hell you say."

"Yes. And therefore — but I forget again. You don't know Latin. Do you?"

"Not intimately. I'm shy on Chinese too." I aimed a Bronx cheer in a sort of general direction. "Maybe we ought to turn this case over to the Heinemann School of Languages. Did Gebert's quotation fix us up on evidence too, or do we have to dig that out for ourselves?''

I overplayed it. Wolfe compressed his lips and eyed me without favor. He leaned back. ''Some day, Archie, I shall be constrained . . . but no. I cannot remake the universe, and must therefore put up with this one. What is, is, including you.'' He sighed. ''Let the Latin go. Information for your records: this afternoon I telephoned Mr. Hitchcock in London; expect it on the bill. I asked him to send a man to Scotland for a talk with Mr. McNair's sister, and to instruct his agent, either in Barcelona or in Madrid, to examine certain records in the town of Cartagena. That means an expenditure of several hundred dollars. There has been no further report from Saul Panzer. We need that red box. It was already apparent to me who killed Mr. McNair, and why, before Mr. Gebert permitted himself the amusement of informing you; he really didn't help us any, and of course he didn't intend to. But what is known is not necessarily demonstrable. Pfui! To sit here and wait upon the result of a game of hide-and-seek, when all the difficulties have in fact been surmounted! Please type out a note of that statement of Mr. Gebert's while it is fresh; conceivably it will be needed."

He picked up his book again, got his elbows on the arms of his chair, opened to his page, and was gone.

He read until dinnertime, but even *Seven Pillars of Wisdom* did not restrain his promptness in responding to Fritz's summons to table. During the meal he kindly explained to me the chief reason for Lawrence's amazing success in keeping the Arabian tribes together for the great revolt. It was because Lawrence's personal attitude toward women was the same as the classic and traditional Arabian attitude. The central fact about any man, in respect to his activities as a social animal, is his attitude toward women; hence the Arabs felt that essentially Lawrence was one of them, and so accepted him. His native ability for leadership and finesse did the rest. A romantic they would not have understood, a puritan they would have rudely ignored, a sentimentalist they would have laughed at, but the contemptuous realist Lawrence, with his false humility and his fierce secret pride, they took to their bosoms. The goulash was as good as any Fritz had ever made.

It was after nine o'clock when we finished with coffee and went back to the office. Wolfe resumed with his book. I got at my desk with the plant records. I figured that after an hour or so of digestion and this peaceful family scene I would make an effort to extract a little Latin lesson out of Wolfe, and find out whether Gebert really had said anything or if perchance Wolfe was only practicing some fee-faw-fum, but an interruption came before I had even decided on a method of attack. At nine-thirty the phone rang.

I reached for it. "Hello, this is the office of Nero Wolfe."

"Archie? Fred. I'm talking from Brewster. Better put Mr. Wolfe on."

I told him to hold it and turned to Wolfe. "Fred calling from Brewster. Fifteen cents a minute."

At that, he stopped to put in his bookmark. Then he got his receiver up, and I told Fred to proceed, and opened my notebook.

"Mr. Wolfe? Fred Durkin. Saul sent me to the village to phone. We haven't found any red box, but there's been a little surprise at that place. We finished with the house, covered every inch, and started outdoors. It's the worst time of year for it, because when it thaws in the spring it's the muddiest time of the year. After it got dark we were working with flashlights, and we saw the lights of a car coming down the road and Saul had us put our lights out. It's a narrow dirt road and you can't go fast. The car turned in at the gate and stopped on the driveway. We had put the sedan in the garage. The lights went out and the engine stopped and a man got out. There was only one of him, so we kept still, behind some bushes. He went to a window and turned a flashlight on it and started trying to open it, and Orrie and I stepped out between him and the car, and Saul went toward him and asked him why he didn't go in the door. He took it cool, he said he forgot his key, then he said he didn't know he'd be interrupting anyone and started off. Saul stopped him and said he'd better come in first and have a drink and a little talk. The guy laughed and said he would and they went in, and Orrie and I went in after them, and we turned on the lights and sat down. The guy's name is Gebert, G-E-B-E-R-T, a tall slender dark guy with a thin nose —''

''Yeah, I know him. What did he say?''

''Not a hell of a lot of anything. He talks but he don't say anything. He says this McNair was a friend of his, and there's some things belonging to him in the place, and he thought he might as well drive out and get them. He ain't scared and he ain't easy. He's a great smiler.''

"Yeah, I know. Where is he now?"

"Why, he's out there. Saul and Orrie have got him —"

"Turn him loose. What else can you do? Unless you're hungry and want to make soup of him. Saul won't get anywhere with that bird. You can't keep him —"

"The hell we can't keep him. I ain't through, wait till I tell you. We had been in there with that Gebert ten or fifteen minutes, when there was a noise out front and I hopped out to take a look. It was two cars, and they stopped by the gate. They piled out and came in the yard after me, and by God if they didn't pull guns. You might have thought I was Dillinger. I saw state troopers' uniforms. I let out a yell to warn Saul to lock the door and then I met the attack. I was surrounded by who do you think? Rowcliff, that mutt of a lieutenant from the Homicide Squad, and three other dicks, and two troopers, and a little runt with spectacles that told me he was an assistant district attorney of Putnam County. Huh? Was I surrounded?''

"Yes. At last. Did they shoot you?''

"Sure, but I caught the bullets and tossed them back. Well, it seems that what they came for was to look for that red box. They went to the door and wanted in. Saul left Orrie there inside the door and went to a window and talked to them through the glass. Of course he asked to see a search warrant and they didn't have any. There was some gab back and forth, and then the troopers announced they were going in after Saul because he was trespassing, and he held the paper that Mr. Wolfe signed up against the window and they put a flashlight on it. There was more talk, and then Saul told me to drive to the village and phone you, and Rowcliff said nothing doing until he searched me for the red box, and I told him if he touched me I'd skin him and hang him up to dry. But I couldn't get the sedan out because Gebert's car was in the driveway and the others blocked the road at the gate, so we declared a truce and Rowcliff took his car and we both came to Brewster in it. It's only about three miles. We left the rest of the gang sitting there on the porch. I'm in a booth in a restaurant and Rowcliff's down the street in a drug store phoning headquarters. I've got a notion to grab his car and go back without him.''

''Okay. Damn good idea. Does he know Gebert's there?''

''No. If Gebert's shy about cops, of course he don't want to leave. What do we do? Toss him out? Let the cops in? We can't go out and dig, all we can do is sit there and watch Gebert smile, and it's as cold as an Englishman's heart and we haven't got a fire. Good God, you ought to hear those troopers talk, I guess out there in the wilds they catch bears and lions with their hands and eat 'em raw.''

''Hold it.'' I turned to Wolfe. ''I suppose I go for a drive?''

He shuddered. I presume he calculated that there must be at least a thousand jolts between 35th Street and Brewster, and ten thousand cars to meet and pass. The lurking dangers of the night. He

298

nodded at me.

I told Fred, ''Go on back. Keep Gebert, and don't let them in. I'll be there as soon as I can make it.''

13

It was a quarter to ten by the time I got away and around the corner to the garage on Tenth Avenue and was sailing down the ramp in the roadster, and it was 11:13 when I rolled into the village of Brewster and turned left — following the directions I had heard Helen Frost give Saul Panzer. An hour and twenty-eight minutes wasn't bad, counting the curves on the Pines Bridge Road and the bum stretch between Muscoot and Croton Falls.

I followed the pavement a little over a mile and then turned left again onto a dirt road. It was as narrow as a bigot's mind, and I got in the ruts and stayed there. My lights showed me nothing but the still bare branches of trees and shrubbery close on both sides, and I began to think that Fred's jabber about the wilds hadn't been so dumb. There was an occasional house, but they were dark and silent, and I went on bumping so long, a sharp curve to the left and one to the right and then to the left again, that I began wondering if I was on the wrong road. Then, finally, I saw a light ahead, stuck to the ruts around another curve, and there I was.

Besides a few rapid comments from Wolfe before I started, I had trotted the brain around for a survey of the situation during the drive, and there didn't seem to be anything very critical about it except that it would be nice to keep the news of Gebert's expedition to ourselves for a while. They were welcome to go in and look for the red box all they wanted to, since Saul, with the whole afternoon to work undisturbed, hadn't found it. But Gebert was worth a little effort, not to mention the item that we had our reputation to consider. So I stopped the roadster alongside the two cars that were parked at the edge of the road and leaned out and yelled:

"Come and move this bus! It's blocking the gate and I want to turn in!"

A gruff shout came from the porch: "Who the hell are you?" I called back:

"Haile Selassie. Okay, I'll move it myself. If it makes a ditch, don't blame me."

I got out and climbed into the other car, open with the top down, a state police chariot. I heard, and saw dimly in the dark, a couple of guys leave the porch and come down the short path. They jumped the low palings. The front one was in uniform and I made out the other one for my old friend Lieutenant Rowcliff. The trooper was stern enough to scare me silly:

"Come out of that, buddie. Move that car and I'll tie you in a knot."

I said, "You will not. Get it? It's a pun. My name is Archie Goodwin, I represent Mr. Nero Wolfe, I belong in there and you don't. If a man finds a car blocking his own gate he has plenty of right to move it, which is what I'm going to do, and if you try to stop me it will be too bad because I'm mad as hell and I mean it.''

Rowcliff growled, ''All right, get out, we'll move the damn thing.'' He muttered at the cossack, ''You might as well. This bird's never been tamed yet.''

The trooper opened the door. ''Get out.''

''You going to move it?''

''Why the hell shouldn't I move it? Get out.''

I descended and climbed back in the roadster. The trooper started his car and eased it ahead, into the road, and off again beyond the entrance. My lights were on him. I put my gear in, circled through the gate onto the driveway, stopped back of a car there which I recognized for the convertible Gebert had parked in front of Wolfe's house the day before, and got out and started for the porch. There was a mob there sitting along the edge of it. One of them got smart and turned on a flash and spotted it on my face as I approached. Rowcliff and the trooper came up and stood at the foot of the steps.

I demanded, ''Who's in charge of this

gang? I know you're not, Rowcliff, we're outside the city limits. Who's got any right to be here on private property?"

They looked at each other. The trooper stuck out his chin at me and asked, "Have you?"

"You're darned tooting I have. You've seen a paper signed by the executor of the estate that owns this. I've got another one in my pocket. Well, come on, who's in charge? Who's responsible for this outrage?"

There was a cackle from the porch, a shadow in the corner. "I've got a right to be here, ain't I, Archie?"

I peered at it. "Oh, hi, Fred. What are you doing out here in the cold?"

He ambled toward me. "We didn't want to open the door, because this bunch of highbinders might take a notion —"

I snorted. "Where would they get it from? — All right, nobody's in charge, is that it? Fred, call Saul —"

"I'll take the responsibility!" A little squirt had popped up and I saw his spectacles. He squealed, ''I'm the Assistant District Attorney of this county! We have a legal right —''

I did some towering over him. ''You have a legal right to go home and go to bed. Have you got a warrant or a subpoena or even a cigarette paper?''

''No, there wasn't time —''

''Then shut up.'' I turned to Rowcliff and the trooper. ''You think I'm being tough? Not at all, I'm just indignant and I have a right to be. You've got a nerve, to come to a private house in the middle of the night and expect to go through it, without any evidence that there has ever been anything or anyone criminal it it. What do you want, the red box? It's Nero Wolfe's property, and if it's in there I'll get it and put it in my pocket and walk out with it, and don't try to play tag with me, because I'm sensitive about coming in contact with people.'' I brushed past them and mounted the porch, crossed to the door and rapped on it:

''Come here, Fred. Saul!''

I heard his voice from inside: "Hello, Archie! Okay?"

"Sure, okay. Open the door! Stand by, Fred."

The gang had stood up and edged toward us a little. I heard the lock turning; the door swung open and a lane of light ribboned the porch; Saul stood on the threshold with Orrie back of him. Fred and I were there too. I faced the throng:

"I hereby order you to leave these premises. All of you. In other words, beat it. Now do as you damn please, but its on the record that you're here illegally, for future reference. We resent your scuffing up the porch, but if you try coming in the house we'll resent that a lot worse. Back up, Saul. Come on, Fred."

We went in. Saul closed the door and locked it. I looked around. Knowing that the joint belonged to McNair, I halfway expected to see some more decorators' delights, but it was rustic. Nice big chairs and seats with cushions and a big heavy wooden table, and a blaze crackling in a wide fireplace at one end. I turned to Fred Durkin:

"You darned liar. You said there was no fire."

He grinned, rubbing his hands in front of it. "I didn't think Mr. Wolfe ought to think we was too comfortable."

"He wouldn't mind. He doesn't like hardship, even for you." I looked around again and spoke to Saul in a lower tone. "Where's what you've got with you?"

He nodded at a door. "In the other room. No light in there."

"You didn't find the box?"

"No sign of it. All cubic inches accounted for."

Since it was Saul, that settled it. I asked him, "Is there another door?"

"One at the back. We've got it propped."

"Okay. You and Fred stay here. Orrie, come with me."

He lumbered over and I led him into the other room. After I closed the door behind us it was good and dark, but there were two dim rectangles for windows, and after a few seconds I made out an outline in a chair. I said to Orrie, "Sing."

He grumbled, "What the hell, I'm too hungry to sing."

"Sing anyway. If one of them happens to glue his ear to a window I want him to hear something. Sing 'Git Along, Little Dogie'."

"I can't sing in the dark —"

"Damn it, will you sing?"

He cleared his throat and started it up. Orrie had a pretty good voice. I went close to the outline in the chair and said to it:

"I'm Archie Goodwin. You know me."

"Certainly." Gebert's voice sounded purely conversational. "You're the fellow who doesn't like scenes."

"Right. That's why I'm out here when I ought to be in bed. Why are you out here?"

"I drove out to get my umbrella which I left here last fall."

"Oh. You did. Did you find it?"

"No. Someone must have taken it."

"That's too bad. Listen to me a minute. Out on the porch is an army of state police and New York detectives and a Putnam County prosecutor. How would you like to have to tell them about your umbrella?"

I saw the outline of his shoulders move with his shrug. "If it would amuse them. I hardly suppose they know where it is."

"I see. You're fancy free, huh? Not a care in the world. In that case, what are you doing sitting in here alone in the dark? — A little louder, Orrie."

Gebert shrugged again. "Your colleague — the little chap with the big nose — asked me to come in here. He was very courteous to me when I was trying a window because I had no key."

"So you wanted to be courteous to him. That was darned swell of you. Then it's okay if I let the cops in and tell them we found you trying to break in?"

"I'm really indifferent about it." I

couldn't see his smile but I knew he was wearing it. "Really. I wasn't breaking in, I was only trying a window."

I straightened up, disgusted. He wasn't giving me anything at all to bargain with, and even if it was a bluff I guessed that he was sardonic enough to go right through with it. Orrie stopped, and I grunted at him to carry on. The conditions were bad for negotiation. I leaned over him again:

"Look here, Gebert. We've got your number — Nero Wolfe has — but we're willing to give you a chance. It's midnight. What's wrong with this: I'll let the cops in and tell them they can look for the red box all they want to. I happen to know they won't find it. You are one of my colleagues. Your name's Jerry. We'll leave my other colleagues here and you and I will get in my car and go back to New York, and you can sleep in Wolfe's house — there's a good bed in the room above mine. The advantage of that is that you'll be there in the morning to have a talk with Wolfe. That strikes me as a good program.''

I could see him shaking his head. ''I live at the Chesebrough. Thanks for your invitation, but I prefer to sleep in my own bed.''

''I'm asking you, will you come?''

''To Mr. Wolfe's house to sleep? No.''

''All right. You're crazy. Surely you've got brains enough to realize that you're going to have to have a talk with somebody about your driving sixty miles to go through a window to get an umbrella. Knowing Wolfe, and knowing the police, I merely advise you to talk with him instead of them. I'm not trying to shatter your aplomb, I like it, I think it's attractive, but I'll be damned if I'm going to stand here and beg you all night. In a couple of minutes I'll begin to get impatient.''

Gebert shrugged again. ''I confess I don't like the police. I leave here with you incognito. Is that it?''

''That's it.''

''Very well. I'll go.''

''To Wolfe's for the night?''

"I tell you so."

"Good for you. Don't worry about your car; Saul will take care of it. Your name's Jerry. Act tough and ignorant, like me or any other detective. — Okay, Orrie, choke it. Come on. Come on, Jerry."

I opened the door to the lighted room and they followed me in. I collected Saul and Fred and briefly explained the strategy, and when Saul objected to letting the cops in I agreed with him without an argument. Our trio was supposed to resume operations in the morning, and in the meantime they had to have some shut-eye. It was settled that no one was to be permitted to enter, and excavations by strangers outdoors were barred. They were to send Fred to the village to get grub, and to phone the office, in the morning.

I went to a window and pushed my nose against the glass and saw that the party was still gathered about the steps. At a nod from me Saul unlocked the door and swung it open, and Gebert and I passed through to the porch. In our rear, Saul and Fred and Orrie occupied the doorsill. We clattered to the edge:

"Lieutenant Rowcliff? Oh, there you are. Jerry Martin and I are going back to town. I'm leaving three men here, and they still prefer privacy. They need some sleep and so do you. Just as a favor, I'll tell you straight that Jerry and I haven't got the red box on us, so there's nothing to gnash your teeth about. — Okay, Saul, lock up, and one of you stay awake." The door shut, leaving the porch in the dark again, and I turned. "Come on, Jerry. If anyone jostles you, stick a hatpin in him."

But the instant the door had closed someone had got smart and clicked on a flashlight and aimed it at Gebert's face. I had his elbow to urge him along, but there was a stir in front of us and a growl: "Now you don't need to run." A big guy was standing in front of Gebert and holding the light on him. He growled again, "Look here, Lieutenant, look at this Jerry. Jerry hell. This is that guy that was at Frost's apartment when I was up there this morning with the inspector. His name's Gebert, a friend of Mrs. Frost's.''

I snickered. ''I don't know you, mister, but you must be cross-eyed. The country air maybe. Come on, Jerry.''

No go. Rowcliff and two other dicks and the pair of troopers all barred the way, and Rowcliff sang at me, ''Back up, Goodwin. You've heard of Bill Northrup and you know how cross-eyed he is. No mistake, Bill?''

''Not a chance. It's Gebert.''

''You don't say. Keep the light on him. How about it, Mr. Gebert? What do you mean by trying to fool Mr. Goodwin and telling him your name's Jerry Martin? Huh?''

I kept my trap shut. Through a bad piece of luck I was getting a kick on the shin, and there was nothing to do but take it. And I had to hand it to Gebert; with that light right in his face and that bunch of gorillas all sticking their chins at him, he smiled as if they were asking him whether he took milk or lemon.

He said, ''I wouldn't try to fool Mr. Goodwin. Indeed not. Anyway, how could I? He knows me.''

''Oh, he does. Then I can discuss the Jerry Martin idea with him. But you might tell me what you're doing out here at the McNair place. They found you here, huh?''

''Found me?'' Gebert looked urbane but a little annoyed. ''Of course not. They brought me. At their request I came to show them where I thought McNair might have concealed the red box they are looking for. But no; it wasn't there. Then you arrived. Then Mr. Goodwin arrived. He thought it would be pleasanter if you did not know I had come to help them, and he suggested I should be Mr. Jerry Martin. I saw no reason not to oblige him.''

Rowcliff grunted. ''But you didn't see fit to mention this place to Inspector Cramer this morning when he asked if you had any idea where the red box might be. Did you?''

Gebert had a cute reply for that too, and for several more questions, but I didn't listen to them with much interest. I was busy taking a trial balance. I shied off because Gebert was being a little too slick. Of course he figured that I would let his story slide because I wanted to save him for Nero Wolfe, but it began to look to me as if he wasn't worth the price. It wasn't an attack of qualms; I would just as soon kick dust in the eyes of the entire Police Department from Commissioner Hombert up in anything that resembled a worthy cause; but it appeared more than doubtful whether Wolfe would be able to squeeze any profit out of Gebert anyhow, and if he couldn't, we would just be giving Cramer another reason to get good and sore without anything to console us for it. I knew I was taking a big risk, for if Gebert had murdered McNair there was a fair chance that they would screw it out of him at headquarters, and there would be our case up the flue; but I wasn't like Wolfe, I was handicapped by not knowing whether Gebert was guilty. While I was making these calculations I was listening with one ear to Gebert smearing it on Rowcliff, and he did a neat job of it; he had smoothed it down to a point where he and I could have got in a car and driven off without even being fingerprinted.

"See that you're home in the morning," Rowcliff was growling at him. "The inspector may want to see you. If you go out leave word where." He turned to me, and you could have distilled vinegar from his breath. "You're so full of lousy tricks I'll bet when you're alone you play 'em on yourself. The inspector will let you know what he thinks of this one. I'd hate to tell you what I think of it."

I grinned at him, his face in the dark. "And here I am all ready with another one. I've been standing here listening to Gebert reel it off just to see how slick he is. He could slide on a cheese grater. You'd better take him to headquarters and give him a bed."

"Yeah? What for? You through with him?"

"Naw, I haven't even started. A little before nine o'clock this evening he got here in his car. Not knowing there was anyone here because the lights were out, he tried to pry open a window to get in. When Saul Panzer asked him what he wanted, he said he left his umbrella here last fall and drove out to get it. Maybe it's in your lost and found room at headquarters; you'd better take him there to look and see. Material witness would do it.''

Rowcliff grunted. ''You were ready with another one all right. When did you think this up?''

''I didn't have to. Fact is stranger than fiction. You shouldn't be always suspecting everybody. If you want me to I'll call them out and you can ask them; they were all three here. I would say that an umbrella that's worth going in a window after is worth asking questions about.''

''Uh-huh. And you were calling this guy Jerry and trying to smuggle him out. Where to? How would you like to come down and look over some umbrellas yourself?''

That disgusted me. I wasn't any too pleased anyhow, letting go of Gebert. I said, ''Poop and pooh. Both for you.

You sound like a flatfoot catching kids playing wall ball. Maybe I wanted the glory of taking him to headquarters myself. Or maybe I wanted to help him escape from the country by putting him on a subway for Brooklyn, where I believe you live. You've got him, haven't you, with a handle I gave you to hold him by? Poops and poohs for all of youse. It's past my bedtime.''

I strode through the cordon, brushing them aside like flies, went to the roadster and got in, backed out through the gate, circling into the road and missing the fender of the troopers' chariot by an inch, and rolled off along the ruts and bumps. I was so disgruntled with the complexion of things that I beat my former time between Brewster and 35th Street by two minutes.

Of course I found the house dark and quiet. There was no note from Wolfe on my desk. Upstairs, in my room, whither I carried the glass of milk I had got in the kitchen, the pilot light was a red spot on the wall, showing that Wolfe had turned on his switch so that if anyone disturbed one of his windows or stepped in the hall within eight feet of his door, a gong under my bed would start a hullabaloo that would wake even me. I hit the hay at 2:19.

14

I swiveled my chair to face Wolfe. "Oh, yes, I forgot to tell you. This may strike a chord. That lawyer Collinger said that they are proceeding with McNair's remains as instructed in his will. Services are being held at nine o'clock this evening at the Belford Memorial Chapel on 73rd Street, and tomorrow he'll be cremated and the ashes sent to his sister in Scotland. Collinger seems to think that naturally the executor of McNair's estate will attend the services. Will we go in the sedan?"

Wolfe murmured, "Puerile. You are no better than a gadfly. You may represent me at the Belford Memorial Chapel." He shuddered. "Black and white. Dreary and hushed obeisance to the grisly terror. His murderer will be

there. Confound it, don't badger me."
He resumed with the atlas, doing the
double page spread of Arabia.

It was noon Friday. I had had less
than six hours' sleep, having held my
levee at eight in order to be ready,
without skimping breakfast, to report to
Wolfe at nine o'clock in the plant
rooms. He had asked me first off if I
had got the red box, and beyond that
had listened with his back as he examined
a bench of cattleya seedlings. The news
about Gebert appeared to bore him, and
he could always carry that off without
my being able to tell whether it was a
pose or on the level. When I reminded
him that Collinger was due at ten to
discuss the will and the estate, and asked
if there were any special instructions, he
merely shook his head without bothering
to turn around. I left him and went down
to the kitchen and ate a couple more
pancakes so as to keep from taking a
nap. Fritz was friendly again, forgiving
and forgetting that I had jerked Wolfe
back from the brink of the Wednesday
relapse. He never toted a grudge.

Around 9:30 Fred Durkin phoned from Brewster. After my departure from Glennanne the night before the invaders had soon left, and our trio had had a restful night, but they had barely finished their stag breakfast when dicks and troopers had appeared again, armed with papers. I told Fred to tell Saul to keep an eye on the furniture and other portable objects.

At ten o'clock Henry H. Barber, our lawyer, came, and a little later Collinger. I sat and listened to a lot of guff about probate and surrogate and so forth, and went upstairs and got Wolfe's signature to some papers, and did some typing for them. They were gone before Wolfe came down at eleven. He had arranged the orchids in the vase, rung for beer, tried his pen, looked through the morning mail, made a telephone call to Raymond Plehn, dictated a letter, and then gone to the bookshelves and returned with the atlas; and settled down with it. I had never been able to think of more than one possible advantage to be expected from Wolfe's atlas work: If we ever got an international case we would certainly be on familiar ground, no matter where it took us to.

I went ahead with a lot of entries from Theodore Horstmann's slips into the plant records.

Around a quarter to one Fritz knocked on the door and followed it in with a cablegram in his hand. I opened it and read it:

SCOTLAND NEGATIVE NUGANT GAMUT CARTAGENA NEGATIVE DESTRUCTION RIOTS DANNUM GAMUT

HITCHCOCK

I got out the code book and did some looking, and scribbled in my book. Wolfe stayed in Arabia. I cleared my throat like a lion and his eyes flickered at me.

I told him, 'If no news is good news, here's a treat from Hitchcock. He says that in Scotland there are no results yet because the subject refuses to furnish help or information but that efforts are being continued. In Cartagena likewise no results on account of destruction in riots two years ago, and likewise efforts are being continued. I might add on my own hook that Scotland and Cartagena have got it all over 35th Street in one respect anyhow. Gamut. Efforts are being continued.''

Wolfe grunted.

Ten minutes later he closed the atlas. ''Archie. We need that red box.''

''Yes, sir.''

''Yes, we do. I phoned Mr. Hitchcock in London again, at the night rate, after you left last evening, and I fear got him out of bed. I learned that Mr. McNair's sister is living on an old family property, a small place near Camfirth, and thought it possible that he had concealed the red box there during one of his trips to Europe. I requested Mr. Hitchcock to have a search made for it, but apparently the sister — from this cable — will not permit it.''

He sighed. ''I never knew a plaguier case. We have all the knowledge we need, and not a shred of presentable evidence. Unless the red box is found — are we actually going to be forced to send Saul to Scotland or Spain or both? Good heavens! Are we so inept that we must half encircle the globe to demonstrate the motive and the technique of a murder that happened in our own office in front of our eyes? Pfui! I sat for two hours last evening considering the position, and I confess that we have an exceptional combination of luck and adroitness against us; but even so, if we are driven to the extreme of buying steamship tickets across the Altantic we are beneath contempt.''

''Yeah.'' I grinned at him; if he was getting sore there was hope. ''I'm beneath yours and you're beneath mine. At that, it may be one of those cases where nothing but routine will do it. For instance, one of Cramer's hirelings may turn the trick by trailing a sale of potassium cyanide.''

''Bah.'' Wolfe upturned a whole palm; he was next door to a frenzy. ''Mr. Cramer does not even know who the murderer is. As for the poison, it was probably bought years ago, possibly not in this country. We have to deal not only with adroitness, but also with forethought."

"So I suspected. You're telling me that you do know who the murderer is. Huh?"

"Archie." He wiggled a finger at me. "I dislike mystification and never practice it for diversion. But I shall load you with no burdens that will strain your powers. You have no gift for guile. Certainly I know who the murderer is, but what good does that do me? I am in no better boat than Mr. Cramer. By the way, he telephoned last evening a few minutes after you left. In a very ugly mood. He seemed to think we should have told him of the existence of Glennanne instead of leaving him to discover it for himself from an item among Mr. McNair's papers; and he hotly resented Saul's holding it against beleaguerment. I presume he will cool off now that you have made him a gift of Mr. Gebert."

I nodded. "And I presume I would

look silly if he squeezed enough sap out of Gebert to make the case jell.''

''Never. No fear, Archie. Mr. Gebert is not likely, under any probable pressure, to surrender the only hold on the cliff of existence he has managed to cling to. It would have been useless to bring him here; he has his profit and loss calculated. — Yes, Fritz? Ah, the soufflé chose to ignore the clock? At once, certainly.''

He gripped the edge of the desk to push back his chair.

We did not ignore the soufflé.

My lunch was interrupted once, by a phone call from Helen Frost. Ordinarily Wolfe flatly prohibited my disturbing a meal to go to the phone, letting it be handled by Fritz on the kitchen extension, but there were exceptions he permitted. One was a female client. So I went to the office and took it, not with any overflow of gaiety, for all morning I had been thinking that we might get word from her any minute that the deal was off. Up there alone with her mother, there was no telling what she might be talked into. But all she wanted was to ask about Perren Gebert. She said that her mother had phoned the Chesebrough at breakfast time and had learned that Gebert had not been there for the night, and after phoning and fussing all morning, she had finally been informed by the police that Gebert was being detained at headquarters, and they had not let her speak with him. She said that Inspector Cramer had told her mother something about Gebert being held on information furnished by Mr. Goodwin of Nero Wolfe's office, and what about it?

I told her, "It's all right. We caught him trying to get in a window out at Glennanne, and the cops are asking him what for. Just a natural sensible question. After a while he'll either answer it or he won't, and they'll either turn him loose or keep him. It's all right."

"But they won't . . ."

She sounded harassed. "You see, I told you, it's true there are things about him I don't like, but he is an old friend of mother's and mine too. They won't do anything to him, will they? I can't understand what he was doing at Glennanne, trying to get in. He hasn't been there . . . I don't think he ever was there . . . you know he and Uncle Boyd didn't like each other. I don't understand it. But they can't do anything to him just for trying to open a window. Can they?"

"They can and they can't. They can sort of annoy him. That won't hurt him much."

"It's terrible." The shiver was in her voice. "It's terrible! And I thought I was hard-boiled. I guess I am, but . . . anyway, I want you and Mr. Wolfe to go on. Go right on. Only I thought I might ask you — Perren is really mother's oldest friend — if you could go down there and see where he is and what they're doing . . . I know the police are very friendly with you . . ."

"Sure." I made a face at the phone. "Down to headquarters? Surest thing you know. Bless your heart, I'd be glad to. It won't take me long to finish my lunch, and I'll take it on the jump. Then

I'll phone you and let you know."

"Oh, that's fine. Thank you ever so much. If I'm not at home mother will be. I . . . I'm going out to buy some flowers . . ."

"Okay. I'll phone you."

I went back to the dining room and resumed with my tools and told Wolfe about it. He was provoked, as always when business intruded itself on a meal. I took my time eating, on to the coffee and through it, because I knew if I hurried and didn't chew properly it would upset Wolfe's digestion. It didn't break his heart if I was caught out in the field at feeding time and had to grab what I could get, but if I once started a meal at that table I had to complete it like a gentleman. Also, I wasn't champing at the bit for an errand I didn't fancy.

It was after two when I went to the garage for the roadster, and there I got another irritation when I found that the washing and polishing job had been done by a guy with one eye.

Downtown, on Centre Street, I parked

at the triangle, and went in and took the elevator. I walked down the upstairs corridor as if I owned it, entered the anteroom of Cramer's office as cocky as they come, and told the hulk at the desk:

"Tell the inspector, Goodwin of Nero Wolfe's office."

I stood up for ten minutes, and then was nodded in. I was hoping somewhat that Cramer would be out and my dealings would be with Burke, not on account of my natural timidity, but because I knew it would be better for everyone concerned if Cramer had a little more time to cool off before resuming social intercouse with us. But he was there at his desk when I entered, and to my surprise he didn't get up and take a bite at my ear. He snarled a little:

"So it's you. You walk right in here. Burke made a remark about you this morning. He said that if you ever wanted a rubdown you ought to get Smoky to do it for you. Smoky is the little guy with a bum leg that polishes the brass railings downstairs at the entrance."

I said, "I guess I'll sit down."

"I guess you will. Go ahead. Want my chair?"

"No, thanks."

"What *do* you want?"

I shook my head at him wistfully. "I'll be doggoned, Inspector, if you're not a hard man to please. We do our best to help you find that red box, and you resent it. We catch a dangerous character trying to make an illegal entry, and hand him over to you, and you resent that. If we wrap this case up and present you with it, I suppose you'll charge us as accessories. You may remember that in that Rubber Band affair —"

"Yeah, I know. Past favors have been appreciated. I'm busy. What do you want?"

"Well . . ." I tilted my head back so as to look down on him. "I represent the executor of Mr. McNair's estate. I came to invite Mr. Perren Gebert to attend the funeral services at the Belford Memorial Chapel at nine o'clock this evening. If you would kindly direct me to his room?"

Cramer gave me a nasty look. Then he heaved a deep sigh, reached in his pocket for a cigar, bit off the end and lit it. He puffed at it and got it established in the corner of his mouth. Abruptly he demanded:

"What have you got on Gebert?"

"Nothing. Not even passing a red light. Nothing at all."

"Did you come here to see him? What does Wolfe want you to ask him?"

"Nothing. As Tammany is my judge. Wolfe says he's just clinging to the cliff of existence or something like that and he wouldn't let him in the house."

"Then what the devil do you want with him?"

"Nothing. I'm just keeping my word. I promised somebody I would come down here and ask you how he is and what his future prospects are. So help me, that's on the level."

"Maybe I believe you. Do you want to look at him?"

"Not especially. I would just as soon."

"You can." He pressed a button in a

row. "As a matter of fact, I'd like to have you. This case is open and shut, open for the newspapers and shut for me. If you've got any curiosity about anything that you think Gebert might satisfy, go ahead and take your turn. They've been working on him since seven o'clock this morning. Eight hours. They can't even make him mad."

A sergeant with oversize shoulders had entered and was standing there. Cramer told him: "This man's name is Goodwin. Take him down to Room Five and tell Sturgis to let him help if he wants to." He turned to me. "Drop in again before you leave. I may want to ask you something."

"Okay. I'll have something thought up to tell you."

I followed the sergeant out to the corridor and down it to the elevator. We stayed in for a flight below the ground floor, and he led me the length of a dim hall and around a corner, and finally stopped at a door which may have had a figure 5 on it but if so I couldn't see it. He opened the door and we went in and he closed the door again. He crossed to where a guy sat on a chair mopping his neck with a handkerchief, said something to him, and turned and went out again.

It was a medium-sized room, nearly bare. A few plain wooden chairs were along one wall. A bigger one with arms was near the middle of the room, and Perren Gebert was sitting in it, with a light flooding his face from a floor lamp with a big reflector in front of him. Standing closer in front of him was a wiry-looking man in his shirt sleeves with little fox ears and a Yonkers haircut. The guy on the chair that the sergeant had spoken to was in his shirt sleeves too, and so was Gebert. When I got close enough to the light so that Gebert could see me and recognize me, he half started up, and said in a funny hoarse tone:

"Goodwin! Ah, Goodwin —"

The wiry cop reached out and slapped him a good one on the left side of his neck, and then with his other hand on his right ear. Gebert quivered and sank back. "Sit down there, will you?" the cop said plaintively. The other cop, still holding his handkerchief in his hand, got up and walked over to me:

"Goodwin? My name's Sturgis. Who are you from, Buzzy's squad?"

I shook my head. "Private agency. We're on the case and we're supposed to be hot."

"Oh. Private, huh? Well . . . the inspector sent you down. You want a job?"

"Not just this minute. You gentlemen go ahead. I'll listen and see if I can think of something."

I stepped a pace closer to Gebert and looked him over. He was reddened up a good deal and kind of blotchy, but I couldn't see any real marks. He had no necktie on and his shirt was torn on the shoulder and there was dried sweat on him. His eyes were bloodshot from blinking at the strong light and probably from having them slapped open when he closed them. I asked him:

"When you said my name just now, did you want to tell me something?"

He shook his head and made a hoarse grunt. I turned and told Sturgis: "He can't tell you anything if he can't talk. Maybe you ought to give him some water."

Sturgis snorted. "He could talk if he wanted to. We gave him water when he passed out a couple of hours ago. There's only one thing in God's world wrong with him. He's contrary. You want to try him?"

"Later maybe." I crossed to the row of chairs by the wall and sat down. Sturgis stood and thoughtfully wiped his neck. The wiry cop leaned forward to get closer to Gebert's face and asked him in a wounded tone:

"What did she pay you that money for?"

No response, no movement.

"What did she pay you that money for?"

Again, nothing.

"What did she pay you that money for?"

Gebert shook his head faintly. The cop roared at him in indignation, "Don't shake your head at me! Understand?

What did she pay you that money for?''

Gebert sat still. The cop hauled off and gave him a couple more slaps, rocking his head, and then another pair.

''What did she pay you that money for?''

That went on for a while. It appeared to me doubtful that any progress was going to be made. I felt sorry for the poor dumb cops, seeing that they didn't have brains enough to realize that they were just gradually putting him to sleep and that in another three or four hours he wouldn't be worth fooling with. Of course he would be as good as new in the morning, but they couldn't go on with that for weeks, even if he was a foreigner and couldn't vote. That was the practical viewpoint, and though the ethics of it was none of my business, I admit I had my prejudices. I can bulldog a man myself, if he has it coming to him, but I prefer to do it on his home grounds, and I certainly don't want any help.

Apparently they had abandoned all the side issues which had been tried on him earlier in the day, and were concentrating on a few main points. After twenty minutes or more consumed on what she had paid him the money for, the wiry cop suddenly shifted to another one, what had he been after at Glennanne the night before. Gebert mumbled something to that, and got slapped for it. Then he made no reply to it and got slapped again. The cop was about on the mental level of a woodchuck; he had no variety, no change of pace, no nothing but a pair of palms and they must have been getting tender. He stuck to Glennanne for over half an hour, while I sat and smoked cigarettes and got more and more disgusted, then turned away and crossed to his colleague and muttered wearily:

"Take him a while, I'm going to the can."

Sturgis asked me if I wanted to try, and I declined again with thanks. In fact, I was about ready to leave, but thought I might as well get a brief line on Sturgis' technique. He stuck his handkerchief in his hip pocket, walked over to Gebert and exploded at him:

"What did she pay you that money for?"

I gritted my teeth to keep from throwing a chair at the sap. But he did show some variation; he was more of a pusher than a slapper. The gesture he worked most was to put his paw on Gebert's ear and administer a few short snappy shoves and then put his other paw on the other ear and even it up. Sometimes he took him full face and shoved straight back and then ended with a pat.

The wiry cop had come back and sat down beside me and was telling me how much bran he ate. I had decided I had had my money's worth and was taking a last puff on a cigarette, when the door opened and the sergeant entered — the one who had brought me down. He walked over and looked at Gebert the way a cook looks at a kettle to see if it has started to boil. Sturgis stepped back and pulled out his handkerchief and started to wipe. The sergeant turned to him:

"Orders from the inspector. Fix him up and brush him off and take him to the north door and wait there for me. The inspector wants him out of here in five minutes. Got a cup?"

Sturgis went and opened the door of a cupboard and came back with a white enamelled cup. The sergeant poured into it from a bottle and returned the bottle to his pocket. "Let him have that. Can he navigate all right?"

Sturgis said he could. The sergeant turned to me: "Will you go up to the inspector's office, Goodwin? I've got an errand on the main floor."

He went on out and I followed him without saying anything. There was no one there I wanted to exchange telephone numbers with.

I took the elevator back upstairs. I had to wait quite a while in Cramer's anteroom. Apparently he was having a party in there, for three dicks came out, and a little later a captain in uniform, and still later a skinny guy with grey hair whom I recognized for Deputy Commissioner Alloway. Then I was allowed the gangway. Cramer was sitting there looking sour and chewing a cigar that had gone out.

"Sit down, son. You didn't get a chance to show us how downstairs. Huh? And we didn't show you much either. There was a good man working on Gebert for four hours this morning, a good clever man. He couldn't start a crack. So we gave up the cleverness and tried something else."

"Oh, that's it." I grinned at him. "That's what those guys are, something else. It describes them all right. And now you're turning him loose?"

"We are." Cramer frowned. "A lawyer was beginning to heat things up, I suppose hired by Mrs. Frost. He got a habeas corpus a little while ago, and I couldn't see that Gebert was worth fighting for, and anyway, I doubt if we could have held him. Also the French consul started stirring around. Gebert's a French citizen. Of course we're putting a shadow on him, and what good will that do? When a man like that has got knowledge about a crime there ought to be some way of tapping him the way you do a maple tree, and draw it out of him. Huh?"

I nodded. "Sure, that'd be all right. It would be better than . . ." I shrugged. "Never mind. Any news from the boys at Glennanne?"

"No." Cramer clasped his hands behind his head, leaned back into them, chewed his cigar, and scowled at me. "You know, I hate to say this to you. But it's what I think. I wouldn't like to see you get hurt, but it might have been more sensible if we had had you down in Room Five all day instead of that Gebert."

"Me?" I shook my head. "I don't believe it. After all I've done for you."

"Oh, don't kid me. I'm tired, I'm not in a mood for it. I've been thinking. I know how Wolfe works. I don't pretend I could do it, but I know how he does it. I admit he never yet has finished up on the wrong side, but you only have to break an egg once. It's just possible that in this case he has got his feet tangled up. He's working for the Frosts."

"He's working for *a* Frost."

"Sure, and that's funny too. First he said Lew hired him, and then the daughter. I never knew him to shift clients like that before. Has it got anything to do with the fact that the fortune belongs to the daughter, but that it has been controlled by Lew's father for twenty years? And Lew's father, Dudley Frost, is a great one for keeping things to himself. We put it up to him that we're investigating a murder case and asked him to let us check the assets of the estate because there might be a connection that would be helpful. We asked him to cooperate. He told us to go chase ourselves. Frisbie up at the D.A.'s office tried to get at it through court action, but apparently there's no loophole. Now why did Wolfe all of a sudden quit Lew and transfer his affections to the other side of the family?"

"He didn't. It was what you might call a forced sale."

"Yeah? Maybe. I'd like to see Nero Wolfe forced into anything. I noticed it happened right after McNair was croaked. All right; Wolfe had got hold of some kind of positive information. Where did he get it from? From that red box. You see, I'm not trying to play foxy, I'm just telling you. His stunt at Glennanne was a cover. Your play with Gebert was a part of it too. I haven't got an iota of proof of anything, but I'm telling you. And I warn you and I warn Wolfe: don't think I'm too dumb to find out eventually what was in that red box, because I'm not.''

I shook my head sadly. ''You're all wet, inspector. Honest to God, you're dripping. If you've quit looking for the red box let us know, and we'll take a shot at it.''

''I haven't given it up. I'm making all the motions. I don't say Wolfe is deliberately covering a murderer, he'd have to get more than his feet tangled before he'd be fool enough to do that, but I do say he's withholding valuable evidence that I want. I don't pretend to know why; I don't pretend to know one damn thing about this lousy case. But I do think it's in the Frost family, because for one thing we haven't been able to uncover any other connection of McNair's that offers any line at all. We don't get anything from his sister in Scotland. Nothing in McNair's papers. Nothing from Paris. No trail on the poison. My only definite theory about the Frosts is something I dug up from an old family enemy, some old scandal about Edwin Frost disinheriting his wife because he didn't like her ideas about friendship with a Frenchman, and forcing her to sign away her dower rights by threatening to divorce her. Well, Gebert's a Frenchman, but McNair wasn't, and then what? It looks as if we're licked, huh? Remember what I said Tuesday in Wolfe's office? But Wolfe is absolutely not a damned fool, and he ought to know better than to try to sit on a lid which sooner or later can be pried off. Will you take him a message from me?"

"Sure. Shall I write it down?"

"You won't need to. Tell him this Gebert is going to have a shadow on him from now on until this case is solved. Tell him that if the red box hasn't been found, or something else just as good, one of my best men will sail for France on the *Normandie* next Wednesday. And tell him that I know a few things already, for instance that in the past five years $60,000 of his client's money has been paid to this Gebert, and the Lord knows how much before that."

"Sixty grand?" I raised the brows. "Of Helen Frost's money?"

"Yes. I suppose that's news to you."

"It certainly is. Shucks, that much is gone where we'll never see it. How did she give it to him, nickels and dimes?"

"Don't try to be funny. I'm telling you this to tell Wolfe. Gebert opened a bank account in New York five years ago, and since then he has deposited a thousand dollar check every month, signed by Calida Frost. You know banks well enough to be able to guess how easy it was to dig that up."

"Yeah. Of course, you have influence with the police. May I call your attention to the fact that Calida Frost is not our client?''

''Mother and daughter, what's the difference? The income is the daughter's, but I suppose the mother gets half of it. What's the difference?''

''There might be. For instance, that young lady up in Rhode Island last year that killed her mother. One was dead and the other one alive. That was a slight difference. What was the mother paying Gebert the money for?''

Cramer's eyes narrowed at me. ''When you get home, ask Wolfe.''

I laughed. ''Oh, come, Inspector. Come, come. The trouble with you is you don't see Wolfe much except when he's got the sawdust in the ring and ready to crack the whip. You ought to see him the way I do sometimes. You think he knows everything. I could tell you at least three things he never will know.''

Cramer socked his teeth into his cigar. ''I think he knows where that red box is, and he's probably got it. I think that in the interest of a client, not to mention his own, he's holding back evidence in a murder case. And do you know what he expects to do? He expects to wait until May 7th to spring it, the day Helen Frost will be twenty-one. How do you think I like that? How do you think they like it at the D.A.'s office?''

I slapped a yawn. ''Excuse it, I only had six hours' sleep. I'll swear I don't know what I can say to convince you. Why don't you run up and have a talk with Wolfe?''

''What for? I can see it. I sit down and explain to him why I think he's a liar. He says 'indeed' and shuts his eyes and opens them again when he gets ready to ring for beer. He ought to start a brewery. Some great men, when they die, leave their brains to a scientific laboratory. Wolfe ought to leave his stomach.''

''Okay.'' I got up. ''If you're so sore at him that you even resent his quenching his thirst occasionally every few minutes, I can't expect you to listen to reason. I can only repeat, you're all wet. Wolfe himself says that if he had the red box he could finish up the case''

— I snapped my fingers — "like that."

"I don't believe it. Give him my messages, will you?"

"Right. Best regards?"

"Go to hell."

I didn't let the elevator take me that far, but got off at the main floor. At the triangle I found the roadster and maneuvered it into Centre Street.

Of course Cramer was funny, but I wasn't violently amused. It was no advantage to have him so cockeyed suspicious that he wouldn't even believe a plain statement of fact. The trouble was that he wasn't broad-minded enough to realize that Wolfe and I were inherently as honest as any man should be unless he's a hermit, and that if McNair had in fact given us the red box or told us where it was, our best line would have been to say so, and to declare that its contents were confidential matters which had nothing to do with any murder, and refuse to produce them. Even I could see that, and I wasn't an inspector and never expected to be.

It was after six when I got home. There was a surprise waiting there for me. Wolfe was in the office, leaning back in his chair with his fingers laced at the apex of his frontal buttress; and seated in the dunce's chair, with the remains of a highball in a glass he clutched, was Saul Panzer. They nodded greetings to me and Saul went on talking:

". . . the first drawing is held on Tuesday, three days before the race, and that eliminates everyone whose number isn't drawn for one or another of the entries. The horses. But another drawing is held the next day, Wednesday . . ."

Saul went on with the sweepstakes lesson. I sat down at my desk and looked up the number of the Frost apartment and dialed it. Helen was home, and I told her I had seen Gebert and he had been rather exhausted with all the questions they had asked him, but that they had let him go. She said she knew it; he had telephoned a little while ago and her mother had gone to the Chesebrough to see him. She started to thank me, and I told her she'd better save it for an emergency. That chore finished, I swiveled and listened to Saul. It sounded as if he had more than theoretical knowledge of the sweep. When Wolfe had got enough about it to satisy him he stopped Saul with a nod and turned to me:

"Saul needs twenty dollars. There is only ten in the drawer."

I nodded. "I'll cash a check in the morning." I pulled out my wallet. Wolfe never carried any money. I handed four fives to Saul and he folded it carefully and tucked it away.

Wolfe lifted a finger at him: "You understand, of course, that you are not to be seen."

"Yes, sir." Saul turned and departed.

I sat down and made the entry in the expense book. Then I whirled my chair again:

"Saul going back to Glennanne?"

"No." Wolfe sighed. "He has been explaining the machinery of the Irish sweepstakes. If bees handled their affairs like that, no hive would have enough honey to last the winter.''

''But a few bees would be rolling in it.''

''I suppose so. At Glennanne they have upturned every flagstone on the garden paths and made a general upheaval without result. Has Mr. Cramer found the red box?''

''No. He says you've got it.''

''He does. Is he closing the case on that theory?''

''No. He's thinking of sending a man to Europe. Maybe he and Saul could go together.''

''Saul will not go — at least, not at once. I have given him another errand. Shortly after you left Fred telephoned and I called them in. The state police have Glennanne in charge. Fred and Orrie I dismissed when they arrived. As for Saul . . . I took a hint from you. You meant it as sarcasm, I adopted it as sound procedure. Instead of searching the globe for the red box, consider, decide first where it is, then send for it. I have sent Saul.''

I looked at him. I said grimly,

"You're not kidding me. Who came and told you?"

"No one has been here."

"Who telephoned?"

"No one."

"I see. It's just blah. For a minute I thought you really knew — wait, who did you get a letter from, or a telegram or a cable or in short a communication?"

"No one."

"And you sent Saul for the red box?"

"I did."

"When will he be back?"

"I couldn't say. I would guess, tomorrow . . . possibly the day after . . ."

"Uh-huh. Okay, if it's only flummery. I might have known. You get me every time. We don't dare find the red box now anyway; if we did, Cramer would be sure we had it all the time and never speak to us again. He's disgusted and suspicious. They had Gebert down there, slapping him around and squealing and yelling at him. If you're so sure violence is inferior technique, you should have seen that exhibition; it was wonderful. They say it works sometimes, but even if it does, how could you depend on anything you got that way? Not to mention that after you had done it a few times any decent garbage can would be ashamed to have you found in it. But Cramer did give me one little slice of bacon, the Lord knows why: in the past five years Mrs. Edwin Frost has paid Perren Gebert sixty grand. One thousand smackers per month. He won't tell them what for. I don't know if they've asked her or not. Does that fit in with the phenomena you've been having a feeling for?''

Wolfe nodded. ''Satisfactorily. Of course I had not known what the amount was.''

''Oh. You hadn't. Are you telling me that you knew she is paying him?''

''Not at all. I merely surmised it. Naturally she is paying him; the man has to live or at least he thinks so. Was he bludgeoned into confessing it?

''No. They screwed it out of his bank.''

"I see. Detective work. Mr. Cramer needs a mirror to make sure he has a nose on his face."

"I give in." I compressed my lips and shook my head. "You're the pink of the pinks. You're the without which nothing." I stood up and shook down my pants legs. "I can think of only one improvement that might be made in this place; we could put an electric chair in the front room and do our own burning. I'm going to tell Fritz that I'll dine in the kitchen, because I'll have to be leaving around eight-thirty to represent you at the funeral services."

"That's a pity." He meant it. "Need you actually go?"

"I will go. It'll look better. Somebody around here ought to do something."

15

At that hour, 8:50 p.m., parking spaces were few and far between on 73rd Street. I finally found one about half a block east of the address of the Belford Memorial Chapel, and backed into it. I thought there was something familiar about the license number of the car just ahead, and sure enough, after I got out and took a look, I saw that it was Perren Gebert's convertible. It was spic and span, having had a cleaning since its venture into the wilds of Putnam County. I handed it to Gebert for a strong rebound, since he had evidently recovered enough in three hours to put in an appearance at a social function.

I walked to the portal of the chapel and entered, and was in a square anteroom of paneled marble. A middle-aged man in black clothes approached and bowed to me. He appeared to be under the influence of a chronic but aristocratic melancholy. He indicated a door at his right by extending his forearm in that direction with his elbow fastened to his hip, and murmured at me:

"Good evening, sir. The chapel is that way. Or . . ."

"Or what?"

He coughed delicately. "Since the deceased had no family, a few of his intimate friends are gathering in the private parlor . . ."

"Oh. I represent the executor of the estate. I don't know. What do you think?"

"I should think, sir, in that case, perhaps the parlor . . ."

"Okay. Where?"

"This way." He turned to his left, opened a door, and bowed me through.

I stepped onto thick soft carpet. The room was elegant, with subdued lights, upholstered divans and chairs, and a smell similar to a high-class barber shop. On a chair over in a corner was Helen

Frost, looking pale and concentrated and beautiful in a dark grey dress and a little black hat. Standing protectively in front of her was Llewellyn. Perren Gebert was seated on a divan at the right. Two women, one of whom I recognized as having been at the candy-sampling session, were on chairs across the room. I nodded at the ortho-cousins and they nodded back, and aimed one at Gebert and got his, and picked a chair at the left. There was a murmur coming from where Llewellyn bent over Helen. Gebert's clothes looked neater than his face, with its swollen eyes and its general air of having been exposed to a bad spell of weather.

I sat and considered Wolfe's phrase: dreary and hushed obeisance to the grisly terror. The door opened and Dudley Frost came in. I was closest to the door. He looked around, passing me by without any pretense of recognition, saw the two women and called to them "How do you do?" so loud that they jumped, sent a curt nod in Gebert's direction, and crossed toward the corner where the cousins were:

"Ahead of time, by Gad I am! Almost never happens! Helen, my dear, where the deuce is your mother? I phoned three times — good God! I forgot the flowers after all! When I thought of it, it was too late to send them, so I decided to bring them with me —"

"All right, dad. It's all right. There's plenty of flowers . . ."

Maybe still dreary, but no longer hushed. I wondered how they managed with him during the minute of memorial silence on Armistice Day. I had thought of three possible methods when the door opened again and Mrs. Frost entered. Her brother-in-law came to meet her with ejaculations. She looked pale too, but certainly not as much as Helen, and apparently had on a black evening gown under a black wrap, with a black satin piepan for a hat. There was no sag to her as she more or less disregarded Dudley, nodded at Gebert, greeted the two women, and went across to her daughter and nephew.

I sat and took it in.

Suddenly a newcomer appeared, so silently through some other door that I didn't hear him do it. It was another aristocrat, fatter than the one in the anteroom but just as melancholy. He advanced a few steps and bowed:

"If you will come in now, please."

We all moved. I stood back and let the others go ahead. Lew seemed to be thinking that Helen should have his arm, and she seemed to think not. I followed along behind with the throttle wide open on the decorum.

The chapel was dimly lighted too. Our escort whispered something to Mrs. Frost, and she shook her head and led the way to seats. There were forty or fity people there on chairs. A glance showed me several faces I had seen before; among others, Collinger the lawyer, and a couple of dicks in the back row. I stepped around to the rear because I saw the door to the anteroom was there. The coffin, dead black with chromium handles, with flowers all around it and on top, was a platform up front. In a couple of minutes a door at the far end opened and a guy came out and stood by the coffin and peered around at us. He was in the uniform of his profession and he had a wide mouth and a look of comfortable assurance by no means flippant. After a decent amount of peering he began to talk.

For a professional I suppose he was okay. I had had enough long before he was through, because with me a little unction goes a long way. If I have to be slid up to heaven on soft soap, I'd just as soon you'd forget it and let me find my natural level. But I'm speaking only for myself; if you like it I hope you get it.

My seat at the rear permitted me to beat it as soon as I heard the amen. I was the first one out. For having admitted me to the private parlor I offered the aristocrat in the anteroom two bits, which I suppose he took out of noblesse oblige, and sought the sidewalk. Some cur had edged in and parked within three inches of the roadster's rear bumper, and I had to do a lot of squirming to get out without scraping the fender of Gebert's convertible. Then I zoomed to Central Park West and headed downtown.

It was nearly ten-thirty when I got home. A glance in at the office door showed me that Wolfe was in his chair with his eyes closed and an awful grimace on his face, listening to the Pearls of Wisdom Hour on the radio. In the kitchen Fritz sat at the little table I ate breakfast on, playing solitaire, with his slippers off and his toes hooked over the rungs of another chair. As I poured a glass of milk from a bottle I got from the refrigerator, he asked me:

"How was it? Nice funeral?"

I reproached him. "You ought to be ashamed. I guess all Frenchmen are sardonic."

"I am not a French! I'm a Swiss."

"So you say. You read a French newspaper."

I took a first sip from the glass, carried it into the office, got into my chair, and looked at Wolfe. His grimace appeared even more distorted than when I had glanced in on my way by. I let him go on suffering a while, then took pity on him and went to the radio and turned it off and came back to my chair. I sipped at my milk and watched him. By degrees his face relaxed, and finally I saw his eyelids flicker, and then they came open a little. He heaved a sigh that went clear to the bottom.

I said, "All right, you richly deserve it. What does it mean? Not more than twelve steps altogether. As soon as that hooey started, you could get out of your chair and walk fifteen feet to it and back again makes thirty, and you'd be out of your misery. Or if you honestly believe that would be overdoing, you could get one of those remote control things —"

"I wouldn't, Archie." He was in his patient mood. "I really wouldn't. You are perfectly aware that I have enough enterprise to turn off the radio; you have seen me do it; the exercise is good for me. I purposely dial the station which will later develop into the Pearls of Wisdom, and I deliberately bear it. It's disipline. It fortifies me to put up with ordinary inanities for days. I gladly confess that after listening to the Pearls of Wisdom your conversation is an intellectual and esthetic delight. It's the tops.'' He grimaced. ''That's what a Pearl of Wisdom just said that cultured interests are. He said they are the tops.'' He grimaced again. ''Great heavens, I'm thirsty.'' He jerked himself up and leaned forward to press the button for beer.

But it was a little while before he got it. An instant after he pressed the button the doorbell rang, which meant that Fritz would have to attend to that chore first. Since it was nearly eleven o'clock and no one was expected, my heart began to beat, as it always does when we're on a case with any kick to it and any little surprise turns up. As a matter of fact, I got proof that I had fallen for Wolfe's showmanship again, for I had a sudden conviction that Saul Panzer was going to walk in with the red box under his arm.

Then I heard a voice in the hall that didn't belong to Saul. The door opened and swung around and Fritz stepped back to admit the visitor, and Helen

Frost walked in. At the look on her face I hopped up and went over and put a hand on her arm, thinking she was about ready to flop.

She shook her head and I dropped the hand. She walked toward Wolfe's desk and stopped. Wolfe said:

"How do you do, Miss Frost? Sit down." Sharply: "Archie, put her in a chair."

I got her arm again and eased her over and got a chair behind her, and she sank into it. She looked at me and said, "Thank you." She looked at Wolfe: "Something awful has happened. I didn't want to go home and I . . . I came here. I'm afraid. I have been all along, really, but . . . I'm afraid now. Perren is dead. Just now, up on 73rd Street. He died on the sidewalk."

"Indeed. Mr. Gebert." Wolfe wiggled a finger at her. "Breathe, Miss Frost. In any event, you need to breathe. — Archie, get a little brandy."

16

Our client shook her head. "I don't want any brandy. I don't think I could swallow." She was querulous and shaky. "I tell you . . . I'm afraid!"

"Yes." Wolfe had sat up and got his eyes open. "I heard you. If you don't pull yourself together, with brandy or without, you'll have hysterics, and that will be no help to all. Do you want some ammonia? Do you want to lie down? Do you want to talk? Can you talk?"

"Yes." She put the fingertips of both hands to her temples and caressed them delicately — her forehead, then the temples again. "I can talk. I won't have hysterics."

"Good for you. You say Mr. Gebert died on the sidewalk on 73rd Street.

368

What killed him?''

''I don't know.'' She was sitting up straight, with her hands clasped in her lap. ''He was getting in his car and he jumped back, and he came running down the sidewalk toward us . . . and he fell, and then Lew told me he was dead —''

''Wait a minute. Please. It will be better to do this neatly. I presume it happened after you left the chapel where the services were held. Did all of you leave together? Your mother and uncle and cousin and Mr. Gebert?''

She nodded. ''Yes. Perren offered to drive mother and me home, but I said I would rather walk, and my uncle said he wanted to have a talk with mother, so they were going to take a taxi. We were all going slow along the sidewalk, deciding that —''

I put in, ''East? Toward Gebert's car?''

''Yes. I didn't know then . . . I didn't know where his car was, but he left us and my uncle and mother and I stood there while Lew stepped into the street to stop a taxi, and I happened to be looking in the direction Perren had gone, and so was my uncle, and we saw him stop and open the door of his car . . . and then he jumped back and stood a second, and then he yelled and began running toward us . . . but he only got about halfway when he fell down, and he tried to roll . . . he tried . . ."

Wolfe wiggled a finger at her. "Less vividly, Miss Frost. You've lived through it once, don't try to do so again. Just tell us about it; it's history. He fell, he tried to roll, he stopped. People ran to succor him. Did you? Your mother?"

"No. My mother held my arm. My uncle ran to him, and a man that was there, and I called to Lew and he came and ran there too. Then mother told me to stay where I was, and she walked to them, and other people began to come. I stood there, and in about a minute Lew came to me and said they thought Perren was dead and told me to get a taxi and go home and they would stay. The taxi he had stopped was standing there and he put me in it, but after it started I didn't want to go home and I told the driver to come here. I . . . I thought perhaps . . .''

"You couldn't be expected to think. You were in no condition for it." Wolfe leaned back. "So. You don't know what Mr. Gebert died of."

"No. There was no sound . . . no anything . . ."

"Do you know whether he ate or drank anything at the chapel?"

Her head jerked up. She swallowed. "No, I'm sure he didn't."

"No matter." Wolfe sighed. "That will be learned. You say that after Mr. Gebert jumped back from his car he yelled. Did he yell anything in particular?"

"Yes . . . he did. My mother's name. Like calling for help."

One of Wolfe's brows went up. "I trust he yelled it ardently. Forgive me for permitting myself a playful remark; Mr. Gebert would understand it, were he here. So he yelled 'Calida.' More than once?"

"Yes, several times. If you mean . . . my mother's name . . ."

"I meant nothing really. I was talking nonsense. It appears that, so far as you know, Mr. Gebert may have died of a heart attack or a clot on the brain or acute misanthropy. But I believe you said it made you afraid. What of?"

She looked at him, opened her mouth, and closed it again. She stammered. "That's why . . . that's what . . ." and stopped. Her hands unclasped and fluttered up, and down again. She took another try at it: "I told you . . . I've been afraid . . ."

"Very well." Wolfe showed her a palm. "You needn't do that. I understand. You mean that for some time you have been apprehensive of something malign in the relations of those closest and dearest to you. Naturally the death of Mr. McNair made it worse. Was it because — but forgive me. I am indulging one of my vices at a bad time — bad for you. I would not hesitate to torment you if it served our end, but it is useless now. Nothing more is needed. Did you intend to marry Mr. Gebert?"

"No. I never did."

"Did you have affection for him?"

"No. I told you . . . I didn't really like him."

"Good. Then once the temporary shock is past you can be objective about it. Mr. Gebert had very little to recommend him, either as a sapient being or as a biological specimen. The truth is that his death simplifies our task a little, and I feel no regret and shall pretend to none. Still his murder will be avenged, because we can't help ourselves. I assure you, Miss Frost, I am not trying to mystify you. But since I am not yet ready to tell you everything, I suppose it would be best to tell you nothing, so I'll confine myself, for this evening, to one piece of advice. Of course you have friends — for instance, that Miss Mitchell who attempted loyalty to you on Tuesday morning. Go there, now, without informing anyone, and spend the night. Mr. Goodwin can drive you. Tomorrow —"

"No." She was shaking her head. "I won't do that. What you said . . . about

Perren's murder. He was murdered. Wasn't he?''

''Certainly. He died ardently. I repeat that because I like it. If you make a conjecture from it, all the better as preparation for you. I do not advise your spending the night with a friend on account of any danger to yourself, for there is none. In fact, there is no danger left for anyone, except as I embody it. But you must know that if you go home you won't get much sleep. The police will be clamoring for minutiae; they are probably bullying your family at this moment, and it would only be common sense to save yourself from that catechism. Tomorrow morning I could inform you of developments.''

She shook her head again. ''No.'' She sounded decisive. ''I'll go home. I don't want to run away . . . I just came here . . . and anyhow, mother and Lew and my uncle . . . no. I'll go home. But if you could only tell me . . . please, Mr. Wolfe, please . . . if you could tell me somethng so I would know . . .''

''I can't. Not now. I promise you,

soon. In the meantime —''

The phone rang. I swiveled and got it. Right away I was in a scrap. Some sap with a voice like a foghorn was going to have me put Wolfe on the wire immediately and no fooling, without bothering to tell me who it was that wanted him. I derided him until he boomed at me to hold it. After waiting a minute I heard another voice, one I recognized at once:

''Goodwin? Inspector Cramer. Maybe I don't need Wolfe. I'd hate to disturb him. Is Helen Frost there?''

''Who? Helen Frost?''

''That's what I said.''

''Why should she be? Do you think we run a night shift? Wait a minute, I didn't know it was you, I think Mr. Wolfe wants to ask you something.'' I smothered the transmitter and turned: ''Inspector Cramer wants to know if Miss Frost is here.''

Wolfe lifted his shoulders half an inch and dropped them. Our client said, ''Of course. Tell him yes.''

I told the phone, ''No, Wolfe can't

think of anything you'd be likely to know. But if you mean *Miss* Helen Frost, I just saw her here in a chair."

"Oh. She's there. Some day I'm going to break your neck. I want her up here right away, at her home — no, wait. Keep her. I'll send a man —"

"Don't bother. I'll bring her."

"How soon?"

"Right now. At once. Without delay."

I rang off and whirled my chair to face the client. "He's up at your apartment. I suppose they all are. Do we go? I can still tell him I'm shortsighted and it wasn't you in the chair."

She arose. She faced Wolfe and she was sagging a little, but then she straightened out the spine. "Thank you," she said. "If there really isn't anything . . . ."

"I'm sorry, Miss Frost. Nothing now. Perhaps tomorrow. I'll get word to you. Don't resent Mr. Cramer more than you must. He unquestionably means well. Good night."

I got up and bowed her ahead and through the office door, and snared my hat in the hall as I went by.

I had put the roadster in the garage, so we had to walk there for it. She waited for me at the entrance, and after she got in and I turned into Tenth Avenue, I told her:

"You've been getting lefts and rights both, and you're groggy. Lean back and shut your eyes and breathe deep."

She said thank you, but she sat straight and kept her eyes open and didn't say anything all the way to 65th Street. I was thinking that presumably I would make a night of it. Ever since she had busted in on us with the news, I had been kicking myself for having been in such a hell of a hurry to get away from 73rd Street; it had happened right there at Gebert's car, parked in front of mine, not five minutes after I left. That had been luck for you. I could have been right there, closer than anyone else . . .

I didn't get to make a night of it, either. My sojourn at the Frost apartment as Helen's escort was short and sour. She handed me her key to the door to the entrance hall, and as soon as I got it open there stood a dick. Another one was in a chair by the mirrors. Helen and I started to go on by, but got blocked. The dick told us:

"Please wait here a minute? Both of you."

He disappeared into the living room, and pretty soon that door opened again and Cramer entered. He looked preoccupied and unfriendly.

"Good evening, Miss Frost. Come with me, please."

"Is my mother here? My cousin —"

"They're all here. — All right, Goodwin, much obliged. Pleasant dreams."

I grinned at him. "I'm not sleepy. I can stick around without interfering —"

"You can also beat it without interfering. I'll watch you do that."

I could tell by his tone there was no use; he would merely have gone on being adamant. I ignored him. I bowed to our client:

"Good night, Miss Frost."

I turned to the dick: "Look sharp, my man, open the door."

He didn't move. I reached for the knob and swung it wide open and went on out, leaving it that way. I'll bet by gum he closed it.

17

The next morning, Saturday, there was no early indication that the detective business of Nero Wolfe had any burden heavier than a feather on either its mind or its conscience. I had my figure laved and clothed before eight o'clock, rather expecting a pre-breakfast summons to some sort of action from the head of the firm, but I might as well have snoozed my full 510 minutes. The house phone stayed silent. As usual, Fritz took a tray of orange juice, crackers and chocolate to Wolfe's room at the appointed moment, and there was no indication that I was scheduled for anything more enterprising than slitting open the envelopes of the morning mail and helping Fritz empty the wastebasket.

At nine o'clock, when I was informed

by the hum of the elevator that Wolfe was ascending for his two hours with Horstmann in the plant rooms, I was seated at the little table in the kitchen, doing the right thing by a pile of toast and four eggs cooked in black butter and sherry under a cover on a slow fire, and absorbing the accounts in the morning papers of the sensational death of Perren Gebert. It was a new one on me. The idea was that when he started to enter his car he had bumped his head against a sauce dish full of poison which had been perched on a piece of tape stuck to the cloth of the top above the driver's seat, and the poison had spilled on him, most of it going down the back of his neck. The poison wasn't named. I decided to finish with my second cup of coffee before going to the shelves in the office for a book on toxicology to glance over the possibilities. There couldn't be more than two or three that would furnish results as sudden and complete as that, applied externally.

A little after nine o'clock a phone call came from Saul Panzer. He asked for

Wolfe and I put him through to the plant rooms; and then, to my disgust but not my surprise, Wolfe shooed me off the line. I stretched out my legs and looked at the tips of my shoes and told myself that the day would come when I would walk into that office carrying a murderer in a suitcase, and Nero Wolfe would pay dearly for a peek. Soon after that, Cramer phoned. He was also put through to Wolfe, and this time I kept my line and scribbled it in my notebook, but it was a waste of paper and talent. Cramer sounded tired and bitter, as if he needed three drinks and a good long nap. The gist of his growlings was that they were on the rampage at the District Attorney's office and about ready to take drastic action. Wolfe murmured sympathetically that he hoped they would do nothing that would interfere with Cramer's progress on the case, and Cramer told Wolfe where to go. Kid stuff.

I got out a book on toxicology, and I suppose to an ignorant onlooker I would have appeared to be a studious fellow buried in research, but as a matter of fact I was a caged tiger. I wanted to get in a lick somewhere, so much that it made my stomach ache. I wanted to all the more, because I had scored a couple of muffs on the case, once when I had failed to bring Gebert away from that gang of gorillas up at Glennanne, and once when I had beat it from 73rd Street three minutes before Perren Gebert got his right there on the spot.

It was the humor I was in that made me not any too hospitable when, around ten o'clock, Fritz brought me the card of a visitor and I saw it was Mathias R. Frisbie. I told Fritz to show him in. I had heard of this Frisbie, an Assistant District Attorney, but had never seen him. I observed, when he entered, that I hadn't missed much. He was the window-dummy type — high collar, clothes pressed very nice, and embalmed stiff and cold. The only thing you could tell from his eyes was that his self-esteem almost hurt him.

He told me he wanted to see Nero Wolfe. I told him that Mr. Wolfe would be engaged, as always in the morning, until eleven o'clock. He said it was urgent and important business and he required to see him at once. I grinned at him:

"Wait here a minute."

I moseyed up three flights of stairs to the plant rooms and found Wolfe with Theodore, experimenting with a new method of pollenizing for hybrid seeds. He nodded to admit I was there.

I said, "The drastic action is downstairs. Name of Frisbie. The guy that handled the Clara Fox larceny for Muir, remember? He wishes you to drop everything immediately and hurry down."

Wolfe didn't speak. I waited half a minute and then asked pleasantly, "Shall I tell him you're stricken dumb?"

Wolfe grunted. He said without turning, "And you were glad to see him. Even an Assistant District Attorney, and even that one. Don't deny it. It gave you an excuse to pester me. Very well, you've pestered me. Go."

"No message?"

"None. Go."

I ambled back downstairs. I thought Frisbie might like to have a few moments to himself, so I stopped in the kitchen for a little chat with Fritz regarding the prospects for lunch and other interesting topics. When I wandered into the office Frisbie was sitting down, frowning, with his elbows on the arms of his chair and his fingertips all meeting each other, properly matched.

I said, "Oh, yes. Mr. Frisbie. Since you say you must talk with Mr. Wolfe himself, can I get you a book or something? The morning paper? He will be down at eleven."

Frisbie's fingertips parted. He demanded, "He's here, isn't he?"

"Certainly. He's never anywhere else."

"Then — I won't wait an hour. I was warned to expect this. I won't tolerate it."

I shrugged. "Okay. I'll make it as easy as I can for you. Do you want to look at the morning paper while you're not tolerating it?"

He stood up. "Look here. This is insufferable. Time and time again this man Wolfe has had the effrontery to obstruct the operations of our office. Mr. Skinner sent me here —"

"I'll bet he did. He wouldn't come again himself, after his last experience —"

"He sent me, and I certainly don't intend to sit here until eleven o'clock. Owing to an excess of leniency with which Wolfe has too often been treated by certain officials, he apparently regards himself as above the law. No one can flout the processes of justice — no one!" The high color had got higher. "Boyden McNair was murdered three days ago right in this office, and there is every reason to believe that Wolfe knows more about it than he has told. He should have been brought to see the District Attorney at once — but no, he has not even been properly questioned! Now another man has been killed, and again there is good reason to believe that Wolfe has withheld information which might have prevented it. I have made a great concession to him by coming here at all, and I want to see him at once. At once!''

I nodded. ''Sure, I know you want to see him, but keep your shirt on. Let's make it a hypothetical question. If I say you'll have to wait until eleven o'clock, then what?''

He glared. ''I won't wait. I'll go to my office and I'll have him served. And I'll see that his license is revoked! He thinks his friend Morley can save him, but he can't get away with this kind of crooked underhanded —''

I smacked him one. I probably wouldn't have, except for the bad humor I was in anyway. It was by no means a wallop, merely a pat with the palm at the side of his puss, but it tilted him a little. He went back a step and began to tremble, and stood there with his arms at his sides and his fists doubled up.

I said, ''They're no good hanging there at your knees. Put 'em up and I'll slap you again.''

He was too mad to pronounce properly. He sputtered, ''You'll re —

regret this. You'll —''

I said, ''Shut up and get out of here before you make me mad. You talk of revoking licenses! I know what's eating you, you've got delusions of grandeur, and you've been trying to hog a grandstand play ever since they gave you a desk and a chair down there. I know all about you. I know why Skinner sent you, he wanted to give you a chance to make a monkey of yourself, and you didn't even have gump enough to know it. The next time you shoot off your mouth about Nero Wolfe being crooked and underhanded I won't slap you in private, I'll do it with an audience. Git!''

In a way I suppose it was all right, and of course it was the only thing to do under the circumstances, but there was no deep satisfaction in it. He turned and walked out, and after I had heard the front door close behind him I went and sat down at my desk and yawned and scratched my head and kicked over the wastebasket. It had been a fleeting pleasure to smack him and read him out, but now that it was over there was an inclination inside of me to feel righteous, and that made me glum and in a worse temper than before. I hate to feel righteous, because it makes me uncomfortable and I want to kick something.

I picked up the wastebasket and returned the litter to it piece by piece. I took out the plant records and opened them and put them back again, went to the front room and looked out of the window onto 35th Street and came back, answered a phone call from Ferguson's Market which I relayed to Fritz, and finally got myself propped on my coccyx again with the book on toxicology. I was still fighting with that when Wolfe came down from the plant rooms at eleven o'clock.

He progressed to his desk and sat down, and went through his usual motions with the pen, the mail, the vase of orchids, the button to subpoena beer. Fritz came with the tray, and Wolfe opened and poured and drank and wiped his lips. Then he leaned back and sighed. He was relaxing after his strenuous activities among the flower pots.

I said, "Frisbie got obnoxious and I touched him on the cheek with my hand. He is going to revoke your license and serve you with different kinds of papers and maybe throw you into a vat of lye."

"Indeed." Wolfe opened his eyes at me. "Was he going to revoke the license before you hit him or afterward?"

"Before. Afterward he didn't talk much."

Wolfe shuddered. "I trust your discretion, Archie, but sometimes I feel that I am trusting the discretion of an avalanche. Was there no recourse but to batter him?"

"I didn't batter him. I didn't even tap him. It was just a gesture of annoyance. I'm in an ugly mood."

"I know you are. I don't blame you. This case has been tedious and disagreeable from the beginning. Something seems to have happened to Saul. We have a job ahead of us. It will end, I think, as disagreeably as it began, but we shall do it in style if we can, and with finality — ah! There, I hope, is Saul now.''

The doorbell had rung. But again, as on the evening before, it wasn't Saul. This time it was Inspector Cramer.

Fritz ushered him in and he lumbered across. He looked as if he was about due for dry dock, with puffs under his eyes, his greying hair straggly, and his shoulders not as erect and military as an inspector's ought to be. Wolfe greeted him:

''Good morning, sir. Sit down. Will you have some beer?''

He took the dunce's chair, indulged in a deep breath, took a cigar from his pocket, scowled at it and put it back again. He took another breath and told both of us:

''When I get into such shape that I don't want a cigar I'm in a hell of a fix.'' He looked at me. ''What did you do to Frisbie, anyway?''

''Not a thing. Nothing that I remember.''

''Well, he does. I think you're done

for. I think he's going to plaster a charge of treason on you."

I grinned. "That hadn't occurred to me. I guess that's what it was, treason. What do they do, hang me?"

Cramer shrugged. "I don't know and I don't care. What happens to you is the least of my worries. God, I wish I felt like lighting a cigar." He took one from his pocket again, looked it over, and this time kept it in his hand. He passed me up. "Excuse me, Wolfe, I guess I didn't mention I don't want any beer. I suppose you think I came here to start a fracas."

Wolfe murmured, "Well, didn't you?"

"I did not. I came to have a reasonable talk. Can I ask you a couple of straight questions and get a couple of straight replies?"

"You can try. Give me a sample."

"Okay. If we searched this place would we find McNair's red box?"

"No."

"Have you ever seen it or do you know where it is?"

"No. To both."

"Did McNair tell you anything here Wednesday before he died that gave you any line on motive for these murders?"

"You have heard every word Mr. McNair said in this office; Archie read it to you from his notes."

"Yeah. I know. Have you received information as to motive from any other source?"

"Now, really." Wolfe wiggled a finger. "That question is preposterous. Certainly I have. Haven't I been on the case four days?"

"Who from?"

"Well, for one, from you."

Cramer stared. He stuck his cigar in his mouth and put his teeth into it without realizing he was doing it. He threw up his hands and dropped them.

"The trouble with you, Wolfe," he declared, "is that you can't forget for one little moment how terribly smart you are. Hell, I know it. Do you think I ever waste my time making calls like this on Del Prtichard or Sandy Mollew? When did I tell you what?''

Wolfe shook his head. ''No, Mr. Cramer. Now — as the children say — now you're getting warm. And I'm not quite ready. Suppose we take turns at this; I have my curiosities, too. The story in the morning paper was incomplete. What sort of contraption was it that spilled the poison on Mr. Gebert?''

Cramer grunted. ''You want to know?''

''I am curious, and we might as well pass the time.''

''Oh, we might.'' The inspector removed his cigar and looked at its end with surprise at finding it unlit, touched a match to it, and puffed. ''It was like this. Take a piece of ordinary adhesive tape an inch wide and ten inches long. Paste the ends of the tape to the cloth of the top of Gebert's car, above the driver's seat, about five inches apart, so that the tape swings loose like a hammock. Take an ordinary beetleware sauce dish, like they sell in the five and ten, and set it in that little hammock, and you'll have to balance it carefully, because a slight jar will upset it. Before you set the dish in the hammock, pour into it a couple of ounces of nitrobenzene — or, if you'd rather, you can call it essence of mirbane, or imitation oil of bitter almonds, because it's all the same thing. Also pour in with it an ounce or so of plain water, so that the nitrobenzene will settle to the bottom and the layer of water on top will keep the oil from evaporating and making a smell. If you will make the experiment of getting into a car the way a man ordinarily does, you will find that your eyes are naturally directed toward the seat and the floor, and there isn't one chance in a thousand that you would see anything pasted to the roof, especially at night, and furthermore you will find that your head will go in within an inch of the roof and you're sure to bump the sauce dish. And even if you don't, it will fall and spill on you the first hole you hit or the first corner you turn. How do you like that for a practical joke?''

Wolfe nodded. "From the pragmatic standpoint, close to perfect. Simple, effective, and cheap. If you had had the poison in your possession for some time, as provision against an emergency, your entire outlay would not be more than fifteen cents — tape, an ounce of water, and sauce dish. From the newspaper account I suspected the nitrobenzene. It would do that."

Cramer nodded emphatically. "I'll say it would. Last year a worker in a dye factory spilled a couple of ounces on his pants, not directly on his skin, and he was dead in an hour. The man I had tailing Gebert handled him when he ran up to him after he fell, and got a little on his hands and some strong fumes, and he's in a hospital now with a blue face and purple lips and purple fingernails. The doctor says he'll pull through. Lew Frost got a little of it too, but not bad. Gebert must have turned his head when he felt it spilling and smelled it, because he got a little on his face and maybe even a couple of drops in his eyes. You should have seen him an hour after it happened.''

''I think not.'' Wolfe was pouring beer. ''For me to look at him could have done him no good, and certainly me none.'' He drank, and felt in his pocket for a handkerchief and had none, and I got him one from the drawer. He leaned back and looked sympathetically at the inspector. ''I trust, Mr. Cramer, that the routine progresses satisfactorily.''

''Smart again. Huh?'' Cramer puffed. ''I'll call the turn again in a minute. But I'll try to satisfy you. The routine progresses exactly as it should, but it don't get anywhere. That ought to make you smack your lips. You tipped me off Wednesday to stick to the Frost family — all right, any of them could have done it. If it was either of the young ones they did it together, because they went together to the chapel. They would have had barely enough time to do the taping and pouring, because they got there only a minute or two after Gebert did. It could have been done in two minutes; I've tested it. The uncle and the mother went separately, and either of them would have had plenty of time. They've accounted for it, of course, but not in a way you can check it up to the minute. On opportunity none of them is absolutely out.''

The inspector puffed some more. ''One thing, you might think we could find some passerby who saw someone making motions with the top of that car, but it could have been done sitting inside with the door closed and wouldn't have attracted much attention, and it was night. We've had no luck on that so far. We found the empty bottles in the car, in the dashboard compartment — ordinary two-ounce vials, stocked by every drug store, no labels. Of course there were no fingerprints on them or on the sauce dish, and as for finding out where they came from, you might as well try to trace a redheaded paper match. We're checking up on sources of nitrobenzene, but I agree with you that whoever is handling this business isn't leaving a trail like that.

''I'll tell you.'' Cramer puffed again. ''I don't think we can do it. We can keep on trying, but I don't believe we can. There's too much luck and dirty cleverness against us. It'll be months before I get in my car again without looking up at the top. We've got to get at it through motive, or I swear I'm beginning to believe we won't get it at all. I know that's what you've wanted too, that's why you said the red box would do it. But where the hell is it? If we can't find it we'll have to get at the motive without it. So far it's a blank, not only with the Frosts, but with everyone else we've investigated. Granted that Dudley Frost is short as trustee of the estate, which he may or may not be, what good does it do him to croak McNair and Gebert? With Lew and the girl, there's not even a hair of a motive. With Mrs. Frost, we know she's been paying Gebert a lot of jack for a long time. She says she was paying off an old debt, and he's dead and he wouldn't tell us anyhow. It was probably blackmail for something that happened years ago, but what was it that happened, and why did she have to kill him right now, and where did McNair fit in? McNair was the first to go.''

Cramer reached to knock ashes into the tray, sat back in his chair, and grunted. ''There,'' he said bitterly. ''There's one or two questions for you. I'm back to where I was last Tuesday, when I came here and told you I was licked, only there's been two more people killed. Didn't I tell you this one was yours? It's not my type. Down at the D.A.'s office an hour ago they wanted to put a ring in your nose, and what I told Frisbie would have fried an egg. You're the worst thorn in the flesh I know of, but you are also half as smart as you think you are, and that puts you head and shoulders above everybody since Julius Caesar. Do you know why I've changed my tune since yesterday? Because Gebert's been killed and you're still keeping your client. If you had run out on the case this morning, I would have been ready and eager to put three rings in your nose. But now I believe you. I don't think you've the red box —''

The interruption was Fritz — his knock on the office door, his entry, his approach within two paces of Wolfe's desk, his ceremonial bow:

"Mr. Morgan to see you, sir."

Wolfe nodded and the creases of his cheeks unfolded a little; I hadn't seen that since I had jerked him back from the relapse. He murmured, "It's all right, Fritz, we have no secrets from Mr. Cramer. Send him in."

"Yes, sir."

Fritz departed, and Saul Panzer entered. I put the eye on him. He looked a little crestfallen, but not exactly downhearted; and under his arm he carried a parcel wrapped in brown paper, about the size of a cigar box. He stepped across to Wolfe's desk.

Wolfe's brows were up. "Well?"

Saul nodded. "Yes, sir."

"Contents in order?"

"Yes, sir. As you said. What made me late —"

"Never mind. You are here. Satisfactory. Archie, please put that package in the safe. That's all for the present, Saul. Come back at two o'clock.''

I took the package and went and opened the safe and chucked it in. It felt solid but didn't weigh much. Saul departed.

Wolfe leaned back in his chair and half closed his eyes. ''So,'' he murmured. He heaved a deep sigh. ''Mr. Cramer. I remarked a while ago that we might as well pass the time. We have done so. That is always a triumph, to evade boredom.'' He glanced at the clock. ''Now we can talk business. It is past noon, and we lunch here at one. Can you have the Frost family here, all of them, at two o'clock? If you will do that, I'll finish this case for you. It will take an hour, perhaps.''

Cramer rubbed his chin. He did it with the hand that held his cigar, and ashes fell on his pants, but he didn't notice it. He was gazing at Wolfe. Finally he said:

''An hour. Huh?''

Wolfe nodded. ''Possibly more. I think not.''

Cramer gazed. "Oh. You think not."
He jerked forward in his chair. "What
was in that package Goodwin just put in
the safe?"

"Something that belongs to me. —
Now wait!" Wolfe wiggled a finger.
"Confound it, why should you explode?
I invite you here to observe the solution
of the murders of Molly Lauck and Mr.
McNair and Mr. Gebert. I shall not
discuss it, and I won't have you yelling
at me. Were I so minded I could invite,
instead of you, representatives of the
newspapers, or Mr. Morley of the
District Attorney's office. Almost
anyone. Sir, you are churlish. Would
you quarrel with good fortune? Two
o'clock, and all the Frosts must be here.
Well, sir?"

Cramer stood up. "I'll be damned."
He glanced at the safe. "That's the red
box. Huh? Tell me that."

Wolfe shook his head. "Two
o'clock."

"All right. But look here. Sometimes
you get pretty fancy. By God, you'd
better have it."

"I shall, at two o'clock."

The inspector looked at the safe again, shook his head, stuck his cigar between his teeth, and beat it.

18

The Frost tribe arrived all at the same time, a little after two, for a good reason: they were escorted by Inspector Cramer and Purley Stebbins of the Homicide Squad. Purley rode with Helen and her mother in a dark blue town car which I suppose belonged to Helen, and Cramer brought the two men in his own bus. Lunch was over and I was looking out of the front window when they drove up, and I stood and watched them alight, and then went to the hall to let them in. My instructions were to take them directly to the office.

I was as nervous as a congressman on election day. I had been made acquainted with the high spots on Wolfe's program. It was all well and good for him to get up these tricky

405

charades as far as he himself was concerned, because he didn't have any nerves, and he was too conceited to suffer any painful apprehension of failure, but I was made of different stuff and I didn't like the feeling it gave me. True, he had stated just before we went into lunch that we had a hazardous and disagreeable task before us, but he didn't seriously mean it; he was merely calling my attention to the fact that he was preparing to put over a whizz.

I admitted the visitors, helped get hats and topcoats disposed of in the hall, and led them to the office. Wolfe, seated behind his desk, nodded around at them. I had already arranged chairs, and now allotted them: Helen the closest to Wolfe, with Cramer at her left and Llewellyn next to Cramer; Uncle Dudley not far from me, so I could reach him and gag him if necessary, and Mrs. Frost the other side of Dudley, in the big leather chair which was usually beside the big globe. None of them looked very festive. Lew looked as if he had the pop-eye and his face had a grey tinge, I suppose from the nitrobenzene he had got too close to. Mrs. Frost wasn't doing any sagging, but looked pale in black clothes. Helen, in a dark brown suit with a hat to match, twisted her fingers together as soon as she sat down and put her eyes on Wolfe, and stayed that way. Dudley looked at everybody and squirmed. Wolfe had murmured to the inspector:

"Your man, Mr. Cramer. If he would wait in the kitchen?"

Cramer grunted. "He's all right. He won't bite anybody."

Wolfe shook his head. "We won't need him. The kitchen would be better for him."

Cramer looked as if he'd like to argue, but called it off with a shrug. He turned: "Go on out to the kitchen, Stebbins. I'll yell if I want you."

Purley, with a sour glance at me, turned and went. Wolfe waited until the door had closed behind him before he spoke, looking around at them:

"And here we are. Though I am aware that you came at Mr. Cramer's invitation, nevertheless I thank you for coming. It was desirable to have you all here, though nothing will be expected of you —"

Dudley Frost blurted, "We came because we had to! You know that! What else could we do, with the attitude the police are taking?"

"Mr. Frost. Please —"

"There's no please to it! I just want to say, it's a good thing nothing will be expected of us, because you won't get it! In view of the ridiculous attitude of the police, we refuse to submit to any further questioning unless we have a lawyer present. I've told Inspector Cramer that! I, personally, decline to say a word! Not a word!"

Wolfe wiggled a finger at him. "On the chance that you mean that, Mr. Frost, I promise not to press you; and we now have another good reason for admitting no lawyers. I was saying: nothing will be expected of you save to listen to an explanation. There will be no questioning. I prefer to do the talking myself, and I have plenty to say. — By the way, Archie, I may as well have that thing handy.''

That was the cue for the first high spot. For me it wasn't a speaking part, but I had the business. I arose and went to the safe and got out Saul's package and put it on the desk in front of Wolfe; but the wrapping paper had been removed before lunch. What I put there was an old red leather box, faded and scuffed and scarred, about ten inches long and four wide and two deep. On one side were the backbones of two gilt hinges for the lid, and on the other a small gilt escutcheon with a keyhole. Wolfe barely glanced at it, and pushed it to one side. I sat down again and picked up my notebook.

There was some stirring, but no comments. They all stared at the box, except Helen Frost; she stuck to Wolfe. Cramer was looking wary and thoughtful, with his eyes glued on the box.

Wolfe spoke with sudden sharpness: ''Archie. We can dispense with notes. Most of the words will be mine, and I shall not forget them. Please take your gun and keep it in your hand. If it appears to be needed, use it. We don't want anyone squirting nitrobenzene around here — that will do, Mr. Frost! I say stop it! I remind you that a woman and two men have been murdered! Stay in your chair!''

Dudley Frost actually subsided. It may have been partly on account of my automatic which I had got from the drawer and now held in my hand resting on my knee. The sight of a loaded gun out in the open always has an effect on a guy, no matter who he is. I observed that Cramer had shoved his chair back a few inches and was looking even warier than before, with a scowl on his brow.

Wolfe said, "This, of course, is melodrama. All murder is melodrama, because the real tragedy is not death but the condition which induces it. However." He leaned back in his chair and aimed his half-closed eyes at our client. "I wish to address myself, Miss Frost, primarily to you. Partly through professional vanity. I wish to demonstrate to you that engaging the services of a good detective means much more than hiring someone to pry up floorboards and dig up flower beds trying to find a red box. I wish to show you that before I ever saw this box or its contents, I knew the central facts of this case; I knew who had killed Mr. McNair, and why. I am going to shock you, but I can't help that.''

He sighed. ''I shall be brief. First of all, I shall no longer call you Miss Frost, but Miss McNair. Your name is Glenna McNair, and you were born on April 2nd, 1915.''

I got a glimpse of the others from the corner of my eye, enough to see Helen sitting rigid and Lew starting from his chair and Dudley staring with his mouth open, but my chief interest was Mrs. Frost. She looked paler than she had when she came in, but she didn't bat an eye. Of course the display of the red box had prepared her for it. She spoke, cutting through a couple of male ejaculations, cool and curt:

''Mr. Wolfe. I think my brother-in-law is right. This sort of nonsense makes it a case for lawyers.''

Wolfe matched her tone: ''I think not, Mrs. Frost. If so, there will be plenty of time for them. For the present, you will stay in that chair until the nonsense is finished.''

Helen Frost said in a dry even tone, ''But then Uncle Boyd was my father. He was my father. All the time. How? Tell me how?'' Lew was out of his chair, with a hand on her shoulder, staring at his Aunt Callie. Dudley was making sounds.

Wolfe said, ''Please. Sit down, Mr. Frost. Yes, Miss McNair, he was your father all the time. Mrs. Frost thinks that I did not learn that until this red box was found, but she is wrong. I was first definitely convinced of it on Thursday morning, when you told me that in the event of your death before reaching twenty-one all of Edwin Frost's fortune would go to his brother and nephew. When I considered that, in combination with other points that had presented themselves, the picture was complete.

Of course, the first thing that brought this possibility to my mind was the fact of Mr. McNair's unaccountable desire to have you wear diamonds. What special virtue did a diamond have on you — since he seemed not otherwise fond of them? Could it be this, that the diamond is the birthstone for April? I noted that possibility.''

Llewellyn muttered, ''Good God. I said — I told McNair once —''

''Please, Mr. Frost. Another little point: Mr. McNair told me Wednesday evening that his wife died, but not that his daughter did. He said he 'lost' his daughter. That of course is a common euphemism for death, but why had he not employed it for his wife also? A man may either be direct or euphemistic, but not often both in the same sentence. He said his parents died. Twice he said his wife died. But not his daughter; he said he lost her.''

Glenna McNair's lips were moving. She muttered, ''But how? How? How did he lose me . . .''

''Yes, Miss McNair. Patience. There

were various other little points, things you told me about your father and yourself; I don't need to repeat them to you. Your dream about the orange, for instance. A subconscious memory dream? It must have been. I have told you enough, I hope, to show you that I did not need the red box to tell me who you are and who killed Mr. McNair and Mr. Gebert and why. Anyway, I shan't further coddle my vanity at your expense. You want to know how. That is simple. I'll give you the main facts — Mrs. Frost! Sit down!''

I don't know whether Wolfe regarded my automatic mostly as stage property or not, but I didn't. Mrs. Edwin Frost had stood up, and she had a fair-sized black leather handbag she was clutching. I'll admit it was unlikely she would be lugging an atomizer loaded with nitrobenzene into Wolfe's office, to have it found if she was searched, but that wasn't a thing to take a chance on. I thought I'd better butt in for the sake of an understanding. I did so:

''I ought to tell you, Mrs. Frost, if

you don't like this gun pointed at you, give me that bag or lay it on the floor."

She ignored me, looking at Wolfe. She said with calm indignation, "I can't be compelled to listen to this rubbish." I saw a little flash back in her eyes from the fire inside. "I am going. Helen! Come."

She moved toward the door. I moved after her. Cramer was on his feet and got in front of her before I did. He blocked her way but didn't touch her. "Wait, Mrs. Frost. Just a minute." He looked at Wolfe. "What have you got? I'm not playing this blind."

"I've got enough, Mr. Cramer." Wolfe was crisp. "I'm not a fool. Take that bag from her and keep her in here or you'll eternally regret it."

Cramer didn't hesitate more than half a second. That's one thing I've always liked about him, he never fiddle-faddles much. He put a hand on her shoulder. She stepped back, away from it, and stiffened. He snapped, "Give me the bag and sit down. That's no great hardship. You'll have all the chance for a comeback you want.''

He reached for it and took it. I noticed that at that juncture she didn't appeal to her masculine relatives; I don't imagine she was very strong on appeals. She wasn't doing any quivering, either. She gave Cramer the straight hard eye:

''You keep me here by force. Do you?''

''Well . . .'' Cramer shrugged. ''We think you'll stay for a while. Just till we get through.''

She walked back and sat down. Glenna McNair sent her one swift glance, and then looked back at Wolfe. The men weren't looking at her.

Wolfe said testily, ''These interruptions will help no one. Certainly not you, Mrs. Frost; nothing can help you now.'' He looked at our client. ''You want to know how. In 1916 Mrs. Frost went with her baby daughter Helen, then only a year old, to the east coast of Spain. There, a year later, her daughter died. Under the terms of her deceased husband's will, Helen's death meant that the entire fortune went to

Dudley and Llewellyn Frost. Mrs. Frost did not like that, and she made a plan. It was wartime, and the confusion all over Europe made it possible to carry it out. Her old friend Boyden McNair had a baby daughter almost the same age as Helen, just a month apart, and his wife was dead and he was penniless, with no means of making a livelihood. Mrs. Frost bought his daughter from him, explaining that the child would be better off that way anyhow. Inquiry is now being made in Cartagena regarding a manipulation of the record of deaths in the year 1917. The idea was, of course, to spread the report that Glenna McNair died and Helen Frost lived.

"Immediately Mrs. Frost took you, as Helen Frost, to Egypt, where there was little risk of your being seen by some traveler who had known you as a baby in Paris. When the war ended even Egypt was too hazardous, and she went on to the Far East. Not until you were nine years old did she chance your appearance in this part of the world, and even then she avoided France. You came to this continent from the west.''

Wolfe stirred in his chair, and gave his eyes a new target. ''I suppose it would be more polite, Mrs. Frost, from this point on, to address myself to you. I am going to speak of the two unavoidable difficulties your plan encountered — one from the very beginning. That was your young friend Perren Gebert. He knew all about it because he was there, and you had to pay for his silence. You even took him to Egypt with you, which was a wise precaution even if you didn't like to have him around. As long as you paid him he represented no serious danger, because he was a man who knew how to hold his tongue. Then a cloud sailed into your sky, about ten years ago, when Boyden McNair, who had made a success in London and regained his self-respect, came to New York. He wanted to be near the daughter he had lost, and I have no doubt that he made a nuisance of himself. He kept to the essentials of the bargain he had made with you in 1917, because he was a scrupulous man, but he made annoying little pecks at you. He insisted on his right to make himself a good friend of his daughter. I presume that it was around this time that you acquired, probably on a trip to Europe, certain chemicals which you began to fear might some day be needed.''

Wolfe wiggled a finger at her. She sat straight and motionless, her eyes level at him, the lips of her proud mouth perhaps a little tighter than ordinary. He went on, ''And sure enough, the need arose. It was a double emergency. Mr. Gebert conceived the idea of marrying the heiress before she came of age, and insisted on the help of your influence and authority. What was worse, Mr. McNair began to get his scruples mixed up. He did not tell me the precise nature of the demands he made, but I believe I can guess them. He wanted to buy his daughter back again. Didn't he? He had made even a greater success in New York than in London, and so had plenty of money. True, he was still bound by the agreement he had made with you in

1917, but I suspect he had succeeded in persuading himself that there was a higher obligation, both to his own paternal emotions and to Glenna herself. No doubt he was outraged by Mr. Gebert's impudent aspiration to marry Glenna and by your seeming acquiescence.

"You were certainly up against it, I can see that. After all your ingenuity and devotion and vigilance, and twenty years of control of a handsome income. With Mr. Gebert insisting on having her for a wife, and Mr. McNair demanding her for a daughter, and both of them threatening you daily with exposure, the surprising thing is that you found time for the deliberate cunning you employed. It is easy to see why you took Mr. McNair first. If you had killed Gebert, McNair would have known the truth of it no matter what your precautions, and would have acted at once. So your first effort was the poisoned candy for McNair, with the poison in the Jordan almonds, which you knew he was fond of. He escaped that; it killed an innocent young woman instead. He knew of course what it meant. Here I permit myself another surmise: my guess is that Mr. McNair, being a sentimental man, decided to reclaim his daughter on her real twenty-first birthday, April 2nd. But knowing your resourcefulness, and fearing that you might somehow get him before then, he made certain arrangements in his will and in an interview with me. The latter, alas, was not completed; your second attempt, the imitation aspirin tablets, intervened. And just in the nick of time! Just when he was on the verge — Miss McNair! I beg you . . ."

Glenna McNair disregarded him. I suppose she didn't hear him. She was on her feet, turned away from him, facing the woman with the straight back and proud mouth whom for so many years she had called mother. She took three steps toward her. Cramer was up too, beside her; and Lew Frost was there with a hand on her arm. With a convulsive movement she shook his hand off without looking at him; she was staring at Mrs. Frost. A little quiver ran over her, then she stood still and said in a half-choked voice:

"He was my father, and you killed him. You killed my father. Oh!" The quiver again, and she stopped for it. "You . . . you *woman!*"

Llewellyn sputtered at Wolfe, "This is enough for her — good God, you shouldn't have let her be here — I'll take her home —"

Wolfe said curtly, "She has no home. None this side of Scotland. Miss McNair, I beg you. Sit down. You and I are doing a job. Aren't we? Let's finish it. Let's do it right, for your father's sake. Come."

She quivered once more, shook off Lew's hand again, and then turned and got to her chair and sat down. She looked at Wolfe: "All right. I don't want anybody to touch me. But it's all over, isn't it?"

Wolfe shook his head. "Not quite. We'll go on to the end." He straightened out a finger to aim it at Mrs. Frost. "You, madam, have a little more to hear. Having got rid of Mr. McNair, you may even have had the idea that you could stop there. But that was bad calculation, unworthy of you, for naturally Mr. Gebert knew what had happened and began at once to put pressure on you. He was even foolhardy about it, for that was his humor; he told Mr. Goodwin that you had murdered Mr. McNair. He presumed, I suppose, that Mr. Goodwin did not know French, and did not know that *calida,* your name, is a Latin word meaning 'ardently.' No doubt he meant merely to startle you. He did indeed startle you, with such success that you killed him the next day. I have not yet congratulated you on the technique of that effort, but I assure you —"

"Please!" It was Mrs. Frost. We all looked at her. She had her chin up, her eyes at Wolfe, and didn't seem ready to do any quivering. "Need I listen to your . . . need I listen to that?" Her head pivoted for the eyes to aim at Cramer. "You are a police inspector. Do you realize what this man is saying to me?

Are you responsible for it? Are you . . . am I charged with anything?"

Cramer said in a heavy official tone, "It looks like you're apt to be. Frankly, you'll stay right here until I have a chance to look over some evidence. I can tell you now, formally, don't say anything you don't want used against you."

"I have no intention of saying anything." She stopped, and I saw that her teeth had a hold on her lower lip. But her voice was still good when she went on, "There is nothing to say to such a fable. In fact, I . . . ." She stopped again. Her head pivoted again, for Wolfe. "If there is evidence for such a story about my daughter, it is forged. Haven't I a right to see it?"

Wolfe's eyes were slits. He murmured, "You spoke of a lawyer. I believe a lawyer has a legal method for such a request. I see no occasion for that delay." He put his hand on the red box. "I see no reason why —"

Cramer was on his feet again, and at the desk. He was brisk and he meant business: "This has gone far enough. I want that box. I'll take a look at it myself —"

It was Cramer I was afraid of at that point. Maybe if I had let Wolfe alone he could have managed him, but my nerves were on edge, and I knew if the inspector once got his paws on that box it would be a mess, and I knew damned well he couldn't take it away from me. I bounced up and got it. I pulled it from under Wolfe's hand and held it in my own. Cramer growled and stared at me, and I returned the stare but I don't growl. Wolfe snapped:

"That box is my property. I am responsible for it and shall continue to be so until it is legally taken from my possession. I see no reason why Mrs. Frost should not look at it, to save delay. I have as much at stake as you, Mr. Cramer. Hand it to her, Archie. It is unlocked."

I crossed to her and put it in her extended hand, black-gloved. I didn't sit down again because Cramer didn't; and I stayed five feet closer to Mrs. Frost than he was. Everybody looked at her, even Glenna McNair. She put the box on her lap with the keyhole toward her, and opened the lid part way; no one could see in but her; she was deliberate, and I couldn't see a sign of a tremble in her fingers or anywhere else. She looked in the box and put her hand in, but didn't take anything out. She left her hand inside, with the lid resting on it, and gazed at Wolfe, and I saw that her teeth were on her lip again.

Wolfe said, leaning a little toward her, "Don't suspect a trick, Mrs. Frost. There is no forgery in the contents of that box; it is genuine. I know, and you know, that all I have said here today is the truth. In any event, you have lost all chance at the Frost fortune; that much is certain. It is also certain that the fraud you have practiced for nineteen years can be proved with the help of Mr. McNair's sister and corroboration from Cartagena, and will be made public; and of course the money goes to your nephew and brother-in-law. Whether you will be convicted of the three murders you committed, frankly, I cannot be sure. It will doubtless be a bitterly fought trial. There will be evidence against you, but not absolutely conclusive, and of course you are an extremely attractive woman, just middle-aged, and you will have ample opportunity for smirking at the judge and jury, weeping at the proper intervals for arousing their compasson; and unquestionably you will know how to dress the part — ah, Archie!''

She did it as quick as lightning. Her left hand had been holding the lid of the box partly open, and her right hand, inside, had been moving a little — not fumbling, just efficiently moving; I doubt if anyone but me noticed it. I'll never forget the way she handled her face. Her teeth stayed fastened to her lip, but aside from that there was no sign of the desperate and fatal thing she was doing. Then, like a flash, her hand came out of the box and went to her mouth with the bottle, and her head went back so far that I could see her white throat when she swallowed.

Cramer jumped for her, and I didn't move to block him because I knew she could be depended on to get it down. As he jumped he let out a yell:

"Stebbins! Stebbins!"

I submit that as proof that Cramer had a right to be an inspector, because he was a born executive. As I understand it, a born executive is a guy who, when anything difficult or unexpected happens, yells for somebody to come and help him.

19

Inspector Cramer said, "I'd like to have it in the form of a signed statement." He chewed at his cigar. "It's the wildest damned stuff I ever heard of. Do you mean to say that was all you had to go on?"

It was five minutes past six, and Wolfe had just come down from the plant rooms. The Frosts and Glenna McNair had long been gone. Calida Frost was gone too. The fuss was over. The chain was on the front door to make it easier for Fritz to keep reporters out. Two windows were wide open and had been for over two hours, but the smell of bitter almonds, from some that had spilled on the floor, was still in the air and seemed to be there to stay.

Wolfe, nodding, poured beer. "That

was all, sir. As for signing a statement, I prefer not to. In fact, I refuse. Your noisy indignation this afternoon was outrageous; furthermore, it was silly. I resented it then; I still do."

He drank. Cramer grunted. Wolfe went on, "God knows where Mr. McNair hid his confounded box. It appeared to me more than likely that it would never be found; and if it wasn't it seemed fairly certain that the proof of Mrs. Frost's guilt would at best be tedious and arduous, and at worst impossible. She had had all the luck and might go on having it. So I sent Saul Panzer to a craftsman to get a box constructed of red leather and made to appear old and worn. It was fairly certain that none of the Frosts had ever seen Mr. McNair's box, so there was little danger of its authenticity being challenged. I calculated that the psychological effect on Mrs. Frost would be appreciable."

"Yeah. You're a great calculator." Cramer chewed his cigar some more. "You took a big chance, and you kindly let me take it with you without explaining it beforehand, but I admit it was a good trick. That's not the main point. The point is that you bought a bottle of oil of bitter almonds and put it in the box and handed it to her. That's the farthest north, even for you. And I was here when it happened. I don't dare put it on the record like that. I'm an inspector, and I don't dare."

"As you please, sir." Wolfe's shoulders lifted a quarter of an inch and fell again. "It was unfortunate that the outcome was fatal. I did it to impress her. I was thunderstruck, and helpless, when she — er — abused it. I used the poisonous oil instead of a substitute because I thought she might uncork the bottle, and the odor . . . That too was for the psychological effect —"

"Like hell it was. It was for exactly what she used it for. What are you trying to do, kid me?"

"No, not really. But you began speaking of a signed statement, and I don't like that. I like to be frank. You know perfectly well I wouldn't sign a statement.'' Wolfe wiggled a finger at him. ''The fact is, you're an ingrate. You wanted the case solved and the criminal punished, didn't you? It is solved. The law is an envious monster, and you represent it. You can't tolerate a decent and swift conclusion to a skirmish between an individual and what you call society, as long as you have it in your power to turn it into a ghastly and prolonged struggle; the victim must squirm like a worm in your fingers, not for ten minutes, but for ten months. Pfui! I don't like the law. It was not I, but a great philosopher, who said that the law is an ass.''

''Well, don't take it out on me. I'm not the law, I'm just a cop. Where did you buy the oil of bitter almonds?''

''Indeed.'' Wolfe's eyes narrowed. ''Do you mean to ask me that?''

Cramer looked uncomfortable. But he stuck to it: ''I ask it.''

''You do. Very well, sir. I know, of course, that the sale of that stuff is illegal. The law again! A chemist who is a friend of mine accommodated me. If you are petty enough to attempt to find out who he is, and to take steps to punish him for his infraction of the law, I shall leave this country and go to live in Eygpt, where I own a house. If I do that, one out of ten of your murder cases will go unsolved, and I hope to heaven you suffer for it.''

Cramer removed his cigar, looked at Wolfe, and slowly shook his head from side to side. Finally he said, ''I'm all right, I'm sitting pretty. I won't snoop on your friend. I'll be ready to retire in another ten years. What worries me is this, what's the police force going to do, say, a hundred years from now, when you're dead? They'll have a hell of a time.'' He went on hastily, ''Now don't get sore. I know a jack from a deuce. There's another thing I wanted to ask you. You know I've got a room down at headquarters where we keep some curiosities — hatchets and guns and so on that have been used at one time or another. How's chances to take that red box and add it to our collection? I'd really like to have it. You won't need it any more.''

"I couldn't say." Wolfe leaned forward to pour more beer. "You'll have to ask Mr. Goodwin. I presented it to him."

Cramer turned to me. "How about it, Goodwin? Okay?"

"Nope." I shook my head and grinned at him. "Sorry, Inspector. I'm going to hang onto it. It's just what I needed to keep postage stamps in."

I'm still using it. But Cramer got one for his collection too, for about a week later McNair's own box was found on the family property in Scotland, behind a stone in a chimney. It had enough dope in it for three juries, but by that time Calida Frost was already buried.

20

Wolfe frowned, looking from Llewellyn Frost to his father and back again. "Where is she?" he demanded.

It was Monday noon. The Frosts had telephoned that morning to ask for an interview. Lew was in the dunce's chair; his father was on one at his left, with a taboret at his elbow and on it a couple of glasses and the bottle of Old Corcoran. Wolfe had just finished a second bottle of beer and was leaning back comfortably. I had my notebook out.

Llewellyn flushed a little. "She's out at Glennanne. She says she phoned you Saturday evening to ask if she could go out there. She . . . she doesn't want to see any Frosts. She wouldn't talk to me. I know she's had an awful time of it, but my God, she can't go on forever without any human intercourse . . . we want you to go out there and talk to her. You can make it in less than two hours.''

"Mr. Frost.'' Wolfe wiggled a finger at him. "You will please stop that. That I should ride for two hours — for you to entertain the notion at all is unpardonable, and to suggest it seriously to me is brazen impudence. Your success with that idiotic letter you brought me a week ago today has gone to your head. I don't wonder at Miss McNair's wanting a temporary vacation from the Frost family. Give her another day or two to accustom herself to the notion that you do not all deserve extermination. After all, when you do get to talk with her again you will possess two newly acquired advantages: you will not be an ortho-cousin, and you will be worth more than a million dollars. At least, I suppose you will. Your father can tell you about that.''

Dudley Frost put down the whiskey glass, took a delicate sip of water with a carefulness which indicated that an overdose of ten drops of that fluid might be dangerous, and cleared his throat. "I've already told him," he declared bluntly. "That woman, my sister-in-law, God rest her soul, has been aggravating me about that for nearly twenty years — well, she won't any more. In a way she was no better than a fool. She should have known that if I handled my brother's estate there would sooner or later be nothing left of it. I knew it; that's why I didn't handle it. I turned it over in 1918 to a lawyer named Cabot — gave him a power of attorney — I can't stand him, never could, he's bald-headed and skinny and he plays golf all day Sunday. Do you know him? He's got a wart on the side of his neck. He gave me a quarterly report last week from a certified public accountant, showing that the estate has increased to date 22% above its original value, so I guess my son will get his million. And I will, too. We'll see how long I can hang onto it — I've got my own ideas about that. But one thing I wanted to speak to you about — in fact, that's why I came here with Lew this morning — it seems to me that's the natural place for your fee to come from, the million I'm getting. If it wasn't for you I wouldn't have it. Of course I can't give you a check now, because it will take time —''

"Mr. Frost! Please! Miss McNair is my client —"

But Dudley Frost was under way. ''Nonsense! That's tommyrot. I've thought all along my son ought to pay you; I didn't know I'd be able to. Helen . . . that is . . . damn it, I say Helen! She won't have anything, unless she'll take part of ours —''

"Mr. Frost, I insist! Mr. McNair left private instructions with his sister regarding his estate. Doubtless —"

"McNair, that booby? Why should she take money from him? Because you say he was her father? Maybe. I have my doubts on these would-be discoveries about parentage. Maybe. Anyhow, that won't be anything like a million. She may have a million, in case she marries my son, and I hope she will because I'm damned fond of her. But they might as well keep all of theirs, because they'll need it, whereas I won't need mine, since there isn't much chance that I'll be able to hang onto it very long whether I pay you or not. Not that ten thousand dollars is a very big slice out of a million — unless it's more than ten thousand on account of the new developments since I had my last talk with you about it. Anyway, I don't want to hear any more talk about Helen being your client — it's nonsense and I won't listen to it. You can send me your bill and if it isn't preposterous I'll see that it's paid. — No, I tell you there's no use talking! The fact is, you ought to regard it as I do, a damned lucky thing that I got the notion of turning the management of the estate over to Cabot —''

I shut the notebook and tossed it on my desk, and leaned my head on my hand and shut my eyes and tried to relax. As I said before, that case was just one damned client after another.

The publishers hope that this Large Print Book has brought you pleasurable reading. Each title is designed to make the text as easy to see as possible. G. K. Hall Large Print Books are available from your library and your local bookstore. Or you can receive information on upcoming and current Large Print Books by mail and order directly from the publisher. Just send your name and address to:

G. K. Hall & Co.
70 Lincoln Street
Boston, Mass. 02111